SQINKS

RUDY RUCKER

Transreal Books

Sqinks

Hardback ISBN: 978-1-940948-65-2
Paperback ISBN: 978-1-940948-59-1
Ebook ISBN: 978-1-940948-60-7

The cover art is *Farmers Market* by Rudy Rucker.

The author photo is © Bart Nagel.

.

For Barb Ash

Transreal Books

Los Gatos, California

www.rudyrucker.com/sqinks

CONTENTS

Sqinks

A Transreal Cyberpunk Love Story

1. OLIVER MEETS CAROL

I'm a writer, not that I get paid anymore. I'm old, almost eighty. My wife is gone. My friends are dropping like flies. We're circling the drain, spiraling into the void.

But hold on. I've got another story to tell!

I'm not necessarily the best financial organizer, which is why I'm living in a shipping container by the San Francisco Bay, down past the city's south-end jumble.

This isn't a tragic, bare, dead-end container, you understand. It's a spray-painted habitat assembled by rogue artists. Younger than me—that is to say, they're middle-aged. I know them through my kids.

The Box Farm includes about six containers, some of them welded together, with windows and skylights butchered in. Pirated water, sewage, and electricity. Sticks of scavenged furniture.

My mattress rests on plywood on four round stones on a painted metal floor. I have a big, bright quilt from my dead wife, Sybil. Cozy, after a fashion. No mail, no bills, no hassle. I have a walled-off corner for my room, a private bathroom, and a lock on my door. My son got it done.

And, even though my royalties have died off, I get social security, plus retirement from when I was a math prof.

To my way of thinking, I've got it made.

I awaken, looking through a skylight at the cloudy gray. The rogue artists threw a Box Farm party last night, and it was fun.

I know a lot of their faces from over the years. They've heard of my books, they've seen me around, and they're nice to me.

I don't drink or do drugs anymore. But I'm high all the time. It's an old man's style of being. So I'm enlightened? I'd like to say that. My head's a crystal ball, wrapping the warp. The world is beautiful.

Except when I'm irked, which is more often than I like. Old fool trembling with impotent rage. The guy I try not to be.

I kept it together at the party last night. Put my best foot forward. I dug the punk/noise music, blended in, danced, and jabbered. A lot of the time, I can't understand what people are talking about. Bad hearing, slow brain, sparse contextual database. The world I think I live in is gone.

I met a woman approximately my age. Makes me happy to think about her. A possible girlfriend? I didn't catch her name, and hardly managed to talk to her. Too noisy. Lost opportunity. And not many chances come by.

I use a tweak that lets me write in my head, actually seeing the pages, and now I flip over to this mode, and begin describing some of last night's scenes in my journal.

Before long, as if summoned by my words, someone scratches on my room's door.

"Hold on," I say, or rather croak. I take a drink of water, repeat what I said, then rock my way off my mattress, find my footing, and shrug on my plaid wool robe. Beneath it, I'm wearing pajamas, old coot that I am: a high-quality pinpoint-polka-dot blue pair from Nordstrom. I buy them myself these days, instead of getting them from dear gone Sybil at Christmas, oh *sob*. But it's been two years now, and in some ways, I'm getting past it. And what *about* that woman at the party last night? I was just writing about her.

Naturally, it's her at my door.

"You slept over," I say.

"In a puddle of vomit on the floor? Just kidding. On a couch. Not easy to get home from here. You don't know my name, do you? Even though I told it to you. I'm Carol Cee, and you're Oliver Strunk."

"Indeed, indeed. Come on in. The others are still asleep?"

"The wee tykes," says Carol Cee. "Still growing." We're old people talking about thirty and forty-year-olds, right. She enters and takes a chair.

She's weathered, but not drugged or insane. Pretty face, tightly curled white hair, blue cashmere sweater, a creamy blouse. Black jeans and a black wool duffle coat. Jewelry here and there. Not penniless. She carries a tan leather knapsack. Good quality. It might be pigskin.

I fill a kettle and put it on my range, a portable unit with two electric burners. "Tea?"

"Love some. Did you catch what Loulou said about sqinks last night? About me bringing food for them?"

I smile. "I don't hear all that well. Particularly at parties. Particularly if there's a band. To some extent, I'm out of it."

"You should use twirlware teep. You know. Wireless telepathy."

"I do use it," I say. "But not for conversation. Too digital."

"I thought you were the big author. And a math prof. Ultra-modern. Sharp as a tack."

"I use twirlware for writing my books in the cloud."

"Twirlware teep isn't really digital," says Carol. "It's more like a meditation practice. You relax into the seemingly imaginary voices in your head. The voices that were always there. And the voices can be real. From other people. If you listen."

"I'd rather write than talk," I say. "I have time to revise. Make it sing. Prose can be poetry."

"I'm sorry, but I haven't read any of your books."

"If we hit it off, I'll give you one." I glance at her, assessing how this lands. "I might be starting to write a new novel."

"That would be nice," says Carol Cee, smoothly returning my serve.

"I like my little worlds," I say, going for a touch of weary pathos. "It's like dreaming while I'm awake."

"What's in the new one?" asks Carol.

I shrug. "This is an interesting scenario I'm living in right now. Maybe this time, the novel writes itself. And all I have to do is copy down what happens. Here we are in the Box Farm. Old writer Oliver Strunk with the mysterious and fetching Carol Cee. Possible plot element: a giant mutant squid."

I point at the skylight overhead and raise my voice as if reciting. "*Crash-tinkle!* The obscene tentacle slimes in, with avid suckers erect. A fleshy loop winds around the waists of the naive peasants within. As the tentacle cinches tight, they moan in—is it ecstasy?"

"*Naive peasants?*" goes Carol Cee. "Thanks a lot. We're the cool kids. That's how it has to be."

The teapot shrieks. I crumble Yunnan Pu-erh tea from a dense puck the size of a plate.

"Perfect," says Carol. "That kind is good for your health. I need that."

I wait for more, but she doesn't say. She sips from her mug and looks around my room, taking my measure.

I have a lot of paintings on the blank, foam-padded walls. A few are by me, most are by Sibyl. I do like painting. You smear it around. Another plus: I can finish a painting in a week, instead of in a year. Not that I'm painting much anymore. I'm stalled on that. Grief has knocked the wind out of my sails. Even so, there's this new novel I might write. Maybe I'll put Carol in it.

"Nice colors in the paintings," she says. "I can tell Sybil's from yours. I like the oriental rugs and old furniture too. Cozy."

"I brought them with me. And the seashells and books and nice plates and silver."

"Class," says Carol. "I worried you'd be pathetic. A homeless addict in a culvert. Loulou told me I could come to the party to get a look at you. I'm Loulou's mother, you know."

"Didn't know," I say. "I like Loulou. She's looking very lively these days."

"I agree," says Carol. "Unusually perky. Do you realize that she wants to fix me up with you?"

"Kind of sensed that," I admit. "How am I doing?"

"I like that you're a homebody," says Carol. "If I can say that. And you're nice."

"The naive peasant finds a place among the reckless bohemians," I say.

"Loulou wonders why you moved in," says Carol. "She and her friends were talking about it last night."

"Well, it's interesting here. My son got me in. Not that he lives here; he has a house in the city. I needed a cheap place because I'm broke. I liquidated all my assets and gave most of my money to my kids. Not that they were asking me to do that. It was my bright idea. Maybe I outsmarted myself. My idea was to stop the leeches from bagging it all when I go into a home."

"Funny how *home* can be good or bad," says Carol.

"Sunday puzzle," I say. "Make a list of autoantonyms."

"Spare me," says Carol. "I've done my time with geeks—I did graphic design for companies, and freelanced at how-to seminars, and then I became a photographer. Let's go look for sqinks. Loulou keeps talking about them. She spells sqink with a Q, by the way. She told me that if I visited, she'd tell us how to find them." She titters. "A get-acquainted activity for you and me."

"Will we be good at it?"

"We're creatives, which ought to help. Photographers have good eyes. We frame the telling details. The pop, the wow, the sigh, the what. I distribute them through stock image banks. I licensed the same photo of a tumbleweed five thousand times."

"Where's your camera?"

"I do most of it with my eye. Thanks to twirlware. Eidetic capture. Without the equipment, I'm selling my taste. How I see." She looks around. "How do you write without a keyboard?"

"I do like you. I write in my head. I can see a twirlware page in front of me. Couples with my brain for storage. That word you used. Eidetic. And you mentioned music?"

"Image-based sounds. Twirlware upgrade. I can sing what I see."

With a charming, languid gesture, Carol leans toward me and says, "Click, click, click." And now she sings, her lips lovely.

A nursery rhyme tune that speeds up, circles around, and segues into the sound of a big band's grand finale. How she's able to get that out of her throat, I have no idea. It's fascinating, and I'm struck still when she's done.

"Well, thanks," I say. "I guess. That's the sound of my look?"

"You're easy on the eyes, Oliver. I don't plan my music. It just grows. I was jamming with the band last night. After your bedtime. Playing my images of the musicians. I kept it slow and drifty. You have to be a pro to look at the right things in the right order, and you feed that to your twirlware. Everyone liked my jam. I was glad."

Perhaps, in my sleep, I'd heard Carol's drones and riffs, overlaid upon my slide into sleep. Slippery sounds, innuendo trombones.

"I'm liking our meet-up," I say, pouring us more tea. "Hooray for Loulou. And what are sqinks?"

"Some critters that Loulou found. She's been making art prints of them. The pictures sell pretty well. They're so *odd*."

"What a creative family," I say. "I think I've seen those pictures around the Box Farm. I didn't know Loulou calls them sqinks. She makes them with the latest twirlware art tool, right?"

"Expensive," says Carol. "She was using the free version, but my ex-husband bought her a pro license. Loulou's father. Acting generous for once in his stingy-prick life."

"Let's hold off on that part. Remind me about how an artist makes twirlware pictures look like something they really see?"

"Trial and error," says Carol with a shrug. "Practice. It's about finding the right prompts. That's the whole art of it. Crafting a prompt can take days or weeks. You need skill and luck. And Loulou—somehow she's turned very lucky. Have you noticed that?"

I'm feeling a little lost. Carol's images seed her songs, and Loulou's phrases seed her prints. Everything flowing together. Nothing really real.

"Sqink luck for Loulou?" I say. "Maybe?"

"Do you notice *anything*?" Carol asks me. "How old are you anyway?"

"Less than eighty."

"Me too. But I'm doing my best to have fun. And so should you. We get ourselves dressed, we wake Loulou, and she tells us where to look for her sqinks."

"I'll feed you first," I suggest.

Carol has expressive eyes, and a charming way of rolling them to one side. Looking things over just now.

"I see eggs, oil, bread, an onion, and green peppers. We'll eat, and bring a snack to Loulou. That helps her mood in the morning. You'll see how healthy she looks."

"I never notice anything," I say. "It's true. I'm functionally deaf and blind."

"Alertness is my specialty," says Carol, sounding like Sybil. I'm in the dark without Sybil, always looking for things, my possessions gliding around my house like leaves on water. I have to buy a new pair of glasses every two months. They run away fast … on those little legs.

"Frying pan," I say, seeing it and picking it up. Getting into Carol's game. A solid object. "Knife and board. I'll chop."

"Denver omelet?" says Carol.

"Smart cookie." Breakfast goes fine.

Fed and clad, we enter the central part of the container. Carol has her mug of tea in one hand, and a plate for Loulou in the other.

Three or four Box Farmers lie sleeping. Subliminally sensing our presence, they shift and sigh like sleeping seals.

Loulou is in a puffy hammock, her bleached hair resembling thistledown, and her sleeping face in a wry twist. Yes indeed, there is a certain … health to her. I wish I looked that good.

Carol wakes her daughter by kissing her. Loulou startles and glares. Like, *leave me alone, Mom.*

Healthy or not, Loulou is in no mood to eat; she sets her plate on the floor for the dogs. But she does drink from Carol's mug. And now she talks a little, lying on her side.

"You two made friends, see?" says Loulou. "I told you, Mom. There's still time. And you want me to tell you and Oliver about the sqinks. Fine. But—" She winces like she has a headache. "I was stupid to run my mouth about the sqinks being real. I mean, sure, I'm selling pictures of them, but I've been saying I made them up. I don't want a bunch of strangers to be slobbering over them." She looks around the room, assessing the slow-breathing forms of her cohorts. "You know, and Oliver. And Tobin knows, too. He says the sqinks could be a huge deal."

"Or very small," says Carol Cee, unable to resist teasing her daughter.

Loulou takes it in stride. "Did you notice which one was Tobin, Mom? Shaved head and a neck wrinkle in the back. Always serious. Such the poser. He went to law school for about ten minutes. Pomposity incarnate. But somehow, he's cute. Like a little boy."

"He's after you, isn't he," says Carol.

"Code red option zebra null," says Loulou. Imitating a sentinel's report of a spy threat.

"Why haven't I ever heard you talking about sqinks?" I ask her.

"It helps not to be deaf," puts in Carol. "And to heed your twirlware teep."

"I'm always busy writing," I say.

"Don't go writing about me and my sqinks," puts in Loulou.

"It's a good story," I say. "How could I not?"

Loulou shakes her head and takes another long swig of the tea. "I totally don't know what the sqinks *are*," she says. "A new species? Elves? Aliens? They started manifesting a month ago. They wriggle out of the ground. The head is like a lizard's, but the body isn't. Here." She reaches over to a table and finds a postcard-sized print. "I'm amazed how easy it is for me to prompt for these pictures. Usually, it's way harder. Lately, I'm in the zone. I'm lucky. This is my sqink friend Doink. He says he's the one giving me good luck."

"The sqinks are leading us down a strange path," says Carol.

Doink resembles a string of balls floating in front of the Bay. A garland. The balls are silver and gold, in alternating sizes. At one end is a gold crocodile head, with glittering eyes. Friendly? Hard to say.

"Tobin hasn't even seen a sqink yet," says Loulou. "But he's already grubbing for a business plan. Bottom-feeder that he is. My friend Sailey and I feed Doink and his sister Flubsy."

"I bet you get more luck than Sailey," puts in Carol.

"Mom," says Loulou. "Don't always imagine I'm special. Back to feeding the sqinks, okay? They never want the same thing twice. We've done cabbages, beets, oranges, lemons, and chicken bones. Always something new.

"And the sqinks give you luck," I say, starting to wonder about angles. I'm thinking like that grubber Tobin. "That's how they pay you for the food?"

"They don't *have* to pay," snaps Loulou. "Sailey and I do it for fun. The sqinks are cute. And they have good vibes. I might let them move in with us. They'd like that."

"They're powerful aliens," says Carol. "Here to live among us. Like anthropologists in a crude backwater." Almost sounds like she knows some facts.

"Don't go yapping about this to everyone," cautions Loulou. "You always overdo it, Mom. Making yourself the center of attention. The sqinks are *mine*, okay?"

"Fine," says Carol. "And look at this, dear. I brought goodies for your sqinks. Like I said I would." She holds up her tan leather sack. The sack is full, but it doesn't look heavy. "Nothing growing in my garden," continues Carol. "And the supermarket produce is ick. So, I found something special in the woods."

"Please don't tell me you're into shrooms again," goes Loulou. "Speaking of magical thinking."

"God no," says Carol. "Give me a break. That was twenty years ago." She opens the flap of her sack. "Chestnut tree buds!" She sets the sack on the floor and makes a *behold* gesture. "Fixing to open! Early birds."

I see pale green buds of folded-up leaves with purple highlights. The buds are attached to sappy, broken branch stubs.

"Doink should like that," allows Loulou. "Bursting with life." Her voice trails off. She's tired, and not up for conversation with old people. "Bye now, lovebirds."

That last word is a dig, but it thrills me. I hide my smile. I dare to pose one more question. "Loulou, you didn't say where we can look for sqinks?"

"Look at the frikkin' ground," mumbles Loulou, snuggling herself in. "Open your eyes."

Carol takes her knapsack of chestnut buds, and we make our way outdoors. It's late March, a misty day, almost raining. I can barely see Oakland across the water. I put my arm around Carol's waist, and she doesn't mind. We walk along the narrow strip of wet and somewhat grotty sand that edges the Bay.

After about fifteen minutes, the Box Farm is small behind us, and we're coming up on the remains of a shipyard, with scattered sheds and outbuildings beside a vast, corroded pier and a monstrous lift. Everything is dark and significant against the pearlescent gray sky. Very WWII. In the silence, I take a moment to look into my mental manuscript and make some notes.

"No sqinks yet," says Carol Cee.

"Turn back?" I suggest. It's raining a little more seriously now.

"Okay," says Carol. "And we move inland."

The beach abuts an unused field with boulders and floppy tussocks. And beyond the field is an abandoned parking lot, with the potholed pavement gray and cracked.

Random plants are everywhere, dotted with tender buds. The winter-stilled world is coming to life.

"In the Middle Ages, March was considered the first month of the year," I tell Carol.

"And you like that because your birthday's in March," she says.

"Stalker much?"

"Know your prey."

"Okay, fine. Glad you cared enough to check. Did you read the reviews of my books?"

Carol laughs. "Don't flatter yourself. We're hunting for sqinks!"

"According to Loulou," I say, "a sqink's head is like a lizard's, but the body, *not*."

"Just look for anything that moves, Oliver."

We proceed cautiously through the field, among briars, soggy spots, and slippery stones. It seems we're holding hands. I'm happier than I've been in a long time.

"Wait, wait!" Carol suddenly exclaims. "I see one! Look, look!"

Of course I see nothing, but she leads me to a low spot, some twenty feet off, where the dank, matted weeds are heaving and forming a gap and—yes!

2. SQINKS

A little snout pokes out. A head several inches long, a miniature crocodile head, with a long mouth that runs along the sides.

Its eyes are shiny black beads with white pupils. Lively and alert. Somehow feminine. Rising above the weeds. Faintly luminous. The black eyes track us. The sqink's head itself is pale violet. And the next segment of her body is a purple sphere, and then a violet one. Alternating back and forth like that, with the purple balls smaller.

"Hello, sqink," says Carol Cee in a sweet baby voice. She crouches, extracts a chestnut-flower bud from her knapsack, and waggles it.

The sqink opens her jaws and pipes a sound.

"Do you hear that?" exclaims Carol, turning to me. "So cute. She said, 'Hello, I'm Lilac.'"

I'm not at all sure about that, but I go, "Hello, Lilac, I'm Oliver Strunk."

I prudently have one hand covering my throat—just in case the thing darts at me. But, no, Lilac the sqink is satisfied with the chestnut bud; she's crunching it right down. She doesn't have teeth. Her mouth is like a long beak with sharp edges.

And Loulou was right; despite the look of her head, Lilac is not like a lizard *at all*. As I say, her body is a string of colored balls, the balls alternating in size like grapes and plums. The little ones are dark purple, and the large ones are pale violet.

More and more of the sqink emerges as Carol Cee keeps the chestnut buds coming. The sqink holds her body erect, like a charmed cobra. The newer segments are bigger than the first ones, that is, the body is wider in the middle.

Carol's motions are dainty and alert—she's keeping her fingers well away from those sharp, snappy jaws.

"Looks almost like a garland for a holiday tree," Carol merrily says. "Isn't Lilac cute?"

Me, I wonder if I shouldn't turn around and run like hell. Like … what happens when Carol has no more chestnut buds? The freaking sqink is nearly a yard high by now, and, oh lord, she's entirely out of the sqink hole. To me, her gleaming eyes have taken on a hard, pitiless air. Like a snake's eyes.

The garland sqink is floating in the air, a series of balls, alternately big and small, and tapering down at either end. Floating, as in levitating? Whatever that means. For sure, Lilac doesn't have wings. It's like her body is repelling the ground. Even the plants beneath her seem to bend down a little bit.

So okay, Lilac is a string of balls hanging in the air, and she has razor-sharp jaws, and we're out of food with which to placate her.

"Our throats," I mutter to Carol. "She'll rip out our throats and eat our flesh. Come on now. Move slowly. Let's get down to the beach where we can run. You go first. I'll protect you." It's not an offer I really want to make, but you know, I have to be polite.

I look around for some kind of protection. "A stick!" I say, "I'll grab that stick and—"

Lilac rocks her head up and down. Makes a warble with a stutter at the end.

"She's laughing at you, Oliver," says Carol. "She says she'd need helpers to eat you all up. I guess that's encouraging?"

"Maybe," I mutter, still wondering how to get out of here.

Lilac rocks and talks some more.

"She talks so fast," says Carol. "Maybe I should use my air guitar. Lilac and I could do a jam. I *think* Lilac just told me that sqinks can learn about things by eating them, and that they can, in fact, rebuild the things afterward. Can you follow what she's saying, Oliver?"

Well, no, I can't, not at all. I wonder if I might honorably take a position behind Carol after all. Keeping her between me and the sqink.

The drizzle is picking up, and the wind is steady. I can't see across the Bay anymore, and even the Box Farm is indistinct. My chic cloth raincoat is soaking through. Carol's heavy wool coat is waterproof, with a nice hood. I'm glad for that.

Before we leave, I want to hit Lilac sqink with our original, as yet unspoken, plan.

"What do we get?" I yell at the hovering garland of balls. "Carol gave you munchies, Lilac. What do you give us?"

"Give us something nice," echoes Carol, right on the beam. "That's how it works, Lilac. Loulou's been getting AI prompts from Doink."

Is Lilac nodding yes? I have no idea what to hope for. A diamond, a bar of gold, a wad of counterfeit cash?

Two chirps from the garland of bobbling balls. And for once, I understand. "Good luck," is what Lilac says. And then she drifts over to Carol and presses herself against Carol's chest. Like a hug. Except Carol winces as if it hurts.

The contact breaks, the sqink whistles farewell, and now, angling into the wobbly wind, she wriggles back to where she came from, beneath the sodden mat of dead weeds. I'm not quite sure what's happened.

It's raining even harder: cats-and-dogs, pineapple-express, atmospheric-river, cyclone-bomb type rain. Idiot that I am, I'm not wearing a hat, and my fashionable trench coat has no hood. The rain streams through my hair, down my face, and down the back of my neck. Around the edges of Carol's hood, stray raindrops bead her curly white hair.

We make our way to the strip of sand by the Bay and blunder along, our shoes squelching. I'm half blind. Carol is holding her hand against her chest as if it hurts. But under it all, I feel a sense of calm good vibes. Lilac's blessing.

Carol picks up on this as well. "The sqink luck," she says. "Lilac is working for us. She's my pet."

And now, sure as shit, here's a nice top hat, tumbling across the field, driven by the wind. It comes to a stop on the shore. In some way, this feels natural. I brush sand off the hat and set it atop my head. A perfect fit. Of course.

"Abraham Lincoln," says Carol. "What about me? Or—"

She comes to a stop. Stands stock still with her hand still on her chest. "It's gone, Oliver. The pain. It's been coming and going for weeks, and it kicked up just now when Lilac touched me. I was scheduled for an operation this week, you know, but—"

Carol fumbles at a toggle on her duffel coat and shoves her hand inside. Bending over to make room, she worms her hand under her sweater and inside her blouse and—

"Yes!" she says, drawing her hand out. Stands straight, stunned. "Oh, thank you, thank you, Lilac! The lump in my breast is gone! I can't believe it. I'm well, Oliver."

She's sobbing and laughing, even dancing around. She reaches under her coat again. "It's really gone! It's over!"

I hug her and hold her, and after a while, I kiss her, which is something I've been wanting to do all morning, or even since last night.

"Lucky," I murmur under the splash of the rain.

"Sqink luck," she says.

And it's back to the Box Farm.

"What happened?" jokes Loulou at the sight of our dripping forms. "Did Doink throw you in the bay?"

"It wasn't Doink," says Carol. "The squink we met today was called Lilac."

"Nice," says Loulou. "Didn't know about her. Don't know how many sqinks there are. Let me give you some dry pants and shoes, Mom. And why not take a hot shower?"

"In a minute," says Carol. "I have to tell you some news." She glances at me, wanting me out of the picture.

I get it. "You two talk while I change."

"I like your hat," Loulou tells me.

"That's part of the news," says Carol. "A small part."

"And listen," I tell Loulou, unable to hold myself back. "Sqink luck is real. It did stuff. And I feel it. Don't you?"

Slowly, Loulou nods.

And then I'm in my room. As I mentioned, thanks to my clever son, I have my own private shower, which is important. There's a limit to how bohemian a guy my age wants to be. I shed my wet rags, and get under the spray.

In my head, sqink scenarios are hurtling at me like oafs in a mosh pit, or like lawyers raising issues. What if, what if?

At the same time, I'm liking the hot water, and I'm so very glad that I kissed Carol. She's the first woman I've truly kissed in two years.

The first year after Sybil died, I picked up two different women at the San Francisco Opera, of all places. And I did kiss those women, kind of, but it never went further. I was too eager, or they didn't like me, or whatever. I tried e-dating as well, but never hit a winner. I gave up.

Maybe Carol will sit in my room and chat with me all afternoon, watching me from the corners of her eyes in that special way she has. It would be cozy. Or, better, we could go to a museum or a café. Get away from the Box Farm posse. It's probably too early to ask for sex.

I'm out of the shower now, drying myself, and admiring the new luster of my sqink-lucky skin. It's like Lilac gave me a spa treatment. But then I flip back into worry mode. Visions of bad scenarios.

Crowds of seekers with grapefruits and rutabagas and radishes. Tobin with a bullhorn, collecting fees. City officials writing up violations. And here come humorless researchers, born-again believers, rabid xenophobes, con artists, invalids, news crews, gunmen, and the long-suffering police.

As for the sqinks—what's their plan for us? Physical invasion? Demonic possession? Random destruction?

Someone's scratching on my door. Cute, ironic scratching. Kittenish, almost.

"Come in, Carol."

Over Carol's shoulder, I can hear Tobin lecturing Loulou. Talking rapidly, with chiaroscuro in his vocal colors. Some dumb-ass plan.

"The hassles begin," I say to Carol.

"He's a moron," says Carol, closing the door behind her. "I hope Loulou is not at all attached to him. But never mind them. I have to see my doctor. To check if the cure is real. I called her, and she said I can come right now."

"Did you drive here?"

Carol shakes her head. Her white curls bounce.

"I'll take you," I say. "I have a nice old car. Non-robotic. I drive it myself."

"I'd like that," says Carol. And she kisses me again. "My new friend."

Yes, I know that you, the younger reader, don't want to read about hideously old people courting, but what can I say? Hope springs eternal. It's never too late for spring. But don't worry—if Carol and I ever get in bed, I'll draw a veil. I'm not out to torment you.

I bundle up, and we go out in the big room, heading for my car. I'm wearing my lucky top hat, and I have an umbrella. Tobin's voice fills the big room like a circling stream.

"Quiet," says lucky Loulou. "I have to talk to Mom."

"Hold on," says Tobin, striking a pose, unwilling to cede the floor. "I'm making the crucial point that—"

Carol darts over and grabs the man by the throat. Her grip appears very strong. Tobin makes a choking noise. For the moment, he's too shocked to strike back. Taking advantage of the man's confusion, Carol gives him an effortless, tai-chi-type shove that sends him flailing backward, and he lands sprawled on the couch. She's stronger than I realized.

"My daughter and I want to talk," says Carol very calmly. "Don't interrupt."

Tobin holds up one hand in a *calm-down* gesture and rubs his throat with the other.

"Tell me more about your good luck with your art," Carol says to Loulou. "I was so busy talking about myself that I forgot to ask for details. I know, I know, I know. I do that."

"Well—if you'll let me tell you—*yes*. I think I told you that my art prompts come faster. I don't have to grope and tweak and iterate. I nail them all at once. Like the Muse whispers them in my ear. And, get this, I found a hundred dollar bill on the sidewalk yesterday." Loulou pauses and looks at Carol.

"Sqink luck!" the two of them say in unison.

"Tell me one of the art prompts," I say, curious.

Loulou gives me an odd look. "Usually, we keep them private," she says. "Like secret formulas. Or magic spells."

"You can trust me," I say, meaning to strike a bluff, jocular tone. "I'm hoping to seduce your mother."

"*Ew!* Sick! You're a disgusting man."

"Oh, let him dream," says Carol. "But don't get cocky, Oliver. Or I'm gone."

Loulou lets out a sudden guffaw. Flipping her mood. "Crazy times. Okay, here's my prompt for an image of my sqink friend Doink: *shuffle skewer floppy dome phonic dumbo eel marry me*

25

wheenk. Weirdly, that just popped into my head. The *wheenk* is crucial, and who knows why."

Kind of a conversation stopper, that.

"You're putting me on?" I finally say. "That's a prompt?"

"Buy a license for the app," Loulou airily says. "Try for yourself, Mister Nosy. Mister big bad motherfucker." Then she starts laughing again.

Carol Cee is laughing, too. Maybe I've overreached myself with these women. We say goodbye to Loulou, and Carol leads me outside.

"Still raining for sure," she says as we walk to my car.

"This is my faithful twenty-seven-year-old Beemer," I tell her. I hold the umbrella over her as she gets in, the rain sounding a lovely, taut, drum-tattoo.

"It's nice," says Carol, comfortably inside with me. Good sqink-luck vibes fill the car. "I know how to drive, too. You hardly see a car like this anymore."

"Sybil bought me this car for my sixtieth birthday," I say. "It was the last year they sold drive-it-yourself models." Probably I shouldn't talk about my dead wife while on a date, if this is a date. But Carol's a level-headed woman of the world. She won't spook all that easily. "Sybil was a professor teaching English as a second language," I continue. "And I was teaching mathematics at San Francisco State. Even though I was writing SF. We needed the money. I had the energy. We were young."

"I'd give anything to be sixty," says Carol with a rueful laugh.

She guides me to a brick building on Potrero Street near 20th. It's hard to park there, so I wait in the car, watching the rain on my windshield, which is something I like to do. Admiring the ambient gnarl.

The world's natural processes are, if you'll forgive an edifying interruption, impossible to predict. Breezes, rocking leaves, flowing water, your body, your mind—all of them are equally complex, all of them are mathematically chaotic. Chaos isn't rare. It's not a disease. It's the norm. It's health.

"Health," says Carol, getting back in the car. She's been gone—forty-five minutes. "They scanned me. I'm clear. They say it's as if I had a holographic radiation treatment."

"Do you think—" I begin.

Carol puts a finger on my lips. "Let's not think. I don't want the luck to go away." She gives me another kiss. I'm very happy.

"Celebrate?" I say. "It's not even two o'clock. Lunch at the SFMOMA café? And we can look at the art."

"Just like you'd do with Sybil?" says Carol, mocking me a little bit. "Don't try to make me into her."

"I don't expect that," I say. "Not at all. It's good that you're different. I like it." A strained pause. "What would you do now if you were with your old husband?"

"Get drunk in a bar on a high building," says Carol. "But, no, I'm trying not to do that as much. I already had a lot last night with Loulou. Isn't that girl something? My little twin. But god forbid I say that. Museum café sounds sweet, Oliver. Intellectual and eager. And yes, I've been to SFMOMA before; I'm not a complete biz drone. Is the food good?"

"Sure. And they sell wine. And they've got paintings I'd love to show you. A giant Rosenquist called *Leaky Ride for Dr. Leaky*, with a lot of pencils and stars and a lipstick mouth, and a car part with a big drop of oil. The oil is sex, you understand."

"Of course."

"My favorite right now is this grid of portraits by Andy Warhol, doctored prints, hung next to each other. One of the best things Andy ever did." I'm heading into town, happy to be getting my way, holding forth, with the water splashing up on both sides of the car, like we're in a speedboat. There's not much traffic today, and it's all self-driving vehicles. Staying out of my way.

"Aaandy," goes Carol, playfully dragging out the first syllable, saying it like *ahh*. "Aaandy. He's a god for graphic artists. Made it over the wall into art land." On a whim, she takes the sentence and extends it into a song. Her voice is rough and vibrant. I'm overwhelmed with lust.

"In a museum like this, there's always a room that's dark because they're showing videos," I say. "One of those rooms might be empty today. Maybe we can find one. You and me."

Carol stops singing. "Why do you say a thing like that? Don't be so forward."

Forward is the word. I press on. "Where do you live, anyway? I can't see us closing the deal in my room at the Box Farm with Loulou right outside."

"You just get worse, don't you," says Carol, slightly amused. "A man on a mission. Like a dog. Where do I live? In a cabin in the mountains near La Honda." She gives me a look. "Alone."

"I don't want to go there today. Freaks. Bikers. Too far in the rain."

"The city's full of hotels with people closing their deals." Carol flicks a glance over at me, teasing. But before I take the bait, she cuts me short. "And it *cannot* be a place where you went with Sibyl."

"Oh, um, yes, wow. Do you know a hotel?"

"Let's be friends first," says Carol. "And if it comes to that, I'd be okay with your room. Assuming that I would consider something physical with such a forward man. And it would be none of Loulou's business. And aside from all that, I do want to check back at Box Farm to see what's next with the sqinks."

"Sqinkageddon. Sqinkathon. Sqinkadelic," I say.

Carol runs with it. "Sqinkorama. Sqinkastic. Sqinka-doo-dle-doo," and now she's into song again. Utterly enchanting.

Someone's honking at me. I guess I cut in front of them. More cars now, clouds of spray. I'm on track for the SFMOMA parking garage. A tricky left turn here, an unexpected right, and, yes, we're on the homeward glide. I hope to god the museum's open. They have these weird, random days off. But, yes, the lights are on inside.

3. WARHOL

The museum is almost empty, and the café is barely open, but they let us order. Carol gets lox and avocado; I get pork in red sauce with polenta and fried Brussels sprouts. I point them out to Carol.

"Cruciferous vegetables," I say, shaking my head. "Do you—"

"I do know that word," she says, forking one of them. "So why did you order this dish if you don't like it?"

"I order anything with polenta."

We're near a window overlooking the rooftop sculpture garden and the buildings beyond. Still raining steadily. Carol is lovely and smooth in the gray light. I like the whorls of her white curls. This woman is wonderful.

If we never do get to sex, maybe I'll be happy just hugging her a lot. I've been lonely for so long. Mammals are meant to snuggle.

"Sizing me up?" says Carol, noting my pensive gaze.

I shrug, embarrassed. I'm not the subtlest person. "You look good," I say, raising my glass of Pellegrino. She clinks with her white wine.

"You don't mind my Einstein look?" she asks.

"It's cute. Nice to touch. *Boing.*"

Soon after that, I drop a really big bite off my fork, my last bite, and it rolls off my lap to end up under the table. Right away, something bumps my leg. I lean over. A fleeting glint of gold and silver. The forkful of food is gone.

"Got a dog down there?" says Carol, laughing.

"No," I slowly say, managing to sit up without bumping my head. "It almost looked like …"

"A sqink is following us around?" Carol exclaims, taking a quick look down there. She sits back up. "Nothing."

"It's hiding?" I say.

"It's like they want to taste everything we like," says Carol. "And to look at what we see. And to figure us out. So, they followed us to the museum. You should think about my idea that they're anthropologists. You should take that seriously."

I keep wondering if Carol knows something I don't know. But how would she? I stick to the situation at hand.

"This sqink I think I saw—I think it might have been Loulou's sqink friend Doink. Silver and gold?"

"Oh, let's drop it, Oliver. We came here to have a nice time, not worry about the aliens. Show me those damn prints. This meal's over."

"Andy's on the fifth floor." I pause, getting my head together. "Andy Warhol, yes. I know it's corny and obvious to look at him, but this particular assemblage is something I'm into this year. And we'll check out Joan Mitchell and Joan Brown. And if we get a chance, the Rauschenberg is over in the old part of the museum."

"Quite the connoisseur for a math teacher," says Carol, calming down. "Know what I'm thinking? *Today is the first day of the rest of my life.* Speaking of corny." Quietly, she laughs. "What a day."

So first, we look at a big abstract painting by 50s artist Joan Mitchell, who's not the same person as the singer. Michell's one of the best; her colors are harmonious and jubilant. And we check the great Joan Brown's series of paintings about the time she tried to swim to Alcatraz. Deeply transreal.

And now we're in the dim Andy portraits room, with twelve canvases on one wall and eight on the other, all the same size, each about two feet tall, silkscreen images of mono photos, black highlights on blank backgrounds with chalky Warhol-painted color blocks on top, hung in three rows. Each of the images is deeply human, practically talking to you. The assemblage is a wonder. Humanity in full flower. Hello, Andy!

"I love them," says Carol. "I like your taste, Ollie."

"Nobody calls me Ollie. Don't do it."

"I could be mean and do it all the time to see if you like me enough to—wait! Look!"

Carol is pointing at a shadowy corner, up by the ceiling where the two walls meet and, oh shit, it's Lilac and Doink up there, truly following us. Bobbling like a box of shiny balls, levitating, and widening their jaws as if in *haw-haw* laughter. Their glinting black eyes watch us.

And now, how strange and awful, they work their way down the wall that has twelve canvases, snipping giant bites from the Warhol masterpieces, jaws moving very fast, *eating* the twelve paintings one by one, as if using a hedge trimmer, working from one side to the other, from top to bottom, with spare canvas shreds drifting to the floor, and the empty frames dropping off the walls, *ka-krak*. Discarded remains.

Voices behind us, stray visitors attracted by the noise, and here's a pair of guards, a woman and a man, all agog. What can they possibly do?

A minute later, the pair of sqinks have eaten a dozen of the Warhol portraits, somehow fitting them into the sqinks' rather small bellies. This uplifting oasis of art has been laid waste.

An alarm hoots. Footsteps trot toward our nook. Excited voices. More guards.

The two bad sqinks wriggle over to Carol Cee and me, touching us, acting like affectionate pets, looping round our necks, worming under our arms and between our legs.

"Not our fault!" Carol tells the guards, all the while trying to push Lilac away. "It wasn't our idea."

"We don't know where they came from!" I cry. "Quick, let's get out of here, Carol!" I push past the guards and into the hall that leads to the elevators and the stairs, towing Carol by the hand.

The guards can readily see that we're guilty. But, no, they won't catch us. We've got our sqinks with us. Our source of sqink luck.

"Sir!" calls the woman guard, drawing closer. Always bad news when a functionary calls you *sir*. Means they're about to bust you. The guard is holding a spray can of art-safe nuisance-person immobilizer.

The purple/violet Lilac leads our way, out in front of me. Lilac is bigger than before. Nourished by the art? Same for her partner sqink, the string of gold and silver balls we call Doink.

"It's time!" Carol calls to the sqinks. "Time to help us get away."

Lilac skirls an incomprehensible phrase, flies a loop, and ends up between Carol's legs. Like an alien Pegasus offering a ride. Doink does the same for me. The puzzled guards fall off their stride, not sure if they should spray.

The hall is glass on one side, with a patio out there. We've reached a side door. Deftly our sqinks snout open the glass doors. We're in a courtyard with no exit, a dead end, but *whoops*, we're rising into the rainy city sky. Sqink levitation.

Up. Up from the shelter of the museum's walls.

"Can't hold on," I wail into the wind. As if understanding me, Doink enlarges himself and tightens the gaps between his segments, forming a rubbery arc. He's like a tyke's bouncy caterpillar toy. And his levitation force seems even stronger than before. Lilac does the same for Carol.

We're low above the city, not much higher than the buildings, weaving an unpredictable path. The rain pelts our faces. We'll need fresh clothes again. Assuming that we make it back to the Box Farm instead of being whisked off to Sqinkland or gunned down by the police. No emergency helicopters are in sight as yet. A plus.

The two sqinks seem to have no sense of crisis; they're happy and fooling around, flying circles around each other. With their guts comfortably full of Warhol masterpieces. What would Andy think? He wouldn't like it. Is there any way to make this right?

We're flying side by side now, slower than before, down near the water of the Bay. It's late afternoon. The splash and mist over the water give us some cover. But I wouldn't say that I'm feeling a lot of sqink-granted good luck.

Fact is, I'm screwed. Like a fool, I used my membership card to enter the museum and my credit card to pay for lunch. The police will find me. They might already be at the Box Farm. And once again, I'm soaked and freezing.

"Wait!" exclaims Carol. She goes with saying this word a lot. In my current mood, it seems annoying. She hammers on Lilac's rubbery body. "Slow down, sqinks. I want to talk to you."

"Give us nice dry clothes," I say, putting in my two cents worth. "Switch them out for what we have on. I bet you can do that. And give us waterproof yellow rain gear and waterproof hats. Like lobstermen."

"Not *bright* yellow," interjects Carol. "We've got to be modest. Me, I'll go for silver-gray."

"Gentle yellows for me," I say.

"A tasteful mélange," goes Carol. "Both of them in a camouflage design. High-fashion neo-punk. Like the Seventies."

I feel a tingling all across my body. As if I'm inside the assembly bin of a 3D printer. My clothes shift and crawl—and then they're new. The sqinks rule. I'm dry. Not quite cozy yet, but I'm getting there.

The rain ticks against my impermeable rain garb, crafted in chic camo tints of yellow. I blend with the hills across the

Bay. And my top hat is still in place. Glad for that. My personal logo. Like the villain in a superhero comic.

Carol is peppy preppy in her palette of grays, in a fashionable cut, and with a big-brimmed hat. Her garb looks nice with the warm shades of her sqink-dehazed skin.

I'm so comfortable that I begin writing notes in my psychic twirlware notebook.

"Topper and Lady Cee," I murmur.

"What?" goes Carol. "Never mind. The plan, Oliver, listen to the plan. It's butt simple. We go back to the museum and replace the Warhols. Apparently, the sqinks swallowed them intact."

"How did the pictures fit?"

"The sqinks made their stomachs bigger," says Carol.

"Oh, of course!" I say, throwing up my hands. "Hyperbolic space. No further discussion needed! But why take those great paintings at all? It's wrong."

The sqinks chirp and twitter. As ever, Carol understands them, and I don't. Face it, I'm full-on deaf and senile. No use even talking to me, most of the time.

"So what'd they say?"

"They like to collect whatever we think is interesting. Their stomachs have lots of room. If you didn't love those paintings, Oliver, the sqinks wouldn't have taken them. It's like web-scraping. They did it to honor Andy Warhol."

"Why doesn't Oliver look glad," says Doink in his creaky, down-home voice. Talking slowly for my benefit.

"Glad?" I exclaim. "You honor things by stealing them?"

"I don't know why you call it stealing," says Carol. "They borrow things so they can show the others. Maybe take things back to their home world for a while. You call your world Sqinkland, right, Lilac and Doink?"

The sqinks make rhythmic, wavery sounds, bucking their heads up and down. Laughter.

The rain rains on. And here I am with Carol, riding on the backs of two aliens, if that's what they really are, aliens, hovering over the SF Bay, all of us in stylish camouflage, hoping we're unseen in the mist. Over near the Box Farm, three cop choppers churn.

"Can you really put the paintings back?" I say to the Doink and Lilac.

The sqinks are in a playful mood. They bob and twist. I nearly fall into the Bay.

"The sqinks can stretch space," says Carol. "They're superhuman."

Again, I wonder to myself: *How is it that Carol knows so much about sqinks?*

"Yes, she's right," says Lilac. "We don't have to stick to that old-school fixed-size routine. We're more flexible."

The crazy talk is making me giddy. "*Bookkeeper* is the only English word that has three double letters," I say, for no good reason at all.

Lilac says something more, but as per usual, I can't properly understand her.

"Having a sqink body is like using a credit card instead of cash," translates Carol. "Virtual money, virtual space."

"So tidy," I say, a bit sarcastically. "Maybe I'll write a popular science book about sqink physics. It'll be one page long, and it'll cost pi dollars. And I'll write it while we're in prison for art theft."

"Lots of convicts write books," Carol brightly says. But then she relents. "Don't look so worried, Oliver! We'll fix this mess. Back to the museum!"

"Yes," I say, taking heart. "I'll call them on our way."

"I'll be the one to call," says Carol. "You're too direct, Oliver. Too vain. Too rude. Too coarse."

"I just hope the cops don't machine-gun us," I put in.

"With Lilac around, we can count on sqink luck," says Carol. "Look how warm-toned we are."

And Lilac does indeed arrange a peace conference with museum director Kelly Tang. She's frantic about the missing paintings. Carol says we're ready to negotiate. Our heist was a type of performance art, Carol explains. We did it in the spirit of Andy himself. Not much response to that.

"We'll come to you now," says Carol. "The museum lobby?"

Next thing I know, Carol, Lilac, Doink, and I are once again in the museum lobby with director Kelly Tang, plus her staff, a team of cops, and a crew of museum videographers.

Our two sqinks have gone back to normal size. Festive garlands of balls, alternating in size and color, about four feet long. The paintings remain inside them. The sqinks drift around the lobby, sniffing thigs like curious dogs.

As for Carol and me, we look sharp with our sqink-tanned skins in our sqink-crafted camo rainwear. The material has a nice rainbow sheen; it's not like any fabric I've ever seen. Carol's taken off her floppy hat, but I'm still sporting my top hat. I tell myself we're heading toward a happy ending of episode one of the Topper and Lady Cee show.

The cops are concerned about the sqinks. They're a SWAT team armed with pistols, shotguns, assault weapons, and zap guns. Tracking the sqinks in their sights. The museum camera crew is getting all this down, come what may. A meeting for the ages.

"Have a seat," says Kelly Tang, gesturing to a couch. She's trim, about forty, in a fashionable blue pantsuit, and bedecked with high-end museum-shop jewelry. She wears light makeup and a firm expression. Unfriendly, I guess you'd say. She glances down at her phone.

"Let's set the scene. You're Oliver Strunk and Carol Cee. Oliver is a retired professor, and Carol's a photographer, no?

And Mr. Strunk, you're known for your speculative fiction as well. Hardly the profiles of criminal terrorists."

"Art lovers," I say. "The problems are caused by *them*." I gesture at our carefree pair of critters.

"Yes," says Kelly Tang. "We saw them on the surveillance cameras. What are they? I assume they're under your control?"

"We call them sqinks," says Carol. "Lilac and Doink." The sqinks jiggle and hum. Doink calls out *Hello*, and Lilac makes a sound.

"They're intelligent," I put in. "Possibly superhuman. We don't know what they are or why they're here."

"Extraordinary," says Kelly Tang, almost smiling, but not. "Not a hoax? Not performance art? Not drones from the Chinese New Year's parade?"

"Oh, the sqinks are real," says Carol. "Very real."

Kelly Tang makes a dismissive hand gesture. She doesn't care to debate our bullshit. "Let's get to the point." She gives us a hard look. "Are you prepared to return the twelve paintings you stole? Where are they now?"

"Inside the sqinks," I blurt. "They can puke them back."

Carol frowns at me. "Don't be coarse, Oliver. The sqinks have warped the space within their bodies, Ms. Tang."

Kelly Tang cocks her head, intrigued but not buying the jive. "Will you return the original paintings or not?"

"It's possible that storage in a space warp leaves a sheen," I suggest. "As if the works have been varnished. Andy would be amused. He was a master of reappropriation."

"I know art history, Professor Strunk," says Kelly Tang. She's losing patience.

"The restored paintings will be a wonder," says Carol. "A delicious outrage. They'll draw huge crowds."

"Just don't press charges against us," I plead. "We never meant for this to occur. And we're making it right."

Kelly Tang shrugs. She truly doesn't like us. "You did what you did," she says. "You'll face the consequences. I'm not in a position to intervene."

"Cough up those damn paintings!" Carol orders the sqinks. "And, Director Tang, have your staff stand back." Carol addresses the head of the SWAT team. "And, please, captain sir, have your officers hold fire. The sqinks behave oddly. Don't mistake their antics for menace."

The show begins.

I'd thought the sqinks might use their snouts like the nozzles on 3D printers, mechanically scanning back and forth, laying down rows and layers of goo, systematically excreting Andy's twelve paintings upon the lobby's marble floor. But it's funkier than that.

Hovering ten feet above the floor, the sqinks hump their bodies as if miming labor. Doink emits gasping breaths. Lilac counters with hoarse moans. Lurching about, the sqinks shudder, widen their mouths beyond all belief, and then—they birth the lumps onto the floor. The shining deposits ooze into rectangular forms whose surfaces clarify into the Warhols, glistening with damp traces of sqink juice.

The smell is astonishing, like nothing I've ever encountered, so strange and pungent that I don't know whether to call it good or bad.

The cops are itching to blow away Lilac and Doink. Heedlessly the sqinks croon and caper. The paintings dry; the canvases gleam. These are Warhol's painted-on prints paintings, yes, polished to perfection by the ministrations of the sqinks.

Kelly Tang is silent. Spellbound.

"You see?" say I.

Kelly glances over her shoulder to check that the video cameras are capturing this incredible spectacle. She gestures for the cameras to come closer. She's realizing this is pure gold, fodder for the art event of the year.

Bewildered and unnerved, the cops draw closer. And now—disaster.

In his excitement, Doink bumps a segment of his body against a cop's cheek. As if by automatic reflex, the man raises his zap gun and zaps the sqink. A powerful electric shock flows through Doink's body.

And now we learn that sqinks are vulnerable to shock attacks. Doink shrills, spasms, and drops dead to the floor, his body shriveling into something like a string of withered crab apples. He's dead for good, or so it would seem.

Lilac surges forward, her menacing jaws agape. She means to rip open the policeman's neck. A police bullet strikes her. One of her body balls puckers, oozes clear jelly, and deflates. But still, Lilac presses on. Another cop raises his zap gun, meaning to finish the job.

Carol Cee jumps into the fray, screaming. She wraps her arms around Lilac, like a mother protecting a child.

I hurry to Carol's side, calling for peace. "No more killing! Lilac's done nothing! You murdered her partner!"

"Stand down," bellows the chief of police.

"Clear the lobby," orders Kelly Ting. "Gather the paintings. And secure the video files. I don't want them going out."

Silence falls. In the hush, Lilac makes steady grating sounds that might be sobs.

"Can we leave?" I ask, addressing both Kelly Tang and the head cop. "My car's in the garage. We've done what we can. Let us drive home."

"No," says Kelly Tang. "Of course not."

"I'll put them in lock up," says the police chief. "And as for this other sqink—best to use the zap gun again. Release that creature, Ms. Cee."

Carol's does no such thing. Instead, she tucks Lilac under her voluminous gray camo coat and whispers something to the sqink. Abruptly, Lilac switches from her sobbing sound to her laughing sound.

Director Kelly Tang's phone is ringing. She's startled—surely, she'd turned the phone off—but it won't let up, not even when she tries to mute it. She makes a *wait-a-minute* gesture to the police chief and speaks to her device. I can only hear her end of it, a string of fragments.

"Hello?"

"Yes, I know who you are."

"We're in the midst of a crisis."

"How is it that you know?"

"An offer?"

"Can you repeat that?"

"This would happen when?"

"Hold on."

Kelly lowers the phone and speaks directly to the police chief. "I think we may be wanting to withdraw our charges against this pair. Oliver Strunk and Carol Cee. And as for that lavender creature—let her be."

Kelly beckons to one of her underlings. Hands him the phone.

"Work out the details, Henry," she quietly says, laying a finger against her lips. "Take the phone into my office. This will be confidential." She turns to the police captain. "Your expenses will be well reimbursed. More than well."

"Saved by the bell!" exclaims Carol. "Just the thing. Do you *feel* it? Attitude adjustment. Come over to the cause, oh ye benighted minions. Thank you, Director Tang and blessings upon our unknown benefactor."

"Benefactor?" I say, not quite getting it.

"Someone is offering her a bribe," says Carol. Director Tang frowns. "A donation," emends Carol. "An amelioration fund. So, um, Kelly, we're free to go?"

"That's correct," says Kelly Tang. "And I'll rehang the paintings."

Oh wow, Kelly's minions begin carrying the Andy paintings to their ancestral home on the fifth floor of this temple of art. Sqink creations are being elevated to the altar. Two of the videographers follow along, documenting, but the others stay down here.

Kelly's assistant, Harry, emerges from the director's office and murmurs in her ear. She shrugs and offers a quick nod.

"Part of the agreement is that we'll upload the complete video files to the museum's site," Kelly calls to her crew. "Starting with what we already have, and showing the rest in realtime. No such thing as bad art publicity, eh? Scandal, scandal, scandal." For the first time, Kelly smiles. She looks giddy and brave, as if diving off a very high tower. "We are going to have one *hell* of a show!"

One of the videographers catches my eye and throws me a cheerful salute.

"Out of here," says Carol. She catches hold of my hand and drags me out the door and into the freshening dusk. The rain is over.

I doff my top hat, and bow. "You're a force for the good, Lady Cee."

"And you, dear Topper. Let us repair to your digs."

Lilac wraps poor Doink's remains in a cloth and tucks the scraps into a pouch of her body. Then rides to the Box Farm with us in my car, the violet-purple sqink nestled against Carol's breast.

4. SQINK LUCK

The Box Farm is abuzz. They cheer when we enter the big room. We're still wearing our outré rain gear, me in my top hat, and Lilac tucked inside Carol's coat.

The gang is watching a realtime videocast from the SFMOMA. Loops and variations of the video of us in the lobby—with the cops, the director, and the hovering sqinks. The tense negotiations, the disgorging of goo, the transformation of the Warhols. Doink's murder, Lilac's wound, the game-changing phone call, and the solemn procession that bears the resurrected Warhols to the higher floors. Almost like the Bible, that part, or like the funeral of a pharaoh.

As I said, the gang at the museum is making an all-night show out of the video, looping in cycles, continually retweaking the view angles and the zoom, unearthing new wrinkles, and folding in surveillance video of Carol and me flying over the city. The voice of Director Tang's caller isn't quite audible, and it may well be that they're obscuring it. Our star hacker can't find any trace of the call online. Whoever or whatever made the call is, as they used to say, clad in dark ice.

Adding to the festive air in the Box Farm, we have three new sqinks: a green-and-yellow one like a lizard, a punk sqink made of balls in shades of white and black, and a big sqink that resembles a floating cuttlefish, complete with beak, bunched tentacles, and a wiggly hula-skirt fin. Her skin ripples with chameleon shades of purple, beige, and green. Her eyes glow.

Lilac pops out from beneath Carol's coat, loudly greeting the three visitors. Her wound seems already to have healed. She looks up at Carol and emits one of the bursts of sound that serve her as speech.

"The cuttlefish is a sqink too," interprets Carol. "She's—a princess. Princess Moo."

"I'm Flubsy," the green and yellow lizard sqink tells me. She has a very long tail. "And the monochrome garland is Skeeze. Maybe he can work with Oliver." Flubsy is well-spoken, with a bit of a hillbilly accent. Not like Lilac, whose voice has the fidelity of a low-energy call from a collapsed coal mine.

"I'm sorry about what happened to Doink," I tell Flubsy.

"Doink was my brother," says Flubsy. "And now he's gone." She turns to Lilac. "Darn shame you didn't rip out that killer cop's throat."

Lilac's incomprehensible response has a "Yes, but" quality.

"I stopped Lilac just in time," puts in Carol, proud of herself. "And then Kelly got her miracle call." Carol nudges Lilac. "Nobody's told me who the call was from?"

Instead of a proper response, Lilac goes into a tedious laugh session. The others join. Six sqinks, including Moo, the cuttlefish. Rocking and warbling.

Although I'm standing with my arm around Carol's waist, I have to admit that I find Moo to be—can I say this? Well, okay, I find the cuttlefish sexually attractive. What can I say? I'm a science-fiction writer. I'm living in a novel.

The lively flow of patterns on the cuttle's plump bod— *muy fabuloso*. The writhing of her tentacles—delectable. The undulations of her fin—to die for. Not that I'm going to do anything about it. Just a minor quirk of mine.

The video is still live, with the museum VJs replaying and analyzing the recorded events. But suddenly, folded in with the files from the afternoon, I'm seeing—wait a minute—live footage of Lilac, the other sqinks, and our party crowd with, wow, me in the picture, and Carol too. Who in here has a camera?

I scan my gathered housemates. Grungers, artists, scavengers, and reality hackers. Wised up, hardcore San Franciscans. A lot of them are into media—but nobody seems to be holding a lens, and I don't think anyone besides Carol is doing twirlware image capture. And I can tell she's not broadcasting.

What about the hovering Moo? Yes, of course she's twirlware teeping her input to the SFMOMA studios. And that's why I don't see her on the video display. An eye doesn't see itself.

Events are getting away from me—and I have no clue where the flow is going. Are the sqinks going to crush us? I take a shot at declaring a unilateral peace.

"Friends!" I call to Moo the cuttlefish, speaking to her as if to a camera. "Let's work together! We're in the same movie! Love, not war!"

"Well said, Ollie," hoots crass Tobin, standing beside me. I really don't like when he calls me that. He should know that by now.

"*And* we can do biz," he continues. "Ollie, me, you, everyone!"

Everyone applauds. Time for fresh drinks.

That lizard sqink Flubsy wriggles over to me. "Doink and I talked about business," she tells me. "Rember, Loulou was feeding us, and we were giving her luck?"

"At first, Loulou didn't understand that," I say.

"We're always learning, aren't we," says Flubsy. For an alien, he has a very good command of our idioms. Even though, as I say, she sounds like a hick. "We're like exchange students. If a sqink okays your vibes, they're apt to move in with ya. We're guests looking for kind hosts. And we lay sqink luck on our pals."

"Money is what matters," brays one-track-mind Tobin, still next to me. "Not luck."

"You don't know what luck is," Carol tells him. "You're a dull, vulgar man."

"You tell him," I put in.

"You be the one to tell him," Carol says to me. "I don't even like to hear his voice."

"Don't be like that with Tobin," protests Loulou. "He's my good friend."

"Listen, man," I tell Tobin. "Luck is totally real. Much realer than money. Money is bullshit marks on paper, to legitimize bullies' thefts."

Princess Moo, the cuttlefish, hovers nearby, digging all the emotion, staring at my face, vignetting me into the SFMOMA broadcast. Local color.

"Washed up unreadable writer," says Tobin.

"Carol fed chestnut buds to Lilac," I say. "And Carol's cancer went away. Money can't buy that. And I got a little luck too. I met Carol, and she kissed me. And I found a great hat, and I rode on the back of a flying sqink, and I'm not dead in jail, and the video streams are casting Carol and me as heroes. We're not bottom feeders like you. We're stars in the eyes of public opinion. Luck, Tobin, my man. Sqink luck is where it's at."

"Room for all of us," says Carol, not wanting a fight. "Money, art, enlightenment, whatever. "Maybe we'll set up, like, a sqink sponsorship site in our field. We collect admission. Tobin's happy! People meet sqinks and give them presents. Sqinks are happy. Sqinks move in with people and make them lucky. People are happy!"

"*Topper and Lady Cee's Sqink Fair*," I say, drawn into Carol's aura of goodwill.

She nods. "Oliver and I are the marquee names. The figureheads. No scut work for us."

"Maybe," goes Tobin. "Admission is good."

"With money in the mix, the commercial permits and the security fall into place. If someone gets prickly, they get a benefactor phone call like Kelly Tang did. *No problema*," says Carol, and then yawns. "Long, crazy day." Another yawn, clearly faked. She turns her alluring eyes my way. "Wilst grant me shelter, my liege?"

Loulou shakes her head and looks away. That's as close as Carol and I will get to having her approval. That chatty cuttlefish Moo is still staring at me, her eyes bright. Most likely, all these details are on live video. Oh well. Carol and I disappear into my room, making sure the cuttle doesn't follow us in. Privacy. I don't have an extra bed.

And here, my dear and modest readers, I draw the veil.

The next morning, the hubbub has begun. Voices in the main room, especially Tobin's. I can't quite hear what he's saying, and I'm glad for that. Looking out my window, I see strangers walking along the bay beach. Carrying bags of gifts. They're looking for sqinks on their own. The tsunami's about to break.

Carol and I have a quick breakfast: coffee, apples, stale rolls. We can't stop smiling at each other. We won't be drawn into low, grubbing tasks. We need to spend some leisure time together.

At this point, I notice that the frikkin' sqink Moo has found her way into my room after all. I recall hearing that a cuttle can squeeze through any opening large enough to fit its beak through. Is the cuttle-cam broadcasting my moments with Carol?

Seeing me staring at her, Moo glides over, lands on my shoulder, and tickles my chin with a long tentacle.

"Hi, Oliver," she says, putting on a low, breathy, movie-star voice. "I saw the way you looked at me last night. You want me."

"I hope you're not broadcasting this conversation," I say. "Makes me look bad."

"No, no," says Moo. "I'm choosy about what I share with the Earth networks. It's a matter of making sqinks look good.

47

And our love chat is off-topic, no? How far would you like to go with me?"

"Go?" I say, playing dumb. "How far?"

"You two are flirting?" exclaims Carol, as if not believing what she hears. "I'm not enough for you, Oliver? You're quite the raunchy catch, aren't you?"

"It's just a goof," I protest, rolling with the punch. "Research for a story. Don't worry. And lighten up, Moo. Sit down on the table so we can admire you. Those are wonderful colors on your back. And look at Moo's eyes, Carol. The pupils are shaped like the letter W. Cephalopods fascinate me."

Carol prods the creature with an extended finger. Moo twines a tendril around Carol's finger in a friendly way. But Moo likes to tease.

"Who knows," she archly tells Carol. "Maybe I'll squeeze your boyfriend down my throat and shape him into a cuttle— so he and I can mate. Like, pass me a spermatophore, darling Oliver! I'm the ultimate tourist!"

"*Ick*!" goes Carol.

"Oliver might like it," coos Moo. "You can't trust men, Carol. They're rotten to the core. As for sqinks, well, that's a long story that I'll …"

"Let's go!" shouts Tobin.

5. TOPPER AND LADY CEE

And now it's off for the fair.

Skeeze tags after us, my self-appointed pet who looks like a punk-rock garland with long jaws. I can sense his attachment to me. I'm a bit of a punk too. Or used to be.

Moo the cuttlefish is in the distance, near the admission table, broadcasting video of gawkers, users, and sqinks.

"It seemed like Moo was about to tell us more about the sqinks and how they got here," I say to Carol. "In my room. And then Tobin horned in."

"How about it, Skeeze?" says Carol. "Why are the sqinks here?"

Skeeze calmly pipes his response. "We keep telling you, but you don't pay attention. We're from a Sqinkland. We're like tourists. Or, no, like exchange students, that's the line. And you, Oliver, you can be my host. I like you."

"Moo said this guy Winston Tropp lured you here? He sent a signal?"

"Winston calls it a *bulk beacon*," says Skeeze. "He thought it was something like a radar. Thought he'd bounce signals off us, and then go after us, and exploit us. Didn't occur to him that he'd be summoning us. So very stupid."

"I hope you're not evil spirits," I say.

"You'll see," says Skeeze, making that sound between a squeal and a laugh. He pauses, then continues. "I'm in a strange mood. I might be about to die."

"What I want to know is how sqinks can do so many cool things?" says Carol.

"You ask me a noob goob question like that?" says Skeeze with a mournful sigh like a homeless newsboy in a 40s black-and-white film. "Me, I'm nearing the end of my road."

"I want the cool things," insists Carol. "Levitation, shape shifting, space warping, and luck. Can we get those powers from Winston Tropp?"

"No," goes Skeeze. "Winston doesn't know jack shit. He made his bulk beacon, and he idiotically summoned us, and here we are. High-quality planet you've got, Carol and Oliver."

"And you want what?"

"Oh, I don't know," Skeeze airily says. "Trade, or tourism, or colonialization, or eating your brains."

"Oh, you," says Carol, as if Skeeze might be joking.

"Did Moo meet Winston right away?" I ask.

"Right there," says Skeeze, pointing. "Half a mile off? That big old wooden warehouse the size of a city block. Winston and his partner live in one end, and the rest of the warehouse is for his lab. With his bulk beacon."

"What's the bulk beacon like?" I ask Skeeze.

"It's four connected columns. Spidery and delicate. Made of waveguides, twirlware, space rocks, and old bones. Expensive. Winston got support from this venture capitalist, Chantal Floonberry. He didn't want to risk every bit of his twirlware money. Chantal funds out-there entrepreneurial projects. She calls her group Nothing Much. And that's enough questions."

Here in the real world, the meadow is big enough that nobody's come near us yet. They can see that Carol and I are talking to a sqink. But maybe they assume there's no more pickings right here.

"Tell the part about Moo meeting Winston," says Carol.

"It was the middle of the night," goes Skeeze. "Moo went and hovered over Winston's bed. Told him to buy a piece of this field, the funky patch near the Box Farm. Because that's where the mouth of Moo's wormhole tunnel is—not that any of you have noticed it. Camouflaged by weeds and briars."

"Wormholes are important," says Carol, as if she knows.

"That's where a bulk world connects to a planet like this," says Skeeze. "Like a vent from an underground gopher colony."

"My mind is *bzzzt*," I say. "Like a safe dropped on my head. Each answer makes things worse."

"Wait," goes Carol. "One thing: how did Lilac fix my cancer?"

"Sqinks have vast mental powers," says Skeeze. "And we make good use of what we've got. You needed holographic radiation treatment, Carol. And your doctors couldn't muster the crunch. But a sqink can. A use case for sqinks."

Out on the bay, a large container ship is slowly turning around. Backing and filling. Great churning of water. Takes a long time. Meanwhile, nobody is bothering us, and Moo is over at the admission table helping Tobin.

"Yesterday a pelican ate me, or she tried to," goes Skeeze. "I wouldn't let her swallow me. I latched onto her bill from the inside, and I stayed there, enjoying the view. What a ride. Eventually she dove into the Bay and rinsed me out. Bottom line? The answers are all around you, if you'll look. Why isn't Moo coming back? She was supposed to tell you all the things I've been saying. Moo's the queen sqink, right? She's top royalty and I'm a peon."

"Moo seemed pretty low-down when she got into that argument with Carol," I say.

"You goaded us into it," says Carol, never one to hold back. "You're a horndog and an idiot."

I let that pass because, well, because basically it's true. "We like listening to you," I reassure Skeeze. "You're very well-spoken."

Skeeze is bobbing in the morning breeze, preoccupied with bending his black and white string of balls into a wreath. Like for a funeral.

"Gonna be a Nobel prize in this jive for Winston Tropp and his sideways gravitons and his bulk beacon," says Skeeze after a while. "If he lives. Big thinker. Golden new chapters in the history of your planet's weak-ass science."

"Your story makes more sense to me all the time," says Carol.

"Carol heard it when she made her private side deal with Winston and Moo," says Skeeze. "The deal to recruit Oliver."

"No idea what you're talking about," cries Carol.

I can tell she's lying. It makes me sad. I thought I was on the inside. But I'm not.

And here comes Moo the cuttlefish, very annoyed. Her body is a dusky red. She's been eavesdropping from afar, and she disapproves of Skeeze spilling the beans.

"Blabber," blubbers Moo, with a wet sound in her voice. She grabs the Skeeze the sqink with a long tentacle, shakes him hard, and throws him to the ground. "Upstart runt. I shouldn't have let you onto my team."

Any kinky longings I had for Moo are quite gone. I whack her with my closed fist, as if serving a volley-ball. Moo sails away. But then she flies back, her body waggling.

"I don't like a little worker like Skeeze to try and tell my story," goes Moo.

"Well, you sure as hell weren't doing it," I say, deflecting my anger onto the sqink.

"I was about to tell the whole story to you and Carol at the Box Farm, but that asshole Tobin broke in," says Moo. "Talk to me, kids. Ask anything you want."

"Okay," says Carol, eager to get away from discussing her treachery. "How do you levitate?"

"We use jets of gravitons," goes Moo. "Easy."

"Got it," says Carol, trying to sound efficient. "And how does sqink luck work? Moo? Skeeze?"

Skeeze is playing with a newly arrived sqink whose segments are striped like the body of a bumblebee. Yellow and black. The new sqink has emerged from the grasses beneath our feet. Like many sqinks, he's a garland of larger and smaller balls. Both kinds of balls are striped the same way, like, as I said, the body of a bumblebee. And he's fuzzy. Quite cute.

Moo wants to answer Carol's question, but Skeeze interrupts.

"I'll take this one," goes Skeeze, ignoring Moo's angry burbles. "Luck means happy coincidences. The world is patterned in two ways. You've got the workadaddy up and down of Time. Cause and effect. That's how you think on Earth. But think about Space. Perpendicular to Time. Everything fitting. All at once. Luck. That's how we sqinks roll. Synchronicity."

"Self-delusion," I say. "Bullshit."

"Telepathy is synchronicity," puts in Moo. "It's not like I *do* something to see into your mind, Oliver. My thoughts and your thoughts resonate with each other. Happens on its own." Moo giggles. Not an attractive sound. "And that's how I knew you were having naughty thoughts about me, yes you were, you bad boy!"

"Oh god," groans Carol. "Moo is so utterly disgusting."

"Enough talk," I tell Moo. "Isn't anything ever going to *happen*?"

"Well, Moo is going to attack me pretty soon," says Skeeze. "Because I don't obey her. Will that make you happy?"

"Oh, sob," says Carol. "Did someone step on your tiny violin?"

Skeeze's new bumblebee-striped sqink friend pipes up. "Greetings, all. My name is Xavier. I have a thought to contribute."

"How do you have even the faintest idea of what we were talking about?" I ask Xavier. "We've only known you for, like, ten seconds."

"In your heart, you understand me," intones Xavier. "And yet, in fear, you deny. This is about more than tourism. Our goal is symbiosis."

"Yes," goes Carol.

"Fine," I say with a sigh. "I'll run with you and the sqinks, Carol. Even if you're a liar. I want to see where the path leads."

"And you'll help with our ad campaign," says Moo. "This field is perfect. And the Box Farm is edgy. And your Loulou is so cheerful and—can I say flaky? The girl next door runs wild. And you two, Carol and Oliver—our closers. Topper and Lady Cee."

"I love that Oliver is an unsuccessful academic and a failed science-fiction writer," says Skeeze. "And that people think he's crazy. Raffish. His unreliability enhances his claims. He wouldn't know *how* to lie."

"I'm really basking in your praise," I snap. "Treasuring every word."

This said, I do in fact appreciate the attention. My most recent and, in my opinion, greatest novel got precisely one review, written by a close personal friend.

"Harken to the world-weary scribe," says Skeeze. "I'll partner with you, Oliver. I bet I can write novels too."

"As if," I say. "But sure, I want a sqink helper. But don't feel like you have to constantly follow me around. If we meet just once in a while, that could be fine."

"Buurn," Moo says to Skeeze, kind of laughing at him.

"Our campaign is live now," says Moo. She gazes past us at the gathering crowds. "Today is for rumors, gossip, buzz. And later this week? Full boil. And probably more sqinks. Maybe a lot more."

"I don't want to be in ads," says Carol. "Don't like the glare. Losers mocking me. And roper Guidos staring at my butt."

"What if Carol and I drop out of sight," I suggest. Whether or not she's been honest with me, I want to be with her. I'm hooked.

"Yes!" says Carol, flashing me a really nice smile. "And the public can be, like, where are Topper and Lady Cee? And we're, like, *ta-ta* goobs!"

"What's a roper Guido?" I ask.

"Means whatever I say it does," says Carol. "I just this minute made it up."

"I enjoy human language," says Moo. "So pliant. And, as you might put it, bailing from this scene would be ausp."

"Ausp?" goes Carol. "Not a word."

"Auspicious," says Moo. "Skeeze and I can help with your exit. But not quite yet."

"Why can't we disappear on our own?" I ask. "Right now. Why do you have to run us?"

"Because you'll need help." goes Skeeze. "There's a riot coming on. Tobin's customers. Supply way, way short of demand. See them over there? Drifters. Investors. Reporters. Cops. Bikers. City officials. Helicopters."

"And roper Guidos," I put in, kind of laughing.

"Oliver and Carol are our stars," says Moo. "The heart of the Winston Tropp sqink sponsorship program. But the mob doesn't quite know you're standing here. Also, they don't know there are only a few free sqinks left to partner with. Tobin way overhyped this. But of course, that's what I told him to do. Tobin's on my team."

"Why can't we just pay everyone to go away?" I say. "Chantal Floonberry did that at the museum, right? Chantal Floonberry, the billionaire who backed Winston? She paid off the director, Kelly Tang. And Kelly split the dough with the city and the cops."

"So do it your way," says Moo. "Hold out your hands, Oliver. I'll let you freelance your escape. Why not."

"Take it!" Carol tells me.

Moo lowers her tentacles onto my palms. Here comes a rustle and a tickle and—my life is a dark fairy tale—I'm holding twenty thousand dollars in packets of hundred-dollar bills. Okay, right. I'm not gonna throw this away. I stuff the money into the pockets of my sqink raincoat.

"If and then," says Skeeze, kind of marveling at what's going down. "Do this, do that. Cause and effect. Like watching a watch."

"See, Oliver, the sqinks can help us," says Carol. "Maybe later Skeeze will be your writing partner. Meanwhile Moo and Skeeze tell us how we get past that crowd before they come over here and crush us."

Indeed, the reporters and fans and enemies and cops and freaks are oozing closer. Like bees in a hive. The one thing distracting them is that there are still a couple of sqinks living in the field.

"Even if you run, they still might catch you," says Skeeze, talking very fast. "How about this. Moo and I stretch our stomachs and swallow you two, and then we go somewhere, and puke you up. Like they did with the Warhols. No sweat. Good as new." Skeeze floats closer, widening his jaws. "Do it now, Moo?" I have a feeling he doesn't know what he's talking about. Like a teenage kid.

"You're horrible," Carol yells at Skeeze, aiming a kick at him. "I hate you."

"Thanks for the suggestion," I politely tell Skeeze. "But, no, we'll just run."

Skeeze hangs in our faces, totally in our way. "It would be cool to try eating a person. Right, Moo?"

"How about I try it on *you*!" cries Moo, completely flipping out. The cuttlefish sqink has a temper.

She grabs Skeeze with her tentacles, and sinks her beak into him with insane fury. Skeeze is screaming, hoarse and wretched, his voice growing weaker.

I slam my elbow into Moo's body and yank Skeeze away from Moo's tentacles. The suckers peel free, one by one, *pop-pop-pop.*

Skeeze is a crooked and chewed punk garland, dripping with Moo's saliva. I cradle Skeeze in my left arm and caress him with my right hand, willing him into life.

Dealing so closely with a sqink seems to have put me into an exalted mental state. I feel energies flowing out from me and into the torn little body. As if I'm a shaman healer.

Skeeze twitches and mutters an obscenity. If he's cursing, that means he's going to live.

A thought strikes me. A few minutes ago, Skeeze told me that Moo would attack him. Skeeze knew this was coming. And yet he played it out. A true stoic, heedless of cause and effect.

The one upside here is that Skeeze's hideous screams slowed the advance of the crowd behind us. We take advantage of the lull, and hurry on again, with Skeeze in my arms.

This field had been a cheerful Easter-egg-hunt scene of users seeking sqinks. But the pickings were quickly exhausted. Even so, a few of the seekers are still bent on meeting Topper and Lady Cee. I'm still wearing that hat. But Carol and I are bent on outdistancing them.

In the distance, the parking lot is packed solid, like a rock concert crowd. A couple of them are happily carrying sqinks. But most are just arriving—and learning they're too late. Fights are breaking out.

Carol and I stretch our legs long, running as fast as we can. Moo whizzes along next to us, apologizing for having lost her temper with Skeeze. Skeeze mutters more curses. When we reach the door of the Box Farm, we want to go inside, but, at least for now, frikkin' Moo is in our way.

Helicopters are landing nearby, with huge, disorienting roars. Police and emergency vehicles are on the scene, sirens whooping and lights flashing. Reporters holler our names through bullhorns. Carol and I are the stars, the focus, the human interest.

Meanwhile cars are driving away from the Box Farm. Our crew is clearing out, bulling their way through the gathering throng. A few of our gang have sqinks, who help them through the traffic. Sqink luck!

Carol and I try to hail a ride, but none of the cars are very close to us. And with all those strangers on foot closing in—what the hell—I elbow roughly past Moo and Skeeze and drag Carol inside the Box Farm, slamming the door behind us, leaving the two sqinks outside.

"Not that they're likely to stay out there," says Carol. "You know how they are."

Anyway, the big main room of the Box Farm is deserted for now, save for our comrades Bety Byte and Smokestack. And they're on the way out, too.

Bety is a solid, level-headed woman. Muscular, maybe 180 pounds. Leather jacket, black jeans, sweatshirt, work boots, and an incongruous flapper-style hairdo with spit curls on the side.

Her girlfriend, Smokestack, is willowy, with the sides of her head shaved and a top shock of flamboyant orange hair. She's in black flannel pajamas and a brocaded bolero jacket, the jammies adorned with bright images of tumbling polyhedra.

"Harsh come-down," rasps Bety. She's holding a duffel bag.

"Box Farm Riot," says Smokestack in her husky contralto voice. "Bety and I are driving crosstown."

"Take us with you," says Carol. "Let us hide in your trunk."

"I'll give you five thousand dollars," I add, handing Bety a packet from my pocket. "If there's a checkpoint, use some to pay them off."

Bety nods. "I'm on it."

"Art theft duo flees," says Smokestack, headline style. It amuses her to talk this way.

"Car's in the garage," says Bety. "An old beater. Belonged to a drug lord. I bought it at a courthouse auction."

The big room abuts a space that serves as a garage for the higher echelons of the Box Farm clan.

"Perfect," says Carol. "High time to blow. *Quelle* zoo."

I throw a few clothes into my pigskin duffel bag, also the rest of the money. Carol adds someone's random crappy makeup from a dresser, and snags a few of Loulou's clothes. We leave our sqink raincoats on the floor, Like shedding skins.

Lilac is resting on the top shelf of our closet. I put my top hat up there for her to use as a nest. She seems to like that.

"Bring her with us?" suggests Carol.

"Leave her be," I say. We've got enough on our hands."

We make our way across the messy big room, entering the garage through a torch-cut hole in the container wall. One last car in there, a wallowing old Chevy.

"Smokestack and I have a pair of pet sqinks ourselves," says Bety. "Zig and Zag. They made themselves small for us. See those stickers on the windshield?"

Two parking-pass-type rectangles are at the bottom of the windshield. The only odd thing is that they're slightly iridescent. Zig and Zag.

"I hope they don't rat us out," I say. "Hope they don't tell the reporters and the seekers."

"Hear that, Zig and Zag?" Bety says in a strict tone. She flicks her finger against one of the rectangles. Flicks it hard. Then flicks the other. The sqinks twitch, but they stay in place.

Carol has a quick, whispered conversation with Smokestack. Telling her to do something. And when Bety opens the Chevy's trunk, Smokestack immediately reaches in and gets a zap gun. Oh oh.

Here comes the action blur. As we'd half-expected, Moo has found her way into the garage. She's hovering three or four feet above us. No sight of Skeeze. Maybe he's outside.

"Get her!" Carol yells to Smokestack.

With a swift, seamless motion, Smokestack whips her arm into the air and zaps Moo. The cuttlefish princess thuds to the floor and lies there, twitching and sizzling. Maybe not quite dead. But for sure she's not broadcasting reports.

Carol and I hop into the trunk of the dealer's heavy car. The trunk has a capacious space beneath a false floor. It's like where you'd put a spare tire, but bigger. Carol and I cram ourselves in there. Smokestack replaces the fake floor.

Bety guns the car's huge engine. The garage door creaks open. Smokestack slams the trunk and hops in the car. The Chevy rocks and humps out of the garage, smooth and low, powering slowly into the sea of people and cars. People pound on our roof and rock the car, but we keep going. We've got some of that sqink luck, thanks to Zig and Zag. But before long, oh no, here's a checkpoint.

No-nonsense cop voices. Bety gets out and opens the trunk. I see a crack of light around the edges of our false floor. Bety mumbles something—and then comes a pause. In my mind's eye, I see Bety slip a cop a sheaf of hundreds, with their hands hidden beneath the trunk's cocked lid.

No hay problema. We roll into thinning traffic. Lefts and rights, stops and starts, across the city.

"Did you have to zap Moo?" I murmur to Carol in our dark, gasoline-fumed nook.

"Safer this way," says Carol. Low, evil laugh. "And it made me glad."

6. MOTEL

Bety and Smokestack drop us at an obscure 50s motel atop a bluff by Ocean Beach. Seal Point Inn. Bety's idea, and a good one. Nobody much around to notice the weirdness of Carol and me floundering out of the trunk.

The women drive away fast, without looking back. Carol and I stand in the lot for a minute, feeling dazed. Pine trees, ocean air. Feels like we've had a very long day but, shit, it's not even two o'clock. Sunny above the pines. The luscious sound of surf pumping in.

"Get a room here?" I ask Carol.

She gives me a hard look. "Did you ever stay here with your wife?"

"Oh Jesus, Carol, give it a rest. Sibyl's dead, okay?"

Carol peers around. Looking somehow crab-like. "Do you think this might be a setup? How well do you know those two girls? They did have those two sqinks, you know."

"Bety and Smokestack are rotten to the core," I say. "Just like us. Nihilists. Enemies of the pig, the gov, the man, whatever you got."

"Okay then," says Carol. "I see a restroom. We go in there and fix our faces."

"You got it, Lady Cee."

I almost think I see something at the edge of the lot. Irregular motions in a clump of pampas grass. A squirrel? A fishing lure? A sqink? Roll with it, Oliver. You've got no choice.

The desk clerk doesn't look up as Carol and I troop in. We two go in the john, and I put my leather duffel on the sink counter. Carol gets to work. Really horrible tan liquid foundation makeup for both of us. Damping any hint of health. Carol puts on grody, greasy lipstick. I'll be sporting blue eyeshadow and heavy magic-marker-type eyebrows. Carol brushes my hair into a pouf, and she slicks hers down with water.

"You do high voice," Carol tells me. "I do low."

"Want some head?" I crow.

"In our room," she rumbles.

We manage to check in. The only available room is the party king, a double-size room on the flat roof. Like a penthouse. It features a very large patio.

"Good for wedding receptions," the clerk says.

"This isn't a wedding," I say.

The clerk shrugs. I pay cash for two nights in advance. Carol tells the man our IDs are in the car, and that our friends drove off, and that they'll be back soon. The guy doesn't care. He barely looks at us. Carol's makeup job is all but wasted.

As we walk to the elevator, the clerk calls, "Have fun." Just a reflex? Or is there mockery in his voice?

The elevator takes us to the roof. Nice view up here, with a breeze across the patio. Our big party king room is dim, with the shades and curtains drawn. It's not till we're fully inside that we notice the man sitting on the bed closest to the door.

The clerk knew.

I want to flee, but, shit, I'm so wiped and freaked that I despairingly let the room's door close behind us. I ask the man some obvious questions.

"I'm Winston Tropp," says the man. "You should know that by now. You and Carol are my knights in armor. And I'm friends with Tobin, too."

I heave a sigh. I'd been counting on a nap with Carol. Mutual trust. A mindless walk on the beach. A hamburger. The sunset. And now this? So tedious. And it's stuffy in here.

"You showing up here is bullshit," Carol boldly tells the guy. "Oliver and I are your allies? My ass."

I keep being surprised at what vulgar language this woman can use. She doesn't look the part. Chic and fit. Well-off. A woman of a certain age.

Haughtily ignoring the man on the bed, Carol strides to the other end of the long room, drawing all the drapes on her way. She swings a window wide open. Something flies in, making a hole in the screen. So, okay, we're going to have this too.

It's Skeeze the punk sqink. He must have leeched onto our escape car's underside while we were zapping Moo. Skeeze has been eavesdropping and, unlike Zig and Zag, he's been messaging people. Winston Tropp in particular. He passed the word as soon as Bety told Smokestack where we were going. And Winston got here before us.

And, yes, I glimpsed Skeeze in the leaves outside the motel. All things considered, I'm surprised how glad I am to have him here.

Skeeze levitates across the room and lands on the lap of Winston Tropp, the misguided scientist whose bulk beacon signals attracted the sqinks in the first place.

Winston fondles Skeeze, toying with the sqink. Winston looks the part of a top techie. Casual clothes of the first water. A tailor-made flannel shirt in a ravishing shade. A featherweight tweed jacket, just so. Wool trousers that somehow lack a baggy ass. Glove-skin loafers. He's tall and slender, with a sculpted, expressive face. Yadda yadda.

"Yadda yadda," Skeeze says. Maybe it's twirlware teep that lets him say the phrase at the moment I think it. Or maybe it's sqink luck.

"My dear little friend," Winston says to Skeeze. And then he turns to Carol and me. "I didn't expect those women to attack Moo," he says, sounding sad. "With a zap gun, no less. My Diana was out of sorts. She's fond of Moo. She said she was fit to be tied. In her Southern style of speech."

"Glad we managed to surprise you," says Carol. "Speaking of accents, Oliver, Winston isn't British at all. He fakes his accent. Talking Brit is a geek thing. Winston is from Iowa."

"Hardly relevant," says Winston, miffed.

Carol flops down against a mound of pillows on a bed by the windows. "Can you go away?" she asks Winston. "And leave us alone?"

"I require your aid," says Winston.

"What for?" I say, settling in beside Carol. "We're nobodies. Outsiders. Old fools." Maybe I'm overdoing it here. Fishing for a compliment.

"You undervalue yourselves," Winston kindly responds. "You and Carol are the low-down streetwise types I need. I have fierce enemies."

"All business, all the time," says Carol. "So boring."

"An outfit named Briefcase Dynamics has tendered an offer to buy Chantal Floonberry's share of my intellectual property," continues Winston. "Chantal's share is, sadly, seventy percent. I agreed to an absurd contract with Chantal when I secured her backing. But it won't do for a company with a silly name to own seventy percent of me."

"And now I'm supposed to ask you about Briefcase Dynamics," I say with a sigh.

"A dummy corporation, distended with Russian mafia cash," says Winston. "With a fake office near Monterey. Captained by one Bengt Oberg. I seek to blight Bengt's harvest."

"And why do people want your intellectual property?" I ask.

"Have you just emerged from a coma? We've executed the strongest publicity gambits since the Pyramid of Giza.

That scene with the sqinks gobbling the Warhols? The Sqink Sponsor Fair riot?"

"Those were my ideas," puts in Carol. "Oliver—he just follows me around."

I let that ride. Why slam a saint of scam? Surely Carol is on my side. Even if she made a side deal with Winston and the sqinks—before she ever met me. Setting these delicate issues aside, there remains one question.

"What's your product supposed to be," I ask Winston. "What do you think you'll be selling? What's your intellectual property?"

"I'll sell sqinks," says Winston. "Like the sqink fair was supposed to be about."

"The sqinks do what they like," I say. "No way you can *sell* them. Is your head so far up your ass that you don't realize that?"

"Ah me," says Winston. "I'm hearing the vulgarity of a delusional flimflam man—the words of an unpublishable author."

"I write made-up bullshit, yes," I allow. "Taking great pains to make it logically consistent. But for this new scam that we're living in, I don't need logic. It's all true."

"I'm not sure we can accept Winston on our team at all," says Carol, flipping the snobbery. "He's deeply uncool." Carol is good at social engineering, that is, good at jiving people.

To put our man further off balance, I wander into a meaningless Irish priest routine. Such moves are perhaps an aspect of my growing senility.

"So, you want to be a-joinin Topper and Lady Cee?" I say in a brogue. "A rum lot. One fella died whilst mounting a sign for them. A construct of uncooked sourdough bread. Meant to swell in the mornin sun. But it had too much yeast." I sadly shake my head. "Strangled the lad."

"Stop," says Carol, cutting me off. "Don't embarrass me." She changes the subject. "Do you think this motel has room service?"

"Hardly likely," says Winston Tropp. "What might the lady require?"

"Eats," Carol flatly says. "And no more biz talk."

"We're fried," I chime in.

For the first time, Winston smiles. "Fried calamari?"

"Not for me," says Carol. "Unless we fry that big sqink Moo."

"Don't mock Moo," says Winston Tropp. "She's extraordinary." The touch of respect makes me like Winston better. He loves that bulging cuttle as much as I do.

"Sushi," suggests Carol. "California rolls with real crab."

"Maguro, avocado, unagi, and salmon," I add. "And some udon."

"Ice cream," puts in Skeeze. "And maple syrup."

"Do sqinks really and truly eat?" I ask, my curiosity piqued. "I know they were accepting food offerings, but—"

"We like sweets," says Skeeze. "That's the only Earth food we truly crave. Those wholesome foods you eat—we have only an anthropological interest in them. But feed us sweets."

"Is it that your metabolism is—" I begin, and then I catch myself. "Don't tell me more, Skeeze. I'm putting a temporary freeze on dialog-based exposition."

"Ah, a writer's wit," goes Carol.

"As for *our* food," says Winston, our out-of-it high-finance techie guru. "I believe there exists a service where one sends a message, and a person delivers the meal."

"Yadda yadda," says Carol. "Remember that Oliver and I are hiding out. At least we *imagine* we're hiding out. But I suppose that if one sqink knows something, all the others do. How many sqinks are left?"

"Nine, including Princess Moo," says Winston, stubbornly ploughing on with more exposition.

"What makes her a princess?" Carol asks.

"She really is a princess on Sqinkland. And her mother, Mumper, is the evil Queen. Moo is the one who noticed my bulk beacon signal. She tracked it to me. Wriggled a wormhole from Sqinkland to Earth. Emerged in the Box Farm field. Brought along nine sqinks, and Doink is dead."

"And how do you know all this?" I ask.

"Moo came to my lab, which is also where I live. I'm exceedingly keen on partnering with Moo. And, as it happens, Moo gets along with my life-long love, Diana."

"Yes, believe it or not, this dry stick Winston has a saucy woman," interrupts Carol. "Diana is a stitch. I know her from high school. Tell Oliver about her, Winston."

Winston gives Carol a look. He can't keep up with her changes. "Enough of this japery." He holds up a hand, declining further inquiries.

"Order that food," Carol tells Skeeze the sqink. "Pay with ChumpChange."

"I'll take a nap while it's on the way," I say. "I'm a hundred years old."

"I'm with you," says Carol. That simple phrase makes me happy.

As we settle into the pillowed bed, Carol can't resist voicing a consumer advisory. "Topper and Lady Cee now in casual embrace, rated G."

I glance over at Skeeze. Instead of doing anything, the punk sqink is floating by a window, savoring the breeze. I goad him. "Message for that food, won't you?"

"Already did," says Skeeze. "So shut your crack."

Rudeness abounds. Carol and I drift off into a nap.

When we wake, the sun is closer to the horizon. No idea what time it is. This is like a holiday weekend, a stretch when clocks don't matter.

Winston has set food on a table, and he's eaten his share. He's in an armchair, mulling things over, thinking genius-type thoughts.

Someone's at the patio's screen door. Bumping against it like a soft fist. I see a bulging outline.

"Enter the princess," says Winston Tropp. "Let her in, Oliver."

And of course it's Moo.

"We'll never get rid of her," groans Carol.

"No hard feelings," says Moo, drifting over to us and tickling Carol's cheeks with her tentacles. "Kiss and make up?"

Despite herself, Carol has to laugh. "Just remember it was Smokestack who shot you with the zap gun, not me."

"Oh, I found the experience refreshing," Moo calmly says. "And now I'm glad I'm here to catch up."

"You're really not so bad, are you?" says Carol.

"I'm supreme," says Moo. "I'm a supersqink. Wait till I show you how far I can stretch a tentacle. Even Winston doesn't know about this move. Skeeze tells me that we want to discourage an investor?"

"This Bengt Oberg wants a controlling interest in my affairs," says Winston. "All of them. Remember that I founded the twirlware industry. And this attracts Oberg. But the word is out: my new discovery could be my greatest. The bulk beacon. That robber Oberg, that nit, that lowlife—he wants to use the bulk beacon for, spare us good lord, faster upload speeds. And he'd block any leakage of my signals into the bulk at large. The leakage being, one understands, the whole purpose of my bulk beacon, which is meant to *view* the bulk. In the manner of radar pings. Obers would ruin it."

"Help them out, Oliver," says Carol. "Spin a scenario for attacking Obert. One of your bonkers, ramshackle, mentally ill plots."

"Well—what kind of guy is this Oberg?"

"Youthful," says Winston. "What you might call a go-getter. A business wonk. Scandinavian. Doesn't understand California. Imagines it's a fitness club. He tones up by paddling a board in Monterey Bay."

A delicious plot pops into my head.

"Great white shark!" I exclaim. "Of course. I'm sure Bengt does his paddling near dusk. An athlete's romance with himself. We hit him right now. This minute."

"How do we get to Monterey?" protests Carol. "How do we rope in a shark?"

I raise my index finger, like Socrates making a philosophical point. "If a man says something in a forest, and no woman hears him, is he still wrong?"

"Good one," goes Moo, as if to take my side against Carol.

"I wish I had that zap gun again right now, Moo," says Carol, never one to hold back.

Genius that he is, Winston focuses on my plan. "Can you reach as far as Monterey?" he asks Moo. "Can you summon a shark?"

"Just watch!" says Moo in a satisfied tone. "I'll stretch a tentacle. How does that work? Scale flip. Hard but easy. Like all great ideas. Ready to watch? Let's go on the veranda. I'll do it slow, so you get the details."

So, we follow Moo outside. Rippling waves of color play across her back. She grows to the size of a car, like a blimp being readied for launch.

"Placing your call," says Moo in a nasal tone.

And then, *whoops*, it's as if the universe turns inside out. Instead of being *outside* of Moo, now we're *inside* of Moo— and so is the rest of the world. Somehow, Moo's outer skin is curved around like a room, and we're all inside that room. And with Moo's innards *outside* the room.

I doubt if anyone but me is understanding this. They're just be seeing shapes and colors. But as an SF writer, I'm pretty quick on the uptake. And it helps that I used to teach math.

The size scales have been switched. Moo's guts are far, but the whole rest of the world is near. Think of Moo as a radius-one sphere around the origin. She swapped the inside with the outside. Each point at distance R was traded with a point at distance 1/R. The points near the origin became points out towards infinity. It's hard but easy.

I'm inside an oval chamber with Moo-skin wallpaper, and with a wad of Moo-tenacles in here too. Moo's two eyes are disks on the inner Moo-wall. Like creepy mirrors.

A *lot* of other stuff is in here with me. Basically, everything except Moo's guts. Even the stars and the Sun and the Moon; they're squeezed into the center of my Moo-room. I feel like I could pretty much touch any of them. This is how Moo "stretches a tentacle."

Slanting away from me is a shape like a couch. It's the coast of California, with a dent in it, and the dent is little old Monterey Bay. I lean over it like a weird wizard, and Moo cranks up the strength of my eyes.

Yes, my long-distance call is going through. I see pale Bengt Oberg on his de-luxe lacquered maple-wood board, energetically wielding his double paddle. Gliding across the gilded ripples of Monterey Bay. A seal swims near him.

"Bring in the shark," I say, assuming that the powerful Moo can do this. "We need the shark."

I hear a sound like a chant. Moo's voice, emerging from the tip of a hundred-and-twenty-mile tentacle. "*Here, sharkie, come sharkie, sharkie bite Bengt's seal.*"

Moo uses her tentacle like a feeler, terribly long and skinny. She pinpoints our target with her trembling tip.

"Go," says Moo.

An upward surge of water explodes. Toothy jaws snap twice: first beheading the seal, and then snapping Bengt's board in two. As intended, Bengt himself escapes. He's dog-paddling in the bloody water. He's sobbing. I lean very, very, very close to him, my lips pursed into a slender horn, and I speak into his ear.

"Don't buy Winston Tropp."

And then, *whoops* again, my image of Moo flips right-side-out, and I'm fully on our motel's roof-top patio, having a convivial time with my friends, and Moo has deflated to her own right size. The tentacle-stretch was a success.

"Smashing!" exults Winston. "Aces. Top shelf."

"When I do a tentacle stretch, people don't notice all the steps," says Moo."

"Can the other sqinks do things like this? I ask.

"Not exactly," says Moo. "But they can make a pair of small, nearby objects exchange positions. And that's important."

"What do you mean by *small*," asks Carol.

"The size of your *brain*," says Moo, sounding mean.

Red flag. But I get back to discussing the business plan. Trying to act like a grown-up,

"Set up a three-way call with you and Bengt and Chantal Floonberry," I tell Winston. "Before Bengt's fear fades. Make sure everyone understands that Bengt's purchase is cancelled. Tell Chantal Floonberry that you're buying a controlling share."

"But—" says Winston.

"Call me if Chantal makes trouble," I chuckle. "We'll find a way."

"Oliver and I are *closers*," adds Carol, getting in on it.

But—" says Winston.

"You'll have the buy-out money," says Moo. "Tomorrow the market will heave. Bigtime. You'll knife in and out. Follow your instincts. You'll have sqink luck."

"Brilliant," goes Winston. "And I'll keep Tobin in the loop, too. He understands business."

Winston, Moo, and Skeeze leave, deep in conversation.

7. Wormhole

Carol and I enjoy a walk on the bluffs, and drink a juice, not talking too much, not quite ready to face the elephant. When we get back, it's night, and we have the room to ourselves. We go on the patio to enjoy the view of the lights down along the coast and the bright half-moon overhead.

"Do you think the moon looks special?" says Carol.

"How do you mean?"

"To me, it looks—shinier. And when the moon looks shiny, it means I'm in love. I hoped—I hoped it might look that way to you."

"I keep having this feeling that you're jiving me," I say. "It's time for The Conversation."

Carol sighs. We go into the room and sit next to each other on the bed, pillows behind our backs, leaning against the wall. Wind in the trees outside, rumbling of the surf, moonlight in the window frame.

"The sqinks say you're in with them," I finally say. "And that you know Winston's partner Diana from high school. I'm thinking Winston paid you to come to that Box Farm party. To make me an agent for Winston and Moo." I'm being calm and logical, but now my voice catches. "I've been alone so long, Carol. I thought we could be happy. But—"

"Don't, Oliver," says Carol, leaning close to me. She wants to kiss me, but I push her away.

"You're a rat," I say.

"Not anymore," says Carol. "I'm for you now, Oliver."

It's nice to hear that, but it's not enough. "Details," I say. "And no more lies."

Carol takes a deep breath. "Okay, yes, I was paid to meet you. And, yes, it was Diana who found me. San Francisco can be a small town. Diana came to my house and told me how she and Winston had met Moo. I didn't understand at all what she was talking about. Like—Moo, the flying cuttlefish showed up in their room one night, hanging over their bed. And Diana tells me that Moo wants me to help with a project. And I'm, like, you're nuts, Diana."

I'm so upset about all the treachery that I'm dabbing my eyes with a corner of the sheet—but I have to smile, imagining that conversation.

Carol continues. "So, we're in my cabin up near Summit Road, and Diana hands me a thousand dollars in cash, and that gets my attention, and I let her keep talking. The flying cuttlefish is named Moo, and Moo wants to do something involving the Box Farm field."

"A huge alien invasion, do you think?" I ask. "Not sure about Moo."

"I don't trust her either," says Carol. "Moo's line is that the sqinks who move in with humans are like foreign exchange students."

"Yeah, I've heard that line too," I say. "Sounds pretty harmless. Maybe there's more."

"Right," says Carol. "Probably I shouldn't be helping the sqinks at all."

"But they paid you, so you went along," I say. "And later, you even pretended to be arguing with Moo. For my benefit. Little sneak. But back up—what's Winston's angle?"

"Well, mainly he wanted to find out about aliens in the bulk. And his bulk beacon worked—a little better than he expected. He didn't realize the aliens would follow the signal and show up here. Seems like Moo has drilled herself a tunnel in the field by the Box Farm. Skeeze was telling us about it."

"Right. And Skeeze told us about Moo hovering over Winston's bed. But how does this connect to you and me?"

"After Winston hears about Moo's tunnel, he hires some private detectives to check out the Box Farm scene. And the gumshoes tell Winston about you, and that you're living there, and that you're semi-famous, so Winston decides to draw you in. Like for eventual promo about the sqinks."

"Me?" I modestly say. "I'm nobody."

"Hey, you're on Wikipedia. And the detective tells Winston how Loulou walks along the bay every morning. So, Moo can plant some sqinks, and Loulou meets them, and that's a start."

"I don't get it."

"Loulou is my daughter, and I'm a friend of Winston's partner Diana, and I'm single, and I'm the right age for you. So, we get Loulou to invite me to a party at the Box Farm, and I meet you—ta da!"

So many layers of weirdness, and coincidence, and jive. With a non-zero possibility of utter catastrophe. Nothing is real. I throw on a sweater and go out to the patio, looking at the night and the fog, with the occasional dim pinprick of a star. It always makes me glad to see the sky. Everything rolling along, no matter how screwed up we humans are.

In the quiet, I write a couple of pages in my head. For the novel that's happening around me. So much to narrate! Such wild and crazy … fun?

I hear Carol come out, softly singing, her vibrant voice rising into the pines, and perhaps to the moon. She stands in front of me and gives me a full-body hug. I'm glad. She puts her face against my chest and talks some more.

"Okay, yes, I helped them at the start, Oliver, but probably it all would have happened anyway. And the key point is that, *no*, I'm not working for them anymore, not taking any orders, and I'm completely on your side. I've seen the error of my devious ways."

"Why?"

"Because now I'm in love with you?"

Well, there is that. And I feel the same way. With song and moonlight, Carol leads me back inside and between the sheets. We laugh about it all, and make love, and it's wonderful, and we have a good night's sleep.

In the morning, we're still alone in our king party room. The rain is gone, and the sky is a blue dome, alive with light. I wake first, and I get in half an hour of writing. The process is good for me; it helps me get a handle on my increasingly weird scene.

Then Carol wakes, and that's even better. After having it out last night, we're feeling friendly, and—god knows why—we even feel optimistic. We take it easy, looking out at the ocean, nibbling from the leftover food, wondering what's in the cards, but not quite wanting to know. More singing from Carol, happy as a bird in the morning light.

Eventually, we flip on the audio news. It's 9 am. The world's gone wild.

The New York stock market has peaked and crashed three times since it opened at 6:30 am California time. Utter chaos. The feds have closed the markets for today, and maybe for longer. Meanwhile, the big-time players have raked off their winnings.

My small part helped spark the surge—I get a mention at least once, as a has-been SF writer living in a group squat near the sqink zone. And somehow they know I'm currently using twirlware to write a transreal novel about my scene.

Winston's nimble doings are a sidelight of the financial news. Known for his work in introducing twirlware and for his invention of the experimental bulk beacon, he has incorporated a project called Sqink Inq. He scored big in this morning's market gyrations, and bought a controlling share of Sqink Inq from his original backer, Chantal Floonberry. Seventy percent.

In other sqink-related stories, two people died yesterday at *Topper and Lady Cee's Sqink Fair*. Most of the violence was caused by disputes over the right to form relationships with the seven or eight sqinks who were present.

The precise nature of the sqinks remains unclear. Supposedly, they bring luck—unless you're beaten to death while trying to get one.

Due to sqink luck, all lotteries and casino games have been suspended along with the markets.

Lightening the mood, the newscaster reads a joking run-through of possible sqink luck results.

Woman finds estranged husband, finalizes her divorce with him, marries his intended.

Missing child finds missing family in missing car under missing freeway ramp.

Oliver Strunk finds a plot for his transreal novel.

Surf god bites hot dog.

Spilled ink reveals face of ink spiller.

And now a non-fictional human-interest story. A *phthisic*, that is, a tubercular man—he ran a mile. Thanks to sqink luck.

Carol and I look at each other. Synchronistic that a random news story would use a random weird word that Tobin said? Or did he feed the story to the station? We're riding a rising tide.

Meanwhile, the newscaster is hung up on the phthisic story. The man's mother brought him to yesterday's sqink fair, and the sqink spent a night with the man in a bed at the Box Farm compound. And this morning, the phthisic ran a mile along the thin, dirty beach by the Bay.

"That bed they shared, I bet it was yours," Carol tells me.

"*Ack.*"

"Sqink luck will disinfect it," says Carol. "Or maybe we buy ourselves a new bed. A bigger one."

"You're already shopping for furniture?" I ask. 'You move fast."

"I feel I've known you a month," says Carol. "This is more excitement than I've had in my whole entire life."

"Me too," I say. "Especially the parts where we make love."

"Dear boy."

The news continues. Up until last week, the ownership of the Box Farm field was murky, with claims by the Navy, a junkyard, a Superfund developer, and the City of San Francisco. But today it was revealed that four days ago, Winston Tropp arranged settlements for all four claims—and acquired a clear title to the property, completely on his own. A big asset for his new Sqink Inq.

Early this morning, shortly after midnight, a fence was constructed around a portion of the Box Farm field. Carried out with remarkable speed. Speculation that the sqinks themselves did the work.

The gates to the fence are guarded by members of the Box Farm commune—or by sqinks. Aerial views of the area are blurred.

"And now for some background," continues the newscaster. "Who *is* Winston Tropp?

Before Carol and I can listen to this, a distraction arrives, in the form of Moo, Skeeze, Xavier, and Winston Tropp. Also, a woman is holding Winston's hand. She's chic, lively, and very California. A bad girl.

"My partner, Diana," says Winston, doing an introduction routine. "Diana, meet my lower companions, Carol Cee and Oliver Strunk. Useful in a pinch."

"You can drop the act," says Carol. "Oliver knows."

"My high school pal," says Diana, smiling at Carol. "Let all be told. Maybe Carol and I can help make this fun. Most of Winston's friends are stumbling goons. Whose side are *you* on, Oliver?"

"How are there sides?" I say. "I don't even know what's happening."

"Chin up, old top," goes Winston. "It's only the first chukker." As if he grew up playing polo in Iowa.

So, we talk things out for a while, and everyone's pretty much okay with where we're at. Maybe *okay* is too mellow a word. But we want to keep it bouncing. We're having too much fun to stop. Maybe *fun* isn't the right word either.

"What's the story on that Chantal Floonberry?" I ask Diana. "What's she like?"

"Tough cookie," says Diana. "Even older than us. Like beef jerky. A lady who lunches … on human remains. I guess you know about Winston buying himself out from under her company. Part of the way. And Winston named his new company Sqink Inq? So silly."

"Droll," says Winston. "Not silly. The name has swagger. Draws the eye."

"Tell me one more time what Sqink Inq is going to sell?" I say.

"As I already told you, I might run something like a dating app," says Winston. "If, that is, the sqink supply grows. And if the sqinks cooperate. People would pay Sqink Inq for the link-up service."

"Instead of having to fight through a riot in the Box Farm field," says Carol.

"And you said you might be licensing out the bulk beacon patent, too?"

Winston makes an ambiguous gesture. "Still pondering that. I might disable my bulk beacon. Not sure that building it was prudent."

"So?" says Diana.

"Don't really want to turn her off," says Winston. "I like the bulk beacon. She's alive, you know. I call her AntnA. A cute palindrome? I enjoy the sound of her signal—*thub thub thub thub thub thub*."

"Can't say as I can ever hear that," Diana tartly says.

"You don't know how to listen," says Winston.

Carol and I shake our heads, starting to wonder about our man Winston.

"Hearing the *thub* is a skill you acquire," says Winston. "You'll learn when you're in the bulk. Like hearing the breaking waves when you're underwater."

"I'll listen for it," I say reassuringly. "If I ever happen to go down there."

Carol gets a fresh thread of conversation going. "What's up with that field by the Box Farm?" she asks.

"It's where Moo hid her wormhole. And now the sqinks have stretched that plot of land to make it bigger. Diana and I are about to tour it."

Noise outside. Reporters.

"A bullhorn in the wilderness," I say.

"Goobs been chawing our butts all morning," says Diana.

"I've always loved how you talk," Carol says to Diana, setting her up for a punch line. "Are y'all from the South?"

"South San Francisco, darlin'. There's this one block of hippie rednecks."

"Carol and I are coming with you to see the tunnel," I tell Winston. "Can Moo carry us all?"

"Moo can do," says Diana. "She flies fast."

We get our stuff, close the patio door, climb onto Moo's back, let her throw some tentacles over us, and—*whee*! We're beside an entrance to the new compound on the Box House field. It looks way different in there.

"A magic forest," says Carol.

Bety Byte and Smokestack are guarding the gate. That is to say, their sqinks are guarding. Each of the women has a bad-ass little sqink perched on her shoulder. The sqinks are new to me. Shaped like donuts, just now, one made of copper, the other made of zinc. I get a sense they can zap very hard. They put me in mind of a Van de Graff generator I saw at my high-school science fair, sixty-five years ago.

"Yo, Oliver!" says Bety. "You made it! Teamed up with Skeeze, huh? These are our sqink buddies, Zig and Zag? They were stickers on my Chevy's windshield, remember?"

"Did you know the motel was a trap?" Carol asks Bety and Smokestack straight up. "Did Zig and Zag squeal?"

"Wasn't them," says Smokestack. "It was Skeeze. He was riding underneath our car. Tunneled up like gopher, I guess. We saw him dart out when we got to the motel. We were worried. But we drove off. Figured you'd find a way to work it out."

"Oh, thanks," I say. "Winston Tropp was waiting in our room."

"The man of the hour," says Bety. "Are you guys going into the glen?"

"Like a new Garden of Eden," says Diana. "Adam, Eve, the snake, and the angry Lord."

"Forget that bullshit," says Bety. "This Eden is more like god threw a hundred gallons of paint against the side of a barn. *Splat*. Action painting is synchronicity."

Moo doesn't take the bait. Just floats there.

"Bety and I are going in with you," says Smokestack. "We don't want to miss this. Don't want to be fascist guards."

"Fine," says Moo. "But maybe we leave your shooter-sqinks to guard the gate. Just for now. Right, Zig and Zag?"

Winston is uneasy about the sqinks as guards. "They're rather diminutive," he says. "One doesn't want reporters streaming in."

"You know damn well that sqinks can shape-shift," says Moo. "Scale is just another axis in the bulk. Let me show you what Zig and Zag can do. Our twin sqinks."

"Twins," says Carol. "How does that happen with sqinks?"

"We reproduce by pinching off buds," says Moo. "Normally, each bud is a little different. But for these two, I made one bud and then split that bud in half. Twin power"

"Could you say that one of them came first?" asks Carol.

"They don't like for people to ask that," says Bety, who knows Zig and Zag better than we do.

As if to confirm Bety's remark, the twins rise up like cobras, perhaps to threaten Carol. They take on different shapes. Zig is a four-foot-tall stack of copper and zinc doughnuts, with a sharp point on the top. Zag is a wireframe tube, hovering near Zig. The sketchy tube is, in effect, the muzzle of a particle-beam gun.

Zig pops small, snapping sparks from her sharp tip. Zag draws the sparks into her tubular body, which begins to glow.

"Go!" says Moo, who knows the drill.

Zag releases her stored energy—which takes the form of a plasma beam directed at the soil next to Carol's feet.

"So never mind who came first!" cries Carol, backing off. "Cancel my question!"

The dirt is too damp to catch fire, but an impressive bank of smoke rolls forth from the targeted spot—the dirt is, in fact, melting like lava. Overhead, a news helicopter is near, broadcasting stupid-ass voices through the customary bullhorn. Zag angles herself so that the killer particle-beam flows close enough to the chopper's windshield to shatter it. With an aggrieved racket, the copter heels to one side and flies away.

"We can blast way harder than that," Zig tells me. "Twin power. We can go thermonuclear on your ass."

"No need for that just now," I caution.

"Enter Eden," says Carol, raising her arms. "Lead us, my dear Moo." So Carol, Winston, Diana, Bety Byte, Smokestack, and I follow Moo in.

"Fabulous," says Carol, admiring the lush, sun-dappled glen. "Our native California trees: buckeyes, willows, laurels, and oaks. Giganticized. A bayside fantasy grove."

"The space is stretched so much in here that I can't see the other side," I say.

A fresh breeze rustles the leaves. We hear the chatter of squirrels. Birds in here too, plenty of them, fluttering about, perching on branches: humming birds, nuthatches, and jays. Skeeze roots in the dirt, then engages a squirrel in a playful tussle.

"We're going to my wormhole," Moo tells us. "It's in the middle of this park."

The Bay feels very far away. Our feet are silent on the forest floor. Streams babble across our path. We edge around a wet spot. I see rabbits and a deer. Woodpeckers rat-tat-tat on the taller trees. Even a few redwoods in here. Moo went all out.

Our group has spread out. Smokestack and Bety Byte have gone off in some completely different direction. Carol and I are holding hands, with Moo just a bit ahead of us. Skeeze flies at Moo's side, orbiting her. Winston and Diana lag behind. He's rapt; she's cracking nervous jokes. The primeval forest is all around.

Carol is focused on the birds, and she's singing along with them, improvising phrases as she goes. Things a bird might say, or things that *Carol* might say if she wasn't shy, not that she's shy once you know her. It's wonderful to hear her sing.

"The world is beautiful," I say to Carol. "The world is so beautiful." I pause, then tell her the rest, which I probably shouldn't. "That was one of the last things Sybil said to me. Our last time walking outdoors. The way she said it—I think

about what it meant. She was wistful that her life was ending. Grateful for what she'd had. Happy with the moment."

"You haven't said much about Sybil," Carol carefully says.

"I don't want to scare you off."

"Just remember that I'm not going to be her."

"Look," I say, forcing a smile. "Sybil and I were married
for fifty-five years. I'm okay with meeting someone *new*. Seriously. You don't have to be like her at all. I'm glad to have you.
A new life, a new love."

Carol smiles.

Zig and Zag cruise by, singing in harmony. They still have
the forms of, respectively, a stack of metal doughnuts, and a
sculpture made of chicken wire. Skeeze darts up to them, sings
a few phrases with them, and returns to Moo.

"They don't want to be gate guards at all," says Skeeze.
"They want to be next to the tunnel. *That's* the spot to guard,
right?"

"Nobody obeys me," says Moo with a sigh. "I'll signal
Xavier and Flubsy to take their place."

Carol, who has been echoing the birdsongs, switches to
speech. "This forest is so beautiful. It makes me think you
sqinks must be good."

Up ahead shines a light, rising from the ground. It's not
cozy; it's *hard* light. More like supernatural rays than like a
candle. Clearly this is the mouth of Moo's tunnel.

"Too spooky," cries Diana from behind us. She's not laughing at all. "I warned you, Winston. You should have said *no*
when that damn cuttlefish Moo showed up. We're getting
the fuck out of here."

Of course, Winston wants to press on. But Diana won't let
up. She drags him back toward the gate, telling him he can get
her out of here, and then come back in. Winston worries that
this moment might be a one-shot chance. But Diana won't
let up. Their quarreling voices fade.

Meanwhile, we've walked to the edge of the hole.

"What's the light?" Carol asks Moo.

"It's okay," says Moo. "The bulk air glows where it meets your air. Inside the bulk, it's fairly dark."

"The tunnel goes straight down?" I uneasily ask.

"It's like a funnel up here, and then it gets narrow like a tunnel to the bulk, and then it opens up. Sort of like an hourglass. It leads to a spot near our Sqinkland. That's where we're going."

"But—" I begin.

Moo makes a sound like a laugh. "Too late to cry about it. You're sliding."

Um, yes, the slope beneath us is unstable dirt and gravel, and no matter how we churn our legs, we keep moving down. Like we're on the sand inside an hourglass.

"A sapling is sliding with us," says Carol. "Grab it!"

The little tree isn't within my reach, but hooray for Carol! She's latched onto it. Stretching her utmost, she grabs me with her other hand.

But … the spindly laurel tree is sliding with the dirt and gravel, sliding like us. For a moment, the tree comes to a halt. We're at the point where the funnel becomes a well shaft, a twenty-foot-wide vertical tube with gleaming walls, arrowing into the bulk, with darkness ahead.

8. SQINKLAND

Moo and Skeeze are down there in the bright/dark tunnel, excitedly circling. Tiny silhouettes riding the ambient energies, insect surfers on choppy waves, tediously vivacious.

Another giant, imaginary Acme safe plummets from the sky and bonks me on the head. Or, putting it differently, that skinny laurel sapling that we're hanging onto—it snaps.

Carol and I are falling down into the glow, following in Moo's and Skeeze's wake. We're terribly afraid and holding each other tight.

"Into the light, my darling," Carol solemnly says. "Go peacefully into the light." Like, she's my death coach?

"Not yet," I say. "Not yet."

"I'll tell you one last time," goes Carol. "I'm really, really sorry I scammed you."

"Oh, forget it," I say. "Things are turning out so wonderfully well."

"Right," goes Carol, getting into my gallows mood. "We're falling into another reality, never to return."

"But, yea, the sacred sqinks shall provide."

We're joking to keep our spirits up, but it's not really working. My thoughts take on a bizarre cast. As if I'm in a horror movie nearing its grisly climax. Carol is a zombie; my hands are a monster's claws. Sheets of electricity envelop us; our hairs stand on end.

Moo and Skeeze have disappeared through the neck of the wormhole and into the dark. We're next. Doom.

It happens, and—the darkness is mellow, at least in a certain sense of that word. We were in hell, and now we're in a velvet black sky. Black, save for the bright mouth of the wormhole above us. We have no real power to direct our motions; presumably we're riding Moo's wake.

An odd, persistent sound fills my ears and resonates in my chest.

thub thub thub

I've entirely lost sight of Skeeze and Moo. Carol remains at my side because we're holding hands.

Amid the darkness, something is coming into focus. A city, far below, as if we're landing in a plane. Even though the sky is dark, and there's no sun, the city is lit. As if it glows from within. It resembles San Francisco.

Hard to see details from this high. The action on the streets and sidewalks down there—indecipherable. And, as I say, it's a very long way down. And we're *not* actually in an airplane. We're free-falling, with the wind whistling ever faster.

"Over there!" cries Carol, pointing. "A ramp!"

We arch our bodies, flexing against the rush of air. The air has a weird feel, as if it's lumpy, like a boba drink. The greater the turbulence, the bumpier the air. Later, I'll hear a sqink claim the effect is caused by insubstantial sqinks who live in the atmosphere's air currents … but you never know. Sqinks say all kinds of things.

Carol and I flounder our way to the ramp. It's slick, and it runs way far down to the ground. With great heaving and grunting, we get ourselves onto it. And, how handy, there's a long, long banister next to the ramp. We catch hold of the railing and sit up, sliding downhill all the while, with Carol in front.

My god, this is the world's longest sliding board, very slippery, but we maintain our balance, slowing ourselves by grasping the handrail. Sliding toward the ground, glad we're alive, and yelling "*Wheeee!*"

We land with a jolt. The *thubs* have faded away. We're beside a bench on a sidewalk. Looks like a bizarro Mission Street. At this moment, the roads and sidewalks are filled with—solid blurs. Like contrails, or like the afterimages of moving hands, or like long-exposure photos. In our state of frozen time, we hear no sounds. Eerie.

And now a shift. The air fills with noise, the congealed traffic resolves into cars, the sidewalk meat-tubes turn into people, and the long banister and the sliding board become— Skeeze and Moo! Laughing at us. The ramp was a time-series of Moo backs; the railing a smear of Skeezes.

"You were angled in time," says Moo. "Easy to get that way in Sqinkland. Nothing stops you from slanting."

I turn my head to look around and, damn, I'm once again angled in time? The street is back to being a silent lattice of spacetime trails. Thank god my brave, smart Carol is still with me. Holding hands, and very uncertain, we two take a few steps down the sidewalk.

I see the frozen front side of a woman in a green shirt, quite nearby. Behind her is a stream of her bodies, with the scalloped arcs of her swinging arms and striding legs. The side of the woman's face is a swath of cheek that's a hundred feet long. I notice a spot in the sequence where the woman opened her mouth, revealing tooth trails, like bars of enamel, framed in snaky ropes of lip.

A slight twitch of my head, and the woman in the green shirt is actively walking toward us, ten feet away. She's smiling as if she knows who we are.

Now it's Carol who's out of synch with me. She's a spacetime mass, about a thousand kilograms, a worm woman with her tail angling into the sky. I touch the stiff sheet of her cheek. Her tilted-time body is fixed in place. I can't budge it. Can't change the past.

But then Carol's timeline swings back to match mine, and she's not a trail, and her cheek is soft. We're parallel. Frightened, excited, and persistently holding hands.

Moo hovers by the bench where we started, "Come here," she burbles.

Crouching a little, moving carefully, Carol and I creep to the bench and sit. The woman in the green shirt takes a seat beside us. She has a hard, symmetric face. A bob of black hair. The scent of a healthy, active person. She looks calm and ruthless. Accustomed to giving orders. Her eyes are dark, and they don't reflect light. No glints. No way to know what she's thinking.

"Welcome, Topper and Lady Cee," says she. "I am Mumper." She chuckles. "Very easy to arrange meetings in Sqinkland. We're all in synch."

"Not many people call me Topper," I say. "I do have a top hat, but I left it on a shelf in my closet in the Box Farm. With Lilac the sqink sitting in it."

"I know," says Mumper. "Meanwhile, I have a mission for you two. You are potential players in a great epic. Hard to be sure. We sqinks have trouble with thinking ahead. That's one reason we enjoy you planet-dwellers. You're refreshingly if-then."

"Just a reminder," Moo says to Carol and me. "Mumper is my mother. She's Queen and I'm Princess. All the other sqinks serve us."

"Serve to a limited extent," says Mumper. "With some debate about our missions to Stok-stok and to Earth."

"It's good for a bulk land to connect to a planet," says Moo. "Especially to an inhabited planet like Earth. I heard Winston's *thub thub*, and I drilled my way in."

"What do you guys to do when you visit a new world?" Carol asks. "I've heard different things."

Mumper lets her head melt into a bunch of tentacles, like the ones on Moo's face, but more of them. She writhes the hundred arms, making jabbing motions in the air. And then the tentacles pull together, sculpting the strong cruel face of before.

"Get it?" says Mumper.

"No," I say. "Not at all."

"Partnerships," says Mumper. "Pairing up with planets."

"Moo drills a tunnel and they send in hordes of sqinks," says Skeeze. "Mumper does bad things, but these days Moo is for doing good. Moo doesn't want Mumper to run Earth. Earth should be like an ecological park. With Moo in charge."

"Moo is too young to run a planet," says the impatient Mumper. "All new planets belong to me, de facto and de jure. And as for you, smart-mouth runt Skeeze—"

Mumper scowls as she talks, and her eyes seem even deader than before. She lengthens a finger into another tentacle. The tip sizzles, sparks and—"

"Don't kill Skeeze!" cries Moo. She interposes herself between Mumper and the punk black-gray-white sqink. "Skeeze is my prize assistant. Yes, he talks too much, and once in a while I try to kill him, but I'm fond of him. Let him be!"

Another spacetime lock-up hits Carol and me. Mumper's frozen-time tentacle is stretched past Moo, and toward where Skeeze *was*, but Skeeze's body trail is a lofty arc, with its end-point very far from Mumper's zappy tip. Skeeze has taken a powder, so to say.

Our timeflow thaws again. Carol elbows me. Skeeze is jeering at Mumper from way up high. Too far for a voice to carry, but twirlware teep works here. Skeeze is calling Mumper every name in the book, or, rather, an alphabetical sampling of the names in the book. Which book? The book you're reading. And I'm the one who wrote it.

"A-hole, butt-head, crap-hound, dumbbell, earthworm, fumbler, grubber, halfwit, idiot, jiller, killjoy, loser, madwoman, numb-buns, ogress, pig, quack, ragamuffin, stink-bomb, turd, ugly-wugly, vermin, wretch, xenophobe, yak-brain, zero!"

With an aggrieved growl, Mumper sends a goodly part of her bodymass into her sparking attack-tentacle, which bloats to the size of a man's leg. The tentacle tip pinches free and flies into the sky, a guided missile meant for Skeeze.

Skeeze flees further, up and up through the dark sky, presumably in the direction of Moo's wormhole to Earth, not that I can see the hole from here. Skeeze's spacetime trail is a towering gyre, patterned with the monochrome shades of the punk sqink's bod.

"I should have claimed Earth immediately," says Mumper. "Sent an army of a thousand, as soon as Moo drilled the wormhole. But I've been waiting to finish my deal with Kanga and Gubb from Mu9. They want to buy a thousand Stok-stok brains, which is what I have on tap in Tiny Town. And I can score a thousand more brains from Earth."

"You should put the Stok-stok brains back in their Stok-stok bodies," says Moo. "When we discover a high-level civilization, we should treat them as equals. Should have done that on Stok-stok, and now I say we *are* gonna do it on Earth. Before it's too late."

"What are you even talking about?" says Carol.

"Why don't you pay better attention?" snaps Mumper. "Here it is, butt-simple. Moo made a wormhole to Earth. Brought along a scout party of sqinks. I want to sell human brains to the Mu9ers in exchange for yump. The Mu9ers will tap the brains for what we call *me-ware*. You can do that about ten times—until the brain gives out. And Moo says it's not *ethical*."

"Good for Moo," I say.

Mumper frowns and shakes her head. "Moo's namby-pamby scouts think that way too. They want to be a small, elite group of participant-observers. They want to be the humans' friends."

"As opposed to being torturers and murderers," says Carol. "That would be your kind of trip, eh, Mumper?"

"Look at Moo's scouts this way," I say to Mumper. "They're like explorers who protect the native tribes from settlers. Like surfers opposed to cruise ships. Hippies against missionaries. Artists against condos."

"Wordy words," sneers Mumper. "Moo and her scouts are selfish jerks. I'm gonna be selling human brains to the Mu9ers, I tell you. The Mu9ers are gonna be huffing me-ware in and out of your brains—and that's final."

In synch with this remark, Moo is struggling with some distant, unseen force. Her tentacles are wrapped tight around her body, and she's flicking the tips of the tentacles as if shooting out precise rays. I hear a distant hiss, like a hot poker doused in water, and I see a flash in the far black sky.

"Shit," goes Mumper, guessing what's happened. Her blank eyes swell with a rare emotion: rage. "Your bright little pioneers melted your wormhole, Moo! Disobeyed you. Weakling! Go drill out that hole again. Is Earth's *thub thub* still working?

Moo cocks her head. "Yes." She looks amused. "You'd almost think that genius Winston Tropp would turn off his *thub* broadcast—and stop inviting us to raid his ass."

"Get on it!" exclaims Mumper.

Moo fixes Mumper with a cold, haughty gaze. "Maybe I will, maybe I won't. You need to understand that I'm not going to give Earth to you! It's mine."

"I'm telling you to reopen the frikkin' wormhole, and kill all those elitist scouts of yours," cries Mumper. "And start by killing Skeeze."

"Like I mentioned, I did in fact tear into Skeeze yesterday," says Moo, laughing. She's enjoying the argument. Standing up to Mom.

"Mumper is slimy!" puts in Carol, taking Moo's side. "Don't lister to her."

"I'm gonna do the right thing," says Moo. "Keep Earth mellow and calm."

"I'll calm those humans all right," yells Mumper. "Ka-ching, ka-ching, ka-ching! Sell their brains for yump!"

"You're a bully," Moo tells Mumper. "A parasite. Deeply unintelligent. A stinky old frog. A—"

"Oh, we don't need to hear the I'm-a-big-girl tantrum again," growls Mumper, perhaps a bit uneasy. "Tell you what, Moo. If you get your scouts to stop busting your wormhole, and if you help me move some product, well then you get half of the yump I score. How does that sound?"

Moo is silent for a full minute. And then she surprises me. "Oh fine, let's call it a deal, Mom. I'll take your offer. I'm sick of arguing with you."

It's a head-snapping U-turn. Is Moo being sarcastic? Or was her talk about saving Earth a negotiation technique—and now she's selling us out?

"What about us?" cries Carol.

"Well, honey, if you help Mom and me, we'll set you up," says Moo in a falsely sweet voice. "Fame, power, money—all of it for you and your man. You'll be running with the big dogs."

"And what would you be asking to do?" I ask.

"Oliver!" exclaims Carol.

"Just wondering."

"Here's a nice detail," Moo tells Mumper. "Each and every scout in my team has teamed up with a friend of Carol's or Oliver's. If they pitch in, we talk everyone around to you way of seeing things, Mom."

"Clever," says Mumper, smiling at Moo. "You're a good daughter."

Moo emits the most vapid and supine giggle imaginable.

Carol makes an impatient gesture, as if waving off gnats. "Can we see some more of Sqinkland?" she demands. "Before we trot home to help Mumper invade Earth? As if we'd ever do that. You sleaze-bag dopes."

As sometimes happens with me, I'm finding a supposedly life-changing negotiation uninteresting. I prefer seeing words be used for fun, and not for power. And more than that, I have a specific need in mind.

"I'm hungry," is what I now contribute to the debate. "Isn't this what you might call the Mission District of Sqinkland, Moo? Any chance I can get a taco? And that it won't kill me?"

"*Is there any chance?*" chuckles Mumper, laying on an affability routine. "Every chance, my boy. Synchronicity, Oliver, synchronicity. Behold. A taqueria is at your side. How convenient. I may even know the sqinks within."

"Uh, cool," I say. No idea where this is going, but I *am* hungry. I turn to Carol. She looks scared and defiant. I can't resist hugging her. Holding her makes me feel safe, even though she's so new to my life. I kiss her cheek.

"I love you," I whisper.

"I love you too, Oliver," she says. "But this isn't really the—"

"Don't like hugging," says Mumper, stepping away from us. "Don't like it at all. Love and kisses—no! Makes me sick. Goodbye for now. I want to ponder my prospects."

Mumper stretches her arms, and shakes, as if in a wild dance. Bits of her body come loose and fall to the ground—just a few bits at first, but then a cascade. Mumper has morphed into a pile of bas-relief tiles, like a Mayan jigsaw puzzle.

"Now Mumper solves herself," says Moo. "A game we royal sqinks like to play. Watch."

The crumbly squares creep about as if in heavy traffic, fitting themselves together, flat on the sidewalk, a square at a time, and then—*ta da*—we've got a thousand-year-old image of, well, it's not exactly Mumper's glassy-eyed face. It's more like a Chichen Itza mural of a god.

Moo hovers low and drizzles an unpleasant fluid onto the bas-relief image. The passers-by become speedy spacetime worms, distancing themselves. Possibly motivated by disgust at Moo.

"Seems like you're ready to rebel," Carol says to Moo. "You were lying about making a deal with Mumper, right? Putting her on?

"There's a toy you humans have," says Moo, dodging the question. "A kaleidoscope? You look into it and you see a pattern. You twist the kaleidoscope, and—*click*—the pattern is different. It all changes at once. No cause and effect. And now we'll experience this effect by entering our capacious taqueria."

"Enough with the cosmo-cryptic jive," I say. "I'm still hungry. You go first, Moo. We'll follow you in."

"My thoughts exactly," says the cuttlefish sqink.

This is a very, *very* large taqueria. Full of motion and mariachi music. Not exactly *people* in here. Some of them are those garlands-of-spheres sqinks we've already seen, a few are cuttlefish like Moo, others are centipedes, and some are good old-fashioned amorphous blobs with fried-egg eyes. And I get the sense that there's small, transparent sqinks in the air current, and a sqink in the hinges of the taqueria's swinging door, and even sqinks in the tables and chairs. They're everywhere.

I'm hungry enough to go over to the counter and begin studying the menu. Not that I can read the squiggles. Or, no, wait—yes, I can.

"Don't even think of it," says Carol, right up against me.

"*Muy bueno*," says a smiling figure behind the counter. He's holding a cuttlefish sqink by the tentacles. He has a butcher's knife. He slaps the cuttle onto a big wooden chopping block, raises the knife and—

Time yaws to one side. Moo is in action again. She darts behind the counter, squirts another icky secretion onto the cook's hand, and pulls the frozen-time cuttle loose from the cook's frozen-time grip. The freed cuttle comes to life and pinballs around the taqueria, wildly squealing.

The cook shifts gears. "Your order, sir?"

"Beans-and-rice taco," I say, wanting to avoid anything that a sqink might call meat.

Instantly the cook hands me my taco … of *course* he knew what I'd want. No surprises in this synchronistic Sqinkland. My wish is his command. By now I'm not really hungry, but now that I've got the taco I might as well open it up and see what's inside. I am sometimes known, after all, as the world's greediest man.

"Cute," says Carol, looking over my shoulder. "The beans are alive. Baby sqinks." She takes the taco and sings to it, melding her fine voice with the many voices around us.

What with me being an SF writer, you'd think I'd be enjoying this, but somehow, it's too much. My knees give way and I fall backwards, not knowing if there's a chair behind me, but of course there is.

Yes—a sqinky chair has trotted over. A table slides over as well. Its scraping legs provoke stuttering screeches from the floor, at least I think it's the floor that's talking, the floor and the table both. I lean forward, retching, with saliva streaming from my mouth.

"Ride it out," says Carol. "A bad trip is a teaching. We're exobiologists."

Carol is doing a little bit of a dance, back and forth. She's set the taco on the tabletop, and the beans are dancing with her, one step forward, one step back, twirl, twirl, twirl. The rice grains in the taco are writhing like insect larvae, and they're singing in chorus. The taco shell, that is, the folded tortilla, it's alive too, and it's flapping like a gabby mouth.

Moo jostles past me and hovers low over the dish. "Are you going eat this?" she asks me.

"Not hardly."

"Perdón," goes Moo, tilting her head down. She brings her beak and tentacles into play. "Nothing like home cooking!"

I look away. This is beyond disgust.

Off in the distance I see endless ranks of cooks, counters, and customers. How can the taqueria be so large? Well, duh, it's that sqink thing of stretchable space. And they warp the time as well. Some of the customers move at a normal pace, others zoom in fast forward, and some are into sideways time, with their bodies forming those spacetime worms.

What are all these sqinks doing here? Maybe these are the thousand sqinks who Mumper enlisted to invade Earth, and this so-called taqueria is a holding room where they pass the spacetime until somebody wedges open that temporarily out-of-order Sqinkland-to-Earth wormhole and gives them the go-go. A barracks of invaders here, a troop ship, a para-trooper plane, a giant U-boat. Disturbed thoughts from a disturbed man.

And now, for whatever reason, that cook who served me is coming around the counter and heading towards me, with his butcher's knife held high. Two knives, actually, one in each hand.

Perhaps he's mad because he knows I'm friends with the skeevy sqink Skeeze who helped close the wormhole to Earth— thereby delaying the invasion Mumper wants to lead.

Or perhaps the cook is mad because I didn't leave him a tip? Well, actually I didn't pay him anything *at all* …

"Time to get out of here," says Carol. "Moo, if you're done being totally disgusting with your food …"

"Hop on my back and hold tight," says Moo. "I'll be flying fast. Taking you to see Tiny Town. Where the brains are stored."

Carol and I mount Moo, she lashes us down with her tentacles, and *zow*, she accelerates to an utterly insane speed.

And then we're hovering above a grassy bluff by an ocean. Carol sings a soundtrack, verbalizing the things we see, somehow mapping the shapes into her figures of sound.

The bluff is rocky in spots, with natural pools filled by waters from hot springs. Spume flies from the crashing waves—and mixes with the steam from the springs. Plants abound: barky redwoods, torrents of orchid vines, drifts of nasturtiums, and tidy garden plots. Like a Big Sur resort.

Glowing blobs inhabit the scene as well, occasionally bouncing off each other. The blobs are like overgrown frog-eggs: rubbery and transparent, enclosing fluids and gels a bit like the arcane liquids seen in lava lamps, or in the psychedelic light shows of yore.

The nearest blob has something inside it.

"A brain is stored in there," says Moo. "That's why we call these things braincozies."

Still atop Moo, I see the nearby braincozies quite clearly. Their motions are playful and purposeful, as if they have lives of their own. But as Moo says, most of them host brains within. To make it weirder, these braincozies have eyes as well, with the eyes set into its surface, and joined by cords to the brains within. Makes sense, in a way.

Moo splashes down into a deep pool of jellied liquid that heaves and jiggles like amniotic fluid. Carol and I slide off Moo and paddle about in the slippery flow, enjoying its vivifying touch.

Carol is playfully singing. It's as if song is her way of seeing the world, or as if she transmutes the world into a form she can understand. I love Carol's voice. I put my arms around her.

A few braincozies bob nearby. The brains inside them—are they truly captives from other worlds?

Before I can fully decipher the scene, I hear the harsh, unwelcome voice of Mumper. An image of her is here—in the form of a flat-topped pyramid adorned by Mayan bas-reliefs. She addresses us in an impatient tone.

"I already told you I don't like that repulsive cuddling, Oliver and Carol. Go back to Earth! Help Moo plead my case to her rebellious crew! You're with me, aren't you, dear daughter Moo? You weren't teasing me, were you? And someday your time to rule will come."

"My time will come when you're finally dead," says Moo.

"Not as nice thing to say, dear daughter," says Mumper. "Let's go back to our bench,"

Moo goes fast again—and again we're at the bench on the Sqinkland version of Mission Street.

"Feels like we've looped to a previous frame," says Moo. "Boring. Let's see if I can get Oliver and Carol home. Even though my tunnel is plugged. And, Mom, when I get back, I'll have my friend Tobin message you. I have a plan for a big step in our campaign. We need you there for the drama."

Mumper nods.

Next thing I know, Moo, Carol and I are in the velvety black bulk. Moo wriggles around, listening for variations in that thub thub, feeling for the path to Earth.

It strikes me that there's a sense in which the bulk isn't dark, no, it's very well-lit, giving me a view akin to what you might see from a deep-sea bathyscaphe that's seven miles down in the Mariana Trench, with jelly log drifters and pukeful tube worms and sharp-toothed gobblers and billowing electric snot-rags—everything shifting and sliding and inside out—and lit by the eldritch, psychic glow of the bulk.

We're getting close.

thub thub thub thub thub thub

Our path leads through dreams and hallucinations, with my thoughts and memories orbiting about me—faces from my youth, mourners at my funeral, events I don't remember because they didn't happen, even though they did. Very deep and freaky. Very ill.

At a conservative estimate, the journey lasts seven hundred and forty-eight years. Carol passes the not-time by crooning a tune that circles around like an Escher staircase.

And then, *yo*, Moo bends her path in a weird way, and just like that we're in the tight-squeezed old wormhole tunnel, except right now the tunnel is full of cold lava—which Moo is steadily zapping aside.

We push upward, as if emerging from a birth canal and—*waah*—we're in the air, floating above the same hole in the ground as before. The hole is all drilled out again, in a pit in the enchanted Eden of the Box Farm field.

Ta da!

Carol and I are exceedingly glad to dismount from Moo, and to stand upon the forest floor. But all the trees within a hundred yards have been reduced to charred stubs.

Skeeze hovers amid the devastation, waiting for us. My pet sqink. Our loyal rebel. He's glad to see me and Moo.

"What happened?" I ask.

"Zig and Zag happened," says Skeeze, waving to these very sqinks, who are sitting on the slope above the charred mouth of the tunnel. They're in their killer cannon mode: a stack of tori, and a wireframe plasma antenna.

"Femtotech bazooka," continues Skeeze. "Disassembling the atoms in Moo's wormhole. Thereby collapsing the rock into lava, all the way down. My idea. I called in Zig and Zag as soon as I got here. I was worried Mumper might be chasing me."

"You little creep," says Moo, more proud than angry. As if Skeeze is her disobedient pupil. "Your instincts were quite right. We don't want Mumper and her thousand sqinks to come through before we're ready. And that was good work, Zig and Zag!"

The cannon sqinks send a blazing blast into the air.

"And you're really not on Mumper's side at all?" Carol says to Moo, wanting to be quite sure.

"Oh, come on," Moo grandly says. "Can't you read me better than that? I was funning. Playing a part. Saying any old thing. Just so Mumper would shut up. She's dead to me, I tell you, dead. I've been down too long. Mother must die."

"Strong words," I say.

"Might not be easy to do," says Skeeze. "Mumper's a sly old sqink. Someone might have to go kamikaze on her ass." He pauses in thought. "Lacking that, we can close Moo's wormhole every damn time she opens it up. It's suicide to leave an open door, Moo, what with Mumper itching to trash Earth."

Moo hesitates, pondering her response, hanging in the air before us, working things out in her mind. Then she rocks from one side to the other, as if shaking her head.

"No need to seal it right now," insists Moo. "You heard me invite Mumper for a visit today. We'll need that. And she's not ready to invade. She's finalizing her big deal with the Mu9ers. And when she does invade, I'll be ready with an ambush. Trust me. Mumper will be my sitting duck."

"So, it's all good?" I say.

"My ambush plan, yes," says Moo. "But if I'm gonna rule, I need to have my *own* army of a thousand sqinks."

"See what I mean?" says Skeeze. "Always another layer with Mumper and Moo. Like Russian eggs."

"Carol and Oliver will be right spang in the middle of the action," says Moo. "But at this moment I need to do some errands before Mumper's visit. Why don't you two lovers go meet Paul Vreed."

"Who is Paul Vreed?" goes Carol.

"I know hm," I say.

"He's friends with a sqink from my scout crew," adds Moo. "A sqink named Doob."

"An artist," I say. "I used to spend a lot of time in his studio. Smoking weed, watching him paint, reading aloud from whatever I was writing. It felt like the way life is supposed to be. Bohemian."

"Tsk, tsk," goes Carol. She prefers the idea of me being sober.

"You go to Paul Vreed, and I'll meet you there," says Moo. "Let's go, Skeeze. And Zig and Zag, keep a lookout, Mumper is going to be coming through fairly soon. Like I told her, we're having a meeting." Moo rises into the air with Skeeze on her back.

"What if Moo *does* bring her army with her?" calls Zig.

"If Mumper pulls that, go femtonuclear on her ass," answers Moo. "But I'm sure she'll be alone. She's curious about the meeting. Bye, all!"

Moo and Skeeze glide past the charred tree-stubs and into the zone of sun-splashed living trees, with Carol and I following on foot. The air turns sweet, with birdsong all around.

Carol and I pause to hug each other as tenderly as if we've just made love. I feel deep warmth when we embrace, as if each of our chests holds half the plutonium for an atom bomb. You might say that Carol and I are generating a chain reaction, but it's a *good* reaction, yielding peace and love, not death and hate. Carol is my safe harbor. The longer and more often I hold her, the better I feel.

9. PAUL AND IRENE

Paul Vreed's apartment building is on busy Guerrero Street at the edge of the Mission. The glassed front door opens onto a flight of stairs to Paul's apartment, which is on the second floor. This front door is locked.

The electric bell stopped working years ago, and the wall-mounted mechanical bell has been ripped off, literally, leaving an unpainted outline on the wall beside the door. I pound the door frame for a while, to Carol's mild disapproval, and then Paul appears on the stairs, genial and ready for company.

He leads us to his cluttered lair. Art everywhere. Velvet paintings of disasters. Plastic toy soldiers with altered heads. Thrift shop paintings with words lettered onto them. Painted images of covers for magazines in unknown tongues. A large and intricate diagram of the tenets of a parody religion that Paul is involved in. A slash-mouthed bowling ball with yellow teeth. Miniature halves of tank-grown beef dangle from the ceiling, with the beef dexterously preserved. Everything is exactly as it was the last time I visited, two or three years ago.

"Meet Carol," I tell Paul. "My new girlfriend."

"Not sure about that word," says Carol. "Partner?"

"Like you two run a business," says Paul. "Dealing sqinks."

"And you got one?" Carol asks Paul.

"I scored my new helper at *Lady Cee and Topper's Sqink Fair*. Her name is Doob. Thanks for making it happen, guys."

It's hard to be completely sure how Paul feels about his sqink. As always, his voice is ironic and modulated, eternally on the edge of laughter.

He leads us into his studio. "Doob herself."

"Well, hiiiii," goes Doob, stretching out the word in a friendly, innocent way. She hovers in the air; a slender cylinder tapered at both ends. Most of her body is smooth and brown, with a lacquered look. She has a small eye at one end, and the other end seems to be dipped in dark blue. Doob is a flying paintbrush.

"Wow," say I. "Sqinks can do anything."

"I'm the boss of her," cautions Paul. "I don't let Doob paint just anything."

"That's not really true," says Doob in her girlish ingenue voice. "I put the veins in the wings of the dragonfly by the pond in Oliver's scene with Sybil. And I added emphasis-lines around the sharp pincers on the dragonfly's rear. You wouldn't have done those, Paul."

"Maybe I was going to paint them later," says Paul, a little annoyed.

"Mmm *hmm*," goes Doob. "I bet."

Paul cleans Doob's brush with a cloth and gives the bristles an affectionate lick.

"Is it love?" asks Carol.

Smilingly Paul shakes his head. "I have no idea what I'm doing. How did you and Carol connect?"

Carol and I look at each other. It's hard to sort out the changes we've been through this week.

Me: "Carol sold me out to the sqinks."

Carol: "I repented."

Me: "We're in love."

"Mumper wants to invade with a thousand sqinks," adds Carol. "Moo plans to stop them."

"I'm against Mumper, and I'm staying that way," says Doob. "I don't feel right about cutting out someone's brain, and stashing the brain in Tiny Town, and letting Mu9ers use the brain to get high."

"Mumper already told us," I say. "It's like a novel I wrote a long time ago. Robots eating brains."

"The Mu9ers don't *eat* the brains," says Doob. "Mumper must have told you that. They tease out a brain's me-ware, and huff it, and get high, and the me-ware drifts back into the brain. And then they huff it again. A strong brain is good for four or five huffs, and then—*pfft*. Flat tire."

"I don't get it," I say. "Why not chew up the brain. Like I wrote in my novel. OG cyberpunk."

"Crude, Oliver," says Paul. "Too obvious."

"Tickle a brain the right way, and that nice, sparkly me-ware oozes out and *huufff*," says Doob. She seems to think our conversation funny.

"That's enough," Paul tells Doob. "Don't bum our guests. They don't need to hear nauseating alien stoner horror tales."

"Yes, I've huffed a brain or two in my time," Doob continues in a comfortable tone. "Don't knock it if you ain't tried it, daddy-o."

"You're skungy," says Carol. "And we saw those horrid braincozy bags in Tiny Town."

Doob darkly chuckles. "I guess you noticed that harvested brains still have their eyeballs? Nice touch, very evocative."

"I said that's enough, Doob," says Paul, giving the sqink a jab with his palette knife. "Time to change the channel. You'll be interested in this, Oliver. As it happens, I'm currently painting the life of you, Oliver Strunk, the man of the hour. Very synchro that you showed up here just now."

Paul leans into his painting, with his Doob-brush under close control. The canvas is round, that is, it's a flat disk. A spiral comic strip. The frames run clockwise, moving in from the edge of the canvas, round and round, getting smaller, heading towards a central vanishing point which is white, or maybe black, with a teensy-weensy eye in the middle, an eye smaller than Doob's physical, organic eye on the tip of her brush handle. Somehow, I feel like the painted eye is an image of Doob's own eye. Miracles and paradoxes abound.

And—this is scary and weird—the comic really *does* depict the story of my life, working its way out from the center. From my low self-esteem childhood, to my college bacchanals, to the joyous event of meeting my wife Sybil at a picnic by a pond with a dragonfly.

And onward through our years of bitter struggle, my bloom as author and professor, Sybil's rise as a painter and scholar— and the birth and growth of our three darling kids.

I have my moment of literary acclaim, we get older, Sybil dies, and then come my tiny days alone in a Box Farm box. But then! Recently brushed in! My cheery meet with Carol, our passage though the black sky of Sqinkland, and our visit to Paul's studio, right here, right now, with Doob's double eye watching all.

"Why isn't there more?" I ask. "More of my life. Don't tell me this is the part where Doob or one of her friends eats my brain?"

"It's not *eating*," corrects Carol raising her voice. "You never listen to anything, Oliver. You sound like you're senile!" For no real reason, she sings a schoolyard taunt: "*Na na, na na, na na—naaah.*"

"The painting stops because this is now," says Doob. "The moment of not yet."

I feel a tickle of curiosity. I'm always on the alert for a new kick—which is a dangerous flaw in my personality. I've gotta ask. "If they take your brain to Tiny Town, are you able to come back?"

"The sqinks always tell the suckers they can come back," says Doob.

Puckish Paul poses a follow-up query. "Do the brains in Tiny Town braincozies get to have sex with each other?"

"Oh sure," says Doob, playing along. "And the brain-huffers watch."

"I hear big, slow, honking laughs from the Mu9ers," goes Paul. "I see a punk Mu9er couple enjoying their evening out."

"Gotta paint that," says Doob. "Boschian detail. Career landmark for you, Paul. Maybe I should take control of your brain. You'll work faster. Your perspective will be tighter."

Paul scowls and makes as if to snap the paintbrush-shaped Doob in half.

"Teasing, teasing, teasing," Doob quickly says.

"I say we do a hyper-gigundo street mural," says Paul. "Wrap it all the way around a building. I see a chance to adorn the outside of Winston Tropp's vintage wood warehouse. I mean, Oliver and Carol are in with him. He'll give the okay. Can you work big, Doob?"

By way of response, Doob stretches her body from one corner of the room to the other, nearly knocking me off my feet.

Paul gives a wheezy chuckle. "We'll *rule*. I've never had the tools and the backup for a mural. A cultural event. Mural by Paul Vreed and his assistant Doob. Dancers and music by Irene Macaw. Poetry. Hookahs and pomegranate juice. Rants against brain theft. Voices raised in unison: *Own Your Brain*! Down With Queen Mumper! Interrogate Queen Moo!"

"I wonder if we can count on Moo or not," says Carol.

"Crazed hipsters fight it out with killer sqinks!" says Paul, deeply into his vision.

Wanting to keep myself in the conversation, I speak up. But, as so often happens these days, my remarks are a bit beside the point.

"Remember what Galileo wrote Kepler when he was on trial for saying the Earth goes around the Sun?" I intone. "*What shall we make of this, Kepler? Shall we laugh, or shall we cry?*"

"Always better to laugh," Paul agreeably says. "When they're burning you at the stake, enjoy the naughty tickle of the kindling between your legs."

"Fun fact," goes Carol. "Oliver and I know every single person who's teamed up with one of Moo's platoon of sqinks. Eight of them still alive."

"How is it that you know exactly those people?" asks Paul.

We just smile at him. Even Paul doesn't fully get it about sqink luck. Nice to have a leg up on this guy for once. Wise-ass art-king that he is.

We head for the street.

Moo and Skeeze are waiting by Paul's front door. Looking sly.

"What's the plan, superman?" I say to Moo.

Moo makes an ambiguous gesture with the fin that encircles her cuttlefish body. "Main thing is that I need an army of one thousand."

"And where are your thousand supposed to be from?" asks Carol.

"I'll get a bunch of sqinks who are stranded on planet Stokstok. Earth might be a good place for them to settle. Plenty of room to reproduce. They'll be loyal, good-humored helpers. As chirpy as Grandma tending Tweety Bird."

"No idea what you're talking about," I say.

Carol speaks. "What I'm hearing is that Moo will block Mumper from invading—so that Moo can invade. And then comes some bullshit about Grandma and Tweety Bird? That's an old cartoon. With Sylvester the Cat."

"I'm an inspirational leader," says Moo. "A fine orator. And now you've got one more sqink to meet. And then a surprise."

"I don't like to hear the word *surprise* from you," I tell Moo. "Don't like that at all."

"True that," goes Skeeze. "Maybe this would be a good time to kill Princess Moo and kill Queen Mumper. Kill both. Zip and Zap could do it."

"All is harmony on team Moo," says Carol.

"We're having a whale of a time," I add.

"Irene Macaw is your next stop," says Moo, ignoring us. "You know where Irene lives, Carol. Skeeze and I will get there later. We have a a side trip. Sorry to be so scattered and mysterioso."

"I bet Oliver knows where we'll be," says Skeeze. "Supposedly he's writing this adventure as novel. Look at your outline, Oliver."

"I never write outlines," I snap. "Outlines suck.".

"Come to think of it, I never see you writing anything at all," shoots back Skeeze.

"I'm writing it in my mind," I say. "As it happens. Do sqinks ever write anything? Do you even have minds?"

No answer. Moo and Skeeze fly off.

"I don't like it," I tell Carol as we walk to my car.

"Irene is my old pal," says Carol. "A zillion years ago, we worked at Hewlett-Packard, designing ads and manuals and brochures. We quarreled over a man. Tig Tucker? I think Irene won. Not sure by now."

"What does your Irene do now?" I ask. "What's she like?"

"These days she works as a choreographer. Designs dances and spectacles. Ballet, gymnasts, choirs, marching bands. Real and virtual. Irene's great. She uses my images in her shows now and then."

Irene's apartment is on the hill above Dolores Park. The streets are slow, even though all the cars but mine are smart. Parking takes forever, with the nimble bot cars always ahead of me. By the time we knock on Irene's door, Moo and Skeeze are done with their errand. They perch in an oak by Irene's house, silently watching. Creepy.

Irene recognizes Carol right away. Theatrical protestations of joy. It's almost like they're singing a duet. Irene is our age, with her hair a pale brick-red. Chic clothes: a ribbed pale-green tee, and flowered pale-yellow lounge-pants. The apartment is vintage, with hardwood floors, abstract rugs, Danish furniture, pastel walls, and framed paintings.

To help Moo eavesdrop, I leave Irene's door open, with the screen closed.

A chrome tube hovers in the living-room.

"Meet my sqink," says Irene. "Do-Re-Mi."

"You got her at the Box Farm sqink fair?" asks Carol.

"You know it," says Irene. "Hauled my booty down there just in time. And learned you were behind it, Carol! You're wilder than ever. Who's this adorable man? I want one too." She takes my hand, as if checking that I'm real.

"I'm Oliver," I say. Truth be told, I feel a bit of instant chemistry with Irene. She's fashionable, with a very attractive face. Something devil-may-care about her. She holds my hand a beat longer than necessary, as if picking up on my thoughts.

"*The* Carol and Oliver," says Irene. "All over the news. So, what brings you my way? Customer satisfaction survey? Selling an upgrade? I thought the sqinks were free."

"Free for *you*, I'm sure," says Carol, smiling. "You never pay for anything."

"No need to," says Irene. "Do-Re-Mi was darting around on her own. Some biker tried to grab her. But I was too fast. I stuffed Do-Re-Mi into my purse." Irene makes her voice into a raucous squawk. "*Come with me, honey, I'll make you a star.*"

"And then?" I ask.

"The biker tried to snatch my purse, and Do-Re-Mi zapped the living shit out of him."

"I *will* be a star," says the hovering Do-Re-Mi, her voice like chimes.

"Both of us," says Irene. "Sqinks are amazing. I'm making better dances than before. Do-Re-Mi puts me on a higher level. Not like those gym-bot exercise routines I've been designing for pay."

"Show me," says Carol. "Let's jam." She looks around, capturing images of the apartment. She breaks into twirlware song. I love Carol's husky voice. And she's jiving funny words.

Yubba wubba wow now wow delight delinsky deedle bump pow yumba fleet squeek orooni jam how.

Irene and Do-Re-Mi conjure up a troupe of virtual dancers. Animated figures in the air, like dragonflies and wasps.

The jam runs for half an hour. Carol is in a chair, and I lie on the floor, looking up, digging it, entranced by the nimble dancers and the aethereal music. They start like rival street gangs, charging and retreating in that trad old way, but then it's a ballroom dance, and now they're herds of game and prey—swirling in whorls, weaving loops and do-si-do scrolls, ceaselessly improvising. They never come close to repeating.

All the while I'm enjoying the play of expressions on the two women's enthralling faces. Carol notices. She doesn't like me looking at Irene.

"It furthers one to cross the great water," I pronounce as the show ends. Once again, I'm trying to be vast and cool. It's an *I Ching* line. I think of "great water" as standing for the changes that the sqinks can bring. I dream we'll cross the water and arrive in a better place. But I don't explain this word-by-word. People don't usually understand what I'm talking about.

As our little party winds down, I pose a question to the sqink Do-Re-Mi.

"Are you for eating human brains?"

"For Christ's sake stop saying *eat* or I'll choke you to death," cries Carol. "They *cut out* the brains and send them to Tiny Town. Nobody literally *eats* the brains at all!"

"What are you talking about?" asks Irene.

"This thing that Oliver and I have been hearing about the sqinks," says Carol, trying to calm her voice.

"I myself would never do such a thing," puts in Do-Re-Mi. "Moo's scouts are kind, and good."

A slobbering giggle drifts in through the screen door.

Do-Re-Mi floats to the open door and raises her voice. "I know you and Skeeze are out there in the tree, Moo. Stop lurking."

"Let's *get* em," says Carol.

She kicks open the screen. Her wasp and dragonfly dancers zoom into the yard and settle onto Moo and Skeeze. They buzz, pinch, sing, and—sting?

"Yikes," goes Moo. "Ow! Quit it. Let's go inside!"

"How does a hologram sting?" I ask.

"A sqink hologram can do most anything," says Do-Re-Mi. "Especially to people who don't applaud our shows."

Moo and Skeeze enter the living-room. We turn off the dancers.

"Good show," Moo belatedly says. "Sorry for no applause. I wasn't sure when it was actually over. And now I'm in a bit of a rush."

"Moo's always in a rush," says Carol. "Unless it's something you yourself want her to do."

Moo wants to do announcer. "And now, behold, Carol and Oliver have met my full gang of eight sqinks. Skeeze, Lilac, Doob, Do-Re-Mi, Xavier, Flubsy, Zig, and Zag."

"Too much to remember," I say. "Too random."

"Never mind," says Moo. "Moving on. Here comes the part when we do our thing with Mumper and Winston Tropp at the Pacific-Union Club on Nob Hill. Tobin worked out the details."

"I don't want to," I say, increasingly suspicious.

"Tell us what it is," says Carol, sounding interested.

"I don't especially like the scenario that we've planned," confesses Moo. "But even so, it's the easiest way to get from here to where we need to be. Please?"

"I still don't—" I begin.

"Oh, let's see what it is," says Carol, cutting me off. "I'm curious. Let's ride there on Moo's back, Oliver. And not bother with your dumb slow car."

I keep grumbling, but Carol is adamant, and then we're in the sky again.

"I saw you drooling over Irene," Carol says to me. "Do you want her more than me?"

"What!" I protest. "She's a nice person, that's all."

"You'll be sorry if you two-time me," says Carol.

"Relax. You're my woman, I'm your man."

"Don't forget it," says Carol, and grants me a slight touch of her hand.

As always, the air on high is nice. The weather's changing, with puffy clouds coming in from the sea.

"We don't have clouds in Sqinkland," remarks Skeeze. He's perched on my knee. "We just have low fog. I guess it has to do with no sun. Maybe you could write a book about that, too."

"You're not much of an assistant," I respond. "You never offer to help with the *actual writing*. You just offer stupid, irrelevant ideas."

"How am I supposed to see into your head and know what you imagine your book is about?" says Skeeze, comfortable with himself.

"You don't even know what writing means," I say.

"Me, I'm an idea man. I get you into situations. Writing is for crazy people. Hard to help with that, huh, Moo?"

"Me, I'm trying to do what's best for everyone," says Moo. "You'll see how it ends."

10. Chrome Axe

The Pacific-Union Club is a cake-like neo-classical brown-stone mansion atop Nob Hill, bounded by a massively sculpted bronze fence.

There has never been the faintest chance of me being invited inside the Pacific-Union. Not ever. But now, here I am. Me, Carol, and Skeeze, ferried here by Moo.

We don't get much of a welcome. A man in black steps out from the rear portico, levels a zap gun, and shoots at Moo. The cuttlefish squeals, dumps us, darts into the sky, and does some kind of writhing body transformation. Not that I follow the details, as I'm busy picking my ass up off the pavement. Moo said the meeting was all set. Looks like this guard didn't get the memo.

He stands there glaring, with his zap gun at the ready. Skeeze shrinks down and takes refuge in my armpit.

With enviable self-assurance, Carol adopts a glam persona and makes as if to flirt with the guard. "We're here for a meeting," she warbles. "Topper and Lady Cee? Huge stars. Our billionaire pal Winston Tropp is already here. And some others. Business meeting, you understand."

"He's going for it," I twirlware-teep to Carol.

"Onward," she declaims.

In the building, we hit the real security, an icy lady who knows exactly who we are and where we rank.

"You're to meet Winston Tropp, yes," she says. "Also, a Tobin, and a Ms. Mumper."

Skeeze crawls down my arm and perches on my wrist. In punk gingerbread-man mode. He looks up at me. As always with a sqink, his expression is hard to read. Two glassy black eyes. His lizard mouth is a wry line.

A sleek man ushers us to a booth in a corner of the club's plush grill. It's late Sunday afternoon. A few members are at early dinner. They glance over, and decide we don't matter.

Winston is in our booth beside Tobin and, yes, Mumper from Sqinkland. The Sqink queen has accepted Moo's invite, perhaps with Tobin acting as a go-between. She's wearing that same green shirt as if it's part of her skin. She's clean and composed, with thin lips and tilted chin.

One might imagine Mumper to be a wealthy Valley investor, here to make a deal with tech wizard Winston Tropp. This said, Mumper still doesn't seem human. She has those dead black eyes. And, hmm, Winston and Tobin have dead eyes too.

"Oh oh," says Carol, nudging me.

Three green braincozies from Tiny Town are sitting on the floor beside the booth. Two of them have pairs of human eyeballs. And you know what *that* means.

"I'm sorry about this," says Skeeze, still on my wrist.

I look around. "Too late to escape?"

"We'll make it right for you later," says Skeeze. "Moo thinks this move is crucial for saving Earth. Tobin and the sqink Flubsy helped set things up."

Light footsteps behind me. Someone shoves my back, quite hard. Almost a jocular shove, as if from a rowdy grade-school pal. It's Moo. So much for my chances of escape.

Moo, by the way, has transmuted herself into a chic society dame. A rich pigeon, as it were. A potential investor. She wears silk and cashmere in shades of taupe and cream.

"Time for our show," Moo tells me. Her voice is the same as ever, burbling and gassy. And her hands are everywhere at once, as if she's still a cuttlefish. She herds Carol and me into the rounded booth. Mumper rises to her feet so I can get an inner seat.

So here we are in this corner booth: Mumper, me, Winston, Tobin, Carol, and Moo. As I say, Winston and Tobin look wrong. Blank, with lifeless eyes. Evidently, their brains are in those two braincozies on the floor, each braincozy with the inhabitant's eyeballs on the side.

Kicker: there's a third braincozy. For now, it's empty. I'm guessing it's for me.

Mumper has a very tight grip on my arm. Skeeze is in front of me on the table. He's changed his shape. More like a largish pear now.

"How can you do this to me?" I ask Moo.

"You're supposed to be our friend!" Carol adds.

And to some extent, our pleas do get to Moo. At least she acts that way.

"Look here," Moo says to Mumper across the table. "I know this was my idea, but I'm not quite sure that—"

Mumper has drawn a small metal axe from beneath the table. A chrome hatchet. Like a trophy that might change hands between two college football teams. Mumper's gripping it. She's about to kill me.

Carol screams and lunges at Mumper—just as Mumper slams her axe into the top of my head, splitting my skull like a coconut. I don't actually see this part happening. Skeeze fills me in on the details a few minutes later.

"Later" means after my brain and eyeballs have been placed into that extra braincozy on the floor.

"Later" also means after the three loaded braincozies have lifted off and have flown at insane speed across town to the

Box Farm, down through Moo's wormhole, and across the bulk to Sqinkland.

And now I'm in sinister Tiny Town, disoriented and nauseated. I'm a brain and pair of eyeballs in a braincozy on the grassy Tiny Town bluff. Here in the gloom with hundreds of other braincozies. And at my side are the two other braincozies from the Club. Two brains, two pairs of eyeballs. Tobin and Winston.

Perhaps the three of us flew down together. I wonder what's happening at the Pacific-Union Club.

"Carol?" I call, projecting my voice via twirlware teep, which is flowing up through Moo's wormhole. "Carol?" No answer. I very much hope Carol won't end up like me.

"Yo, Oliver," comes Tobin's voice from the nearest braincozy.

I don't answer. I can't bear the thought of talking with him. The go-between.

"What a burn," continues Tobin. "Wasn't counting on Mumper and that rotten Flubsy taking me down like the rest of you. I thought they'd be bagging Carol for their third. I thought I had immunity."

"Immunity because you're pals with Moo and Mumper and Winston, and you helped organize the meeting?" I say. "Immunity because you set me up?"

"*I'm* the party to blame," puts in Winston. "I shouldn't have trusted them." His brain and eyeballs are, as I said, in the second braincozy over. His voice is as calm and logical as ever.

"More fool I," continues Winston. "Tobin called on me and said he was to set up the meeting. He said he'd bring his sqink helper Flubsy. I said I'd bring my sqink friend Xavier. It all seemed like a good idea. Hah! Moo said it would help save Earth. So, I reserved us a booth at the Club."

"Well done," I say.

Winston projects a sound of rueful laughter. "I took a class on negotiation at the Stanford business school. I imagined

Moo and I would get the better of Mumper. I assumed Flubsy and Xavier would be loyal to us."

"Flubsy was dazzled by Moo," puts in Tobin. "And gung-ho to live in my skull."

"In what way was this supposed to help Moo's higher plan?" I cry.

"I suppose she wants agents down here," Winston tells me. "You, Tobin, and I—living as brains in braincozies. I suppose there's a twisted logic to it. But, yes, I'm angry. Sad and angry."

My mind is boggling—if I can even say that I have a mind anymore. I fumble out some words. "Xavier is in your skull at the Pacific-Union Club, and Skeeze is in my skull, and Flubsy is in Tobin's?"

Winston's voice catches. "Xavier and I had fascinating technical talks about the cohomolgy symmetry groups of the bulk. I felt we were colleagues. Friends."

"And Skeeze was my little pal," I groan. "He kept saying I'd be helping to save Earth. Fat effing chance." I pause. "How long have we been down here, Winston?"

"Just a few minutes," says Winston. "Quick trip."

"Did they axe you and Tobin too?"

"Xavier and Flubsy swapped out our brains with short-distance hyperjumps. It's a 4D move. 2D analogy: you're on a sheet of paper, inside a circle. You hop up into 3D, glide to the outside of the circle, and land there. But, yeah—Mumper cracked your skull with his axe. Boom!"

"This is not what I deserve," I groan.

"Actually, the axe was my idea," says Tobin. "To make Mumper happy. So dramatic. So visual."

"Did Moo tell you they were filming a new ad?" asks Winston.

"I don't know," I mutter. "Maybe she mentioned it. But, my god, an ad for what? What would you sell with an ad like *that*?"

"An ad for Mumper's cause," says Tobin, kind of chuckling. "An ad for why everyone should surrender and not get treated like Oliver Strunk!" He guffaws. Man, do I hate this guy.

Looking at Tobin and Winston in their braincozies, I think of the French existentialist play, *Huis Clos*, or *No Exit*, about three damned souls whose hell-world is an eternity of living together. And bickering.

But maybe this is different? What about all the other braincozies? Our natural allies, right? And what's that light over the sea? Not a sunset. Far as I know, there isn't any sun at all in the Sqinkland sky.

I take a few minutes to write some pages about what's happening. Fortunately, my twirlware cloud-texting powers are intact. And as always, writing calms me down. Puts me outside of myself. Makes my life seem funny.

But then it's back to frantic worrying. Like: *Where's my Carol?* I call out for her again.

Skeeze's twirlware teep voice is what answers in my mind. "Carol's okay. I'm still at the Pacific-Union Club. Living inside your body, dude. I shaped myself into a functional emulation of the Oliver brain. Working fine. And we sqinks have some goo that healed your skull right up. Only prob is that my eyes look empty. But they work fine. Go ahead and look through them."

Via Skeeze, I see Carol with her face in her hands. She's sobbing. Winston and Tobin are of, course, as dead-eyed as before. Mumper is wiping the tabletop with a really large kerchief, almost the size of a bed-sheet, cleaning up the blood, quite a bit of it.

Lots of hubbub in the lounge—shouts, screams, chairs falling over, as if Mumper's assault just happened. Time is a little bit out of joint.

Mumper's chrome axe is out of sight. Moo still has her club-lady look. She doesn't seem all that surprised about anything that's going on. Well, why *would* she be surprised. She planned it.

"Do you like where you're at?" Skeeze asks me.

"Are you fucking kidding?" I snap. "Of course I don't like it. I'm a brain in a jelly egg with nobody but Tobin and Winston for company. Oh, and we've got a bunch of alien brains in braincozies nearby. And meanwhile you, Skeeze, you've taken my body. And I have the worst headache of my life."

"No surprise about the headache," says Skeeze. "Mumper cut into your brain a little bit when she split your skull. She lost her aim because Carol was all over her."

"This keeps getting better."

"You'll heal," says Skeeze. "They say braincozy treatment is highly salutary. It's like you're in a spa."

I let that pass. "Is Moo going to take Carol's brain?"

"Don't think so," says Skeeze. A growing clatter of noise in the background. Sirens. "The situation here is, um, dynamic, dude."

Carol's beloved features rush in at a crazy angle. She's close to my body's face, my body slumped in that corner booth at the Pacific-Union grill.

"Poor Oliver," she says, as if she knows I can hear. "Moo and I will come get you. Moo has this ridiculous plan about recruiting an army to help her run Earth. That's why you're down there. You'll see. If it works. Oh, and Tobin thought they were filming a viral dark web commercial to make people scared of Mumper and Moo, but—"

Carol lurches back out of view. She's shouting at someone, and people are yelling back.

The visuals slew to one side. My Earth body has fallen out of the booth and onto the ground. Skeeze still doesn't have smooth control. My body is on its back, staring upward.

Oddly enough, despite my desperate condition, a part of me is twirlware-writing notes as fast as I can.

Society-lady Moo is standing on the table. She's shrieking at Mumper, who has the chrome axe in play again. The brief Moo-Mumper alliance has broken down. Mumper is taking swings at Moo's legs. But Moo's too fast. She dodges the swings, and kicks Mumper in the head, over and over again, meanwhile trying to grab the axe. Moo's arms are getting longer; they're well on their way to being tentacles.

"Bring the zap guns!" Carol yells to the Club's security guards.

"Murder Mumper!" squeals Moo, as always having trouble getting her voice right. Mumper finally scores a hit, chopping off one of Moo's legs. But the leg grows right back, this time as a full-on tentacle. These sqink queens are tough.

"Don't listen to any of them," bellows Flubsy/Tobin, groping for a cover-up. "They're all drunk!"

The Skeeze/Oliver body is trying to stand up. And he manages to be looking the wrong way when the zap guns begin to fire. But then he gets his eyes on the action. He's steadily twirlware teeping the sound and video to me, and I'm grateful for that.

The guards sizzle old Mumper's ass but good. Yes, they crisp our queen like she's a tortilla in a blast furnace. She's an ashen ghost of herself, with the ashes studded by crystals of sqink-goo. The guards keep zapping till the crystalized goo is busted to dust too.

"Mumper's gone!" exults Carol.

"Not so fast," says Moo. "We sqinks are more soulful than you know. Mumper no longer has her bod together at all, I grant you that. But see the hot dot over there? Darting and flickering? That's sqink me-ware, my lady. Like a soul. Very hard to destroy. Mumper's me-ware doesn't like it in here. And now—zip! There she goes out the window. Perhaps to be seen again."

"Well, I'll tell you one thing," says stout-hearted Carol. "Mumper's been evicted from the Pacific-Union Club grill, and that's for ding-dang sure!"

The abandoned chrome axe spins on our booth's table like a game token. Most of the early-bird-special geezers are long gone, but a few linger at the fringes of the lounge, enthralled by our insane spectacle. Somehow the actual police aren't here. They're mustering forces? Making a plan? Paid off to leave the Pacific-Union Club alone?

As if hoping to impress someone, Flubsy/Tobin makes a belated glory-hog dive across the floor, trying to tackle a guard who crisped Mumper, even though Mumper is gone, and thus in no need of help. The guard has no trouble dodging clumsy Tobin. That's the kind of idiot the guy is, even with a sqink running his body.

At this point remember that Winston and Xavier were—and perhaps still are—friends. And be aware that Winston's braincozy-stored brain has gone a little screwy.

So now, Winston in the braincozy uses his twirlware teep to prevail upon Xavier/Winston at the Club to snatch up that chrome axe, spring forward, split the Tobin body's head wide open—and pry the sqink Flubsy from within the Tobin body's skull. As if removing a cancer tumor from an otherwise healthy man.

Moo and Carol stand to one side watching—Carol tense, and nice-old-lady Moo amused.

Acting as one, the guards fry the pried-out Flubsy into ashes, and then they fry the crystals among the ashes, like they did with Mumper. Doesn't take long. The ashes drift away. But this time, the guards have their zap guns fully on task. The moment that the bright dot of Flubsy's me-ware is seen, the guards' highly intelligent zap-guns overlay three different laser-like beams onto that one same moving spot that is perhaps Flubsy's soul and—

zzzt zzzt zzzt

Flubsy is gone forever.

The violent action has gotten good to braincozy Winston at a crude level that I didn't know the scholarly man had. Flubsy is gone, but the bloody Tobin body is still at the Club, and Winston doesn't like it.

At braincozy Winton's remote nudging, the Xavier/Winston body works out with that chrome axe for true, fully disassembling the Tobin body, with Xavier/Winston cackling and drooling and crying out as if in ecstasy.

A pause. Winston and I are watching all this from our braincozies in Tiny Town.

"Did you come?" I ask him.

"Can't you be civil?" snaps Winston. "Vulgar cad."

Meanwhile the Pacific-Union Club guards have accepted the murderous Xavier/Winston as a full blood-brother. There will be no criminal charges against this man. The guards are chuffed with death lust. One of their number aims her zap gun at Skeeze/Oliver.

"Let's kill this one too!"

From down in Tiny Town, I send a frantic shriek to Skeeze—who passes it to Moo—who flips fully into flying cuttlefish mode. She uses three tentacles to snatch up Carol, and uses three other tentacles to grab Skeeze/Oliver.

Always one for the grand gesture, Moo speeds along the walls of the Club grill like a tweaker motorcyclist at a county-fair Motor Drome show, circling the room at increasing velocity, and on the third pass, she shatters the grill's large stained-glass window, tumbles free into the cool March air, and ascends into the brilliant sky.

"Your turn now," goes Skeeze's voice in my brain. "Help Moo save your goddam Earth like you're supposed to. Do something in Tiny Town, asshole."

"Where's Moo taking you two?" I ask Skeeze, momentarily ignoring his rudeness.

"Um, I'll have her drop me off at Irene's," says Skeeze. "I think I have a chance with Irene. Don't think I'd have much of a chance with Carol."

I hear Carol's voice in the background.

"I dare you to try, Skeeze."

And then Skeeze tunes me out.

11. TINY TOWN

It takes me a minute to focus back on where I am. It's like awaking in a stranger's bed. Ah, yes, Tiny Town. I'm a brain inside a jellied ball atop a cliff overlooking a sea gilded with anomalous light.

And I'm amid hundreds of alien brains from Stok-stok. We're in braincozies. In the rough on a bluff. Welcome to Tiny Town in fabuloso Sqinkland.

Tobin and Winston are near at hand. That is to say, the brains of my two landsmen are nearby. Tobin is deeply pissed-off. It's the matter of Winston destroying Tobin's Earthside body.

But remember that Tobin laughed about *my head* getting axed. I have zero sympathy for the dude. His eyes are set into the side of his braincozy, with nerve stalks leading to his brain inside. Such resentment in those eyes. Such ill will.

He speaks: "Happy now, Ollie?"

I don't answer. I'll go nuts if I keep talking to this enemy. Turning my attention inward, I find something new. My recent experiences have loosened me up. It's as if the fates are potter's hands, kneading the lump of clay that was Oliver Stunk. I'm not the man I used to be. I'm more.

Some of Skeeze's sqink essence has entered into me. I have new powers. Falling into a meditation, I give the powers a try.

The process hinges upon iterated introspection. I look into myself as if I'm looking at a sqink. And then I look into the imaginary mind of the imaginary sqink, and then I look at that sqink looking at me, and I look at myself looking at the sqink looking at me—bouncing the process back and forth through multiple stages. Seventy-eight steps seems like enough.

I visualize the steps as nested thought-balloons, and I arrange them into a painter's perspective that recedes toward a vanishing point on an imaginary horizon. And—*aha!* I can visualize a handle on the horizon, a curved handle like on a walking-stick. I tentacle-stretch my arm, and grasp it.

And now, ahem, I'm controlling a universal sqink emulation tool. Don't ask me how or why.

First order of business is to work my braincozy into human-oid form. I rush the job, and I end with a grotesque, rudimentary man, little more than a ragdoll. But my brain is inside the little man's head, and my eyes are set into the front of his head where they're supposed to be. My sqink flesh is translucent, and I only have three fingers on each hand, but, oh well. At least I feel better than before.

"Mathematically sound," intones Winston, who's been closely watching my process. "You used an iterated transformation to find a fixed point in sqink phase space—and that point's neighborhood is, in and of itself, a sqink emulation tool."

"I might be the only captive in Tiny Town who ever found it," I say. "And it's not math that got me here, Winston. It's transreal narration. That's why Moo sent me. It takes a science fiction writer for the really hard jobs."

With a bit of coaching, Winston manages to imitate my moves, and he takes on a human form as well—although his body is seemlier than mine. Well, of course it is, given that the guy is riding on my coattails. One goof: Winston's handmade body has a flat Brit chauffeur's cap grown right onto his scalp. Which is totally gross.

This said, Winston's hat reminds me of my top hat on the top shelf of my closet at Box Farm—perhaps with Lilac still sitting in in it. Her nest. Speaking of the top hat—I'm so tuned into my sqink emulation tool that *pop* here's a copy of it, and it's small, like a party hat, and it's grown right onto my *own* ill-favored nob. I'm as ugly as Winston. Oh, well.

Back to the business at hand. I'm going to use my universal sqink emulation tool against the traitor turd Tobin. "Watch this," I say to Winston. "Do unto others as they wouldst do unto you. Do it fast, and do it first."

My sqink emulation tool extrudes a shrill rapier of light from my stubby forefinger. Note in passing that "shrill" is precisely the word I want to use here. It has an alternate meaning as a specific sqink concept, to be found in the operating manual of the universal sqink emulation tool, said instruction document to be found in the reaches of my racing mind.

I swing my shrill rapier. Tobin's braincozy screams, sizzles, and pops. The braincozies are, after all, living sqinks in their own right. Goo drizzles from Tobin's dying braincozy. The man's defenseless brain plops to the ground, wanting to twitch, but unable to.

"Come, come," interrupts Winston, using his upper-crust voice. "Does the poor sod deserve this? Haven't we revenged ourselves enough?"

"You trashed his meat body at the Pacific-Union Club!" I exclaim. "Chopped it up with the chrome axe."

"Granted," says Winston. "I did so do. But only as a lark. A whim. But at some point—"

"Look," I say. "Tobin sold out the human race. And he laughed at me. I don't like that."

"Quite so," says Winston. "Yet—we're among strangers in Tiny Town. One wants to put one's best foot forward."

"Get me another braincozy," wails Tobin's voice in my head. "Don't kill me. I'll do whatever you say."

The man's torment is a rising tide. *Be a mensch, Oliver.* I'm on the point of fetching Tobin a fresh braincozy when …

An alien is walking toward us, picking her way through the cluttered Tiny Town landscape. She's an elfin woman four feet tall. Not exactly a woman. A Mu9er! Like a feckless imp in a dark fairy tale. Her face is seamed and worn. Given what I've heard about the Mu9ers, I assume the aging is from years of unbridled sensual pleasure. Even so, the imp's eyes are bright and intent, like bird eyes, constantly flicking from one spot to the next.

It seems safe to say that this Mu9er has witnessed far madder scenes than Tiny Town. She has an aura of being streetwise to the extreme. Her skin is dark green, with dim yellow tattoos, constantly moving. She regards Winston and me, sizing us up.

We hang back, uneasy. And now the new imp speaks, her voice low and scratchy in our heads, her grammar shaped by hipster idioms.

"Kanga from Mu9. Thanks for peeling your pal's brain." With little ceremony, she produces a sparkling, flexible tube with a mouthpiece at one end. A type of pipe.

"A fresh huff, hey?" continues Kanga. "We might be putting human brains on the market. Where the hell is Gubb?" Kanga looks around, annoyed. "Always getting lost. Always fried."

Kanga throws back her head and ululates a wandering warble. Her companion appears, stumbling through the clusters of braincozies. Gubb. He too is a dark, twitchy elf. His tattoos are magenta. He's yet more weathered than Kanga, and again I have a sense that the wear and tear is self-inflicted.

"One senses that they're ready to kill us at any moment," murmurs Winston.

"Yep," says Kanga, overhearing. "Gubb's the hard cop. Less intelligent. Depraved. An attack dog."

"Screw you," Gubb rasps to his partner. He glares at Winston, his eyes squeezed small. "I'd kill this guy first."

"Is it something about our minds that offends you," I say, trying for a bantering touch. "Too artsy, intellectual, hoity-toity?"

No response. I have no idea what the Mu9ers are thinking. Or if they *do* think in the usual sense of the word.

"Ready to huff?" Kanga asks Gubb. She taps Tobin's naked brain with her pipe.

"Yah, mon," goes Gubb. His lips twist as he gloats over what's to come.

"Mumper's been hyping the shit out of human brains," Kanga says to Gubb. She's ready for business.

Gubb shoots another hard glance at Winston and me. "Hope you goobs don't want in on this. Stash is small."

"And don't try to defend that brain," says Kanga. "If you run any tribal shit, you're dead."

"No, no," I say, wanting this be over, and possibly consigning my soul to hell. "Not at all. Huff Tobin's brain."

"We'll watch," adds Winston.

"Prissy deeves," says Kanga, once more sizing us up. "Skronky. An ugly dream."

Look who's talking, is what I want to say. But I hold my tongue.

"Let's blast," says Gubb.

Kanga closes her thin lips on the mouthpiece of her pipe, and she flicks the pipe's free end in the air. A feathery, nearly transparent fan grows from its free end. The strands writhe.

And, by the way, maybe shouldn't really call the huffing tube a *pipe*, as nothing's going to be burning. But the word feels right.

With precise motions, Kanga runs the pipe's end along the stem of poor Tobin's cerebellum, and then across the lobes, as if sweeping fine debris into a dustpan. Gubb is in synch with Kanga, with his own huffing pipe in play, shadowing his partner's sinister moves.

Tobin senses what's afoot—this being, after all, his brain. In my head, by way of twirlware teep, I hear Tobin's wild twirlware shrieks of terror. I feel horrible. But I don't intervene.

"Dig the screams," says Gubb. Kanga chuckles.

They redouble the caresses of their fans, herding Tobin's psychic biocomputation process out of his physical brain. The huffing pipe's strands writhe deep and deeper into the brain's wrinkles and folds.

The brain lies passively still, even as wild currents rattle the circuits within, shaking Tobin's mind free of his wetware. The brain's very stillness makes the torment more horrible. In my head, Tobin's cries are rhythmic, steady, utterly out of control, unpleasantly orgasmic. As the climax approaches, a singular transition occurs.

You might say that a huffing pipe pries out the soul—whatever that word means to you or me. A glowing pattern rises free of Tobin's flesh. His thought processes have become a living plasma, if you will. And something about the arcane huffing process has made the pattern visible. Akin to the bright, busy jelly beans we saw above the slain sqinks in the Pacific-Union Club. Tobin's me-ware mind is wholly free of his physical brain.

"The me-ware," Gubb rasps in a confrontational tone. "You and the sqinks are lucky to have me-ware."

Paired with Kanga in his unwholesome delight, Gubb brings the fronded end of his huffing pipe close to the pulsing little blob of Tobin's me-ware. Dramatically, he inhales.

Gubb gasps with pleasure. Judging from the motions of the Mu9er's head, I get the impression that the me-ware is circling the inside of his skull—once, twice, three times. And then, with a sob, Gubb breathes it out again.

But now Gubb no longer looks pleased. He looks nauseated. This means nothing to Kanga. She's been closely watching, eyes glazed in anticipation. And now—never mind about Gubb's reaction—it's Kanga's turn.

The me-ware is still afloat. Before it can slip back inside Tobin's brain, Kanga inhales it up with her huffing tube. Like Gubb, she rolls her head as the me-ware zooms round the interior of her skull. And then—*whoosh*—Kanga releases Tobin's me-ware.

Tobin's teep remains silent. Can his me-ware wake him? Perhaps, but the me-ware hesitates, bobbing free in the air, as if enjoying itself, and wanting to fly off on its own, and ready to shuffle off its mortal coil. Perhaps sensing this, Tobin teeps the faintest sound of a groan.

Moved by—sympathy?—the me-ware settles back into Tobin's bare brain, sinking in like a setting sun.

Meanwhile the Mu9ers are stridently bitching. Kanga has thrown her huffing pipe to the ground. Her features are contorted in disgust. She bends and retches uncontrollably, heaving out the contents of her lean gut. A moment later, Gubb follows suit, vomiting more copiously.

In my head, I hear Tobin's voice again. Sobbing in relief, grateful to be alive, begging for mercy. Poor man, poor man, poor man.

"Nobody's buying *this* shit," says Kanga, slowly straightening up. "Stok-stok brains are the only kind we'll be buying today. Who the fuck does Mumper think she is, trying to deal this human crap to us. So nasty. Tastes like—would you call it piss?"

"Yes and no," says Gubb, mulling it over. The conversation is comfortably within his field of expertise. "The human me-ware ... it's coarse. Scrapes on your receptors. In human terms, it's like fingernails on a blackboard. Or, yes, like the taste of piss. Earthy, and with a sour note."

"How can it be a sound and a taste?" says Kanga.

"*Synesthesia*," says the learned Gubb. "Like smelling a noise. Hearing a color."

"Keep it simple," says Kanga, shaking her head. "Human me-ware tastes like piss. And that's the end of it. We're not buying human brains. Our deal with Mumper is off."

"Mumper was trying to burn us," agrees Gubb.

"If she's low on Stok-stok brains, she can sell us sqinks instead," says Kanga. "We'll huff sqinks, why not? Don't need to cut the brain out of a sqink. They're all brain, more or less. Like an octopus, with neurons in all its suckers."

"Like no brain at all," says Gubb. "Stupid turds."

"My Gubb is all brain, too," Kanga fondly says.

Off to the side, Winston and I observe this high-level planning session with interest. Watching the big dogs run.

"Mumper hands over a bunch of sqinks," says Gubb, warming to the subject. "Her subjects or slaves or whatever. Sqinks like to act all high and mighty. But they're just another alien for us to huff."

"Tell Mumper he owes us the sqinks, and if she won't deal, *skzzt*." Kanga pauses. "One thing—have any of us ever huffed a sqink?"

"Huffing sqinks has been on my to-do list for a long time," says Gubb, with a slow, evil cackle. "And no need to talk with Mumper. She's passed her sell-by date. We're with Moo now. Moo will kill Mumper, done deal."

"Got it," says Kanga. "And Moo gives us a sample huff of sqink right away."

"On neutral ground," says Gubb. "In San Francisco."

"Love it, Gubby. You've got octopus tentacles in your brain."

Hysterical laughter. They're still riding that huff lift. They turn to leave.

"Wait," I cry. "I still don't get it about the me-ware. The writhing light."

"Objective correlative for a soul," says Gubb. "To get philosophical on your lank ass. Sometimes the me-ware goes back into the host. Sometimes it don't. And that would be the woo-woo thing about transcending your mortal form, dig?"

"And what do you do if the me-ware goes back inside the host?" I say. "You let the host recuperate before you try and huff them again, right?"

"What are we?" says Gubb. "Nurses or some shit?"

With no further farewell than that, the Mu9ers drift away, cheerful about their plan to huff sqinks. They touch down here and there, deploying their huffing pipes and sampling the Stok-stok brains on the lot.

"Exit Kanga and Gubb, stage left," says Skeeze's voice in my head. He's talking to us from Earth. Making like he's narrating a play. It's all a game for him.

"Charming couple, what?" continues Skeeze. "I'd call this a big win. Mu9ers don't enjoy huffing human brains. A big, big win for your crowd. And, by the way, that's terrific work you and Winston did on finding a sqink emulation tool."

"Full credit to Oliver," says Winston. He's back to being a gentleman.

"Oliver's the man," says Skeeze.

"When do Winston and I get out of here, Skeeze?" I demand, my voice rising. I have a sense that we've been in Tiny Town for several days. Or even weeks? No way to tell.

Meanwhile, naked-brain Tobin's voice is still whimpering for help.

"Hang on," I teep to Tobin, feeling bad. "Just a sec."

"Moo still wants her army," says Skeeze. "That's the reason you're here. You, Oliver, you and your huge and wonderful personality, you will recruit a thousand sqink followers for Moo."

"How?" I ask.

"You get the stokkers to help."

"Huh?"

"The folks from Stok-stok," says Skeeze. "They're called stokkers. There's more than a thousand stokker brains in Tiny Town. Each of those brains was evicted by a sqink who's living on Stock-stok. Get it?"

"No."

"You lead the stokker brains to Stok-stok, idiot. Swap their sqinks back out. And enlist said sqinks in Moo's army!"

"We can do it," says Winston.

"And step lively," says Skeeze. "Not that I myself am in any particular hurry. I like it Oliver's body. A feast of sensory inputs and—*aaah*, the wetware. The hormones, neurotransmitters, and pheromones. Has it every occurred to you that the sexual climax is a form of quantum collapse?"

"You keep your slimy mitts off Carol," I say.

"Those would be *your* slimy mitts, no?" says Skeeze. "Carol is very jealous about my affair with Irene. That's a factor."

"*Grrrr.*"

Once again Skeeze tunes out.

Tobin is still talking. "I want to go home," he begs.

"You don't have a body on Earth, old top," says the heartless Winston. "Seems I rather damaged it. Perhaps you'd best stay here for a time. A naked brain lying on the ground. One hopes no one steps on you. Oliver and I will return anon."

"Stop picking on Tobin," I tell Winston. "The guy has paid his dues. And then some." I turn to Tobin. "Hang on, man. I'm finding a braincozy for you right now. And I'll make your braincozy look human. It'll work for you back on Earth. Everything will be fine."

Sure enough, I do find an unoccupied braincozy nearby, and I fit Tobin's brain inside it. The man is excessively grateful. It's heartbreaking.

"I'm sorry about everything we did to you," I tell Tobin. "I'll get you back into the game. Relax now. Can you feel how the braincozy is healing you? And now get this."

Using my sqink emulation tool, I humanize the braincozy's shape, doing a better job than I did on my own braincozy. I'm making Tobin look, well, like a regular guy, more or less.

"And now we'll need Moo to take you home," I tell the weary Tobin.

"Thanks, Oliver," Tobin says, lying flat on his back, very weak. "I always admired you."

And then, oh shit, he dies. No twirlware teep coming out. No electrical signals. Total flatline. All this has been too much for the guy. And it's my fault. For a moment, I wish I was dead too. What did Tobin ever do that was so bad? I'm a horrible person.

"Turn the page," says low-empathy Winston, nudging me. "Let's hobnob with our new mates. It's an unprecedented opportunity for xenoanthropology."

It takes me a while. I'm sobbing. Yadda yadda.

Winston gets me back in motion. We only have to walk about twenty yards until we connect.

"I'm Randa," says a braincozy near me. "A femme from poor old Stok-stok. We've been watching your antics. Too bad about your friend. But show me how to change my shape."

I heave a sigh. Or something to that effect, given that I'm a brain inside a glob of mystery gel.

"Don't let this story end," says Randa, very precisely calibrating my mood. "We stokkers need help too."

So alright, I feign a merry mood. And, strutting players on a stage that we humans are, I begin to feel it.

"Mental tango," I tell Randa. I dance back and forth on my stubby rag-doll legs. "You dream you see a sqink. You dream that she see you. You look her in the eye. The eye she look at you. Your yump begins to bump, your mug begins to glub, you tango to and fro, your vibe she start to flow." I pump my short arms as if I'm running.

Randa's braincozy rocks to my rhythm. For now, she's still just a bouncing blob, but she's circling me, getting the hang of the thang.

"You see me, me see you, sqink in you, she do it too," I chant. When the moment is ripe, I throw back my head and yell. "Bop boppity *bop*!"

"Tally ho!" cries Winston.

Randa's braincozy dimples, bends, and takes on a rag-doll form like mine. But Randa doesn't stop there.

She has style, and she morphs better than Winston or I were able to do. Her features and her limbs refine themselves, making Randa into an eloquent Black fashion model with pale lipstick.

Randa and I link arms and do a tango double strut.

"That's it!" exults Randa. "This is how I'm supposed to be." She turns to the stokker braincozy next to her. "Pinchly! You do it too!"

The Pinchly braincozy morphs into something like a dog, a cream-white dog with a brown patch, faceted eyes, antennae, and a large pair of mandibles. Maybe he's more like an ant than a dog.

"*Wooph*," says Pinchly.

"I'm Dazz," announces a third stokker in a braincozy. "Dazz stands for dazzler."

Her voice is smooth and melodious, and she picks up fast on the craft of sqink-tool body-morphing. Her braincozy becomes a radiant ziggurat, with a single eye on top. An eye with eyeshadow, eyeliner, and mascara—as if lifted from a glam dancer.

Pinchley, Randa, Winston, and I cheer Dazz on.

"I was in an elite stokker clan ... before the invasion," says Dazz. "A caste of witty intellectuals," she says. "We were at the top. The eye on the pyramid. Pinchly and Randa wish they'd been in my scene, but they were too straight, and they're jealous of me. And now they look like a human and an antdog? Pish."

"The hell we're jealous of you," says the deep-voiced Randa.

"Let's ask my sister about that," says Dazz, extending a gleaming ray toward a fourth braincozy.

"No, no!" interrupts Winston, raising a flat hand of *nay*. "Three stokker lieutenants is enough.

"What's that light above the sea?" I interrupt. "I can't figure it out."

"The glow is the wormhole that Moo dug to Stok-stok," says Pinchly. "Like a mineshaft through the boundary of the bulk, leading to our home planet? Mumper and Moo used the tunnel to invade us."

"Maybe my friends and I can undo the Stok-stok invasion," I suggest, understanding that this is what Moo wants. "We'll evict the sqinks who are squatting in your skulls on Stok-stok. We'll put you exiled stokker brains back in. We'll act for the good."

"Um, we saw you standing back and watching while your friend Tobin got his me-ware huffed," says Pinchly. "And then he died. And you began doing the tango. Is that your idea of acting for the good?"

"You didn't know Tobin," says Winston. "He was a problem."

"So you let him die," says Pinchly.

"Stop it," says Winston. "Or I'll kill you too."

Again I do something like heaving a sigh.

"Please," I say. "We really want to help you stokkers. You'll ask what's in it for us? I'll tell you straight up. We want to conscript those sqinks who now occupy Stok-stok. Gather them into an army for our friend Moo. An army for peace."

"And of course if you screw up, it's us Stok-stok folks that take the rap," says Dazz.

"Things can only get worse if you stay in Tiny Town," puts in Winston. "Waiting for Mu9ers to huff you."

"Eventually they'll be huffing you humans too," snaps Dazz. "Even though you taste wack."

"I understand that you two are bitter and suspicious," Randa tells her companions. "But right now these two humans are the only friends we've got. Don't push them away."

Somewhere in the background I'm hearing a woman singing the Queen of the Night's aria from Mozart's *Magic Flute*. Is that Carol?

I press forward. "Take us to Stok-stok," I tell the three stokkers. "I *will* get your bodies back. My powers are vast."

"Your ego is what's vast," says Carol, gliding in on Moo's back.

I've never in my life been so glad to see anyone as Carol just now. I wish I could lie right down on top of her, and make mad, crazy love. But, sadly, I'm a rubbery gingerbread man, of no great physical appeal.

Carol senses both my hubris and my dejection. She bursts out laughing.

"True or false: men are an unnecessary evil," she says. I guess this is a joke, or a paradox. Its meaning is hard to process. Whatever. I see empathy in my Carol's beloved face.

"You're wonderful," I babble. "Thank you for coming, my darling."

"Where's Diana?" demands Winston. As if he's entitled to a conjugal visit, too.

"She's in Oakland, working with Paul on his mural," goes Carol. "And Irene's organizing a dance performance for the anti-Mumper demonstration. By the way, that icky Skeeze-possessed Oliver body is with Irene all the time. I hate them so much. Even though I can get that fake Oliver back in a minute, whenever I want to. But never mind that. Here I am to help you." She giggles. "Hate to tell you, Oliver, but your body here doesn't even have a dick."

"I'll make myself better," I protest. "I can edit this body."

"Oh, don't bother. Introduce me to your new friends?"

"Meet the brains of three Stok-stok citizens," says Winston.

"Oliver claims he'll get us back into our bodies," says Pinchly. "And he'll enlist the sqinks who have been living in those bodies."

"Just as I wanted," says Moo. "My army."

"Who are you exactly?" asks Randa.

"I'm the mighty Princess Moo. Come, come, you know all about me, from the time of the invasion. I imagine that Oliver's been praising me to the skies. And, yes, sadly, it was I who drilled the wormhole to your world. Accept my apologies."

"That and a nickel will buy you a penny," says Dazz.

"It's Queen Mumper who bears the blame for brain thefts," continues Moo. "I'll kill Mumper soon. As the new Queen, I'll rule with justice for all. And yes, my champions, Carol and Oliver, will restore your brains to your bodies. Before long, all will be well on Stok-stok once more."

"Doubt it," says Pinchley.

The memory of Tobin's tortured death edges back into my mind. What if my plans for Stok-stock fare just as badly?

"Oliver's odds of succeeding are better when I'm around," puts in Carol, as if sensing my thoughts. "So, how do we get to Stok-stok so we can fix it? The mouth of the wormhole is that glow over the sea?"

"It's a wide highway," says Pinchly. "Mumper ran a thousand sqinks through there. More than enough to get the brain harvest rolling. And I hear that the sqinks are reproducing. As if they wanted to bag every single stokker brain. It's a Beeson-Pearce predation loop with no damping."

"Love the old-school chaos jive," I say. "How would you know so much about Earth?"

"Large language model," says Randa. "She that hath ears, let her hear. Let's get going. I'm the top stokker her, okay? So I'll ride up to Stok-stok with Moo. And of course you and Carol ride along."

"Me and Dazz will fly on our own," says Pinchley. "Brain-cozies are *mobile*."

"We won't be on our own, my dear," says Dazz. "We'll be leading a legion. A horde. Top lieutenants that we are. Or no, Pinchley, you be a sergeant."

"The other stokkers!" exclaims Pinchley," catching up with the conversation.

"All the other stokker brains in their cozies," says Dazz. "You can drill them on the niceties of the sqink emulation tool, Sergeant Pinchley. Be gruff. And then—off we go!"

"What about me?" Winston forlornly says.

"Oh, you just stay here," says Randa. "You're a poser. That accent you use—right away I knew it's fake. Even though I don't speak English."

We're talking via twirlware teep, of course. And the twirlware take care of translation. But somehow the reek of Winston's Brit accent comes through.

But right now, galled by the suggestion that he's the only one who can't come to Stok-stok, Winston's not using the accent at all.

"I gotta be there!" he screams. He has tears in his eyes. "Don't bully me, Randa. I'm a regular guy."

"Oh, I *say*," I say.

"Fuck you," hollers Winston. "Eat shit. You suck."

"Our pupa splits his character armor," says Carol. "What manner of moth doth emerge?"

"Stiff upper lip," I tell Winston. "As you were. I'll vouch for you. Top shelf." I turn to Randa. "Winston is smarter than you can possibly know. He weaves his own neural nets."

"So let him ride on Moo too," grates Pinchley. "I'm guessing the whole thing will be a fiasco anyway."

12. STOK-STOK

Carol and I hop onto Moo's back, with Randa and Winston behind us—and the thousand stokkers preparing to fly on their own. Moo soars forward above the crinkled sea, bending our course toward the glow. Carol and I look upward, our visages illuminated by the wormhole radiance.

"You look horrible," Carol says again. "Like a brain inside a condom. I can see your cortical folds. And your sad, add-on eyes! And that stupid hat. Oh darling. I'm so sorry for you." She bends forward as if to kiss me, but pulls back. She can't bring herself to do it. But, still wanting to be kind, she hums a bit of a lullaby.

"I feel sort of normal," I insist. "How's my body doing on Earth? With that damn Skeeze running it."

"He kept wanting to sleep with me, but then he moved in with Irene, and that's hard for me to handle." Carol's voice cracks, but she manages a tough-girl shrug. "Men are dogs."

"We'll set things right," I say, fighting back an alluring image of the Oliver body in bed with Irene.

"You just have to lose that rubber rag-doll look," says Carol. "And that pathetic little top hat in your flesh—ditch it right this minute."

"I'll take it," breaks in Moo. She pinches off my top-hat tumor with her beak, then chews and swallows.

"What is your problem?" I snap at Moo. "How can you do a thing like that?"

"At a sqink-luck level that meat hat was synced to your top hat in your closet," replies Moo. "The hat where Lilac broods. You'll see what I mean."

I let that one go.

Once we're directly beneath the Stok-stok wormhole, we rise upwards. Beneath us swirls the great throng of exiled stokkers. Each of them has tweaked their enveloping brain-cozy in their own particular way. I'm a bit frightened of them. Might they attack?

"Counting on you to get their real bodies back," says Carol. "They believe in you!"

I'm proud, but uneasy. What if I fail?

"Lead on," says Randa. "Let my people go."

Stok-stok is in fact a planet in Earth's universe. So the wormhole leads from the multidimensional bulk into normal space. Inevitably, such an arcane passage involves unpredictable side effects.

Just for starters, I begin seeing see bright-line mesh images of household objects—lamps, doors, vases, daffodils, rugs, toothbrushes, tubs. pills, pillows. And many of the objects are completely unfamiliar.

"I don't see how this cloud of icons is a planet," I tell Randa.

"Not there yet," says Randa. "What you're seeing is existential echoes from our nearby world."

"A self-generating epistemology?" inquires Winston. "Or, no, one might better call it a mirror phenomenology."

"Yadda yadda," goes Randa. "Logical thought is a fence that blocks the view. You look through the knotholes to see the real." Randa makes a lattice of her fingers and peers at me through the cracks.

"Nonplussed," murmurs Carol, entranced by the tumbling wireframe objects around us. Deep-space night lies beyond them, with bright specks of stars.

"Going through a wormhole is a psychic process," continues Randa. "Not a physical motion. And here's your in-flight entertainment." She makes baroque hand gestures, and chants a stream of surreal anagram poetry.

"Good dog, I eye, go ogre, Stok-stork, emit time, apocalypse psychospace, boring robing, sqink kink, dank candy, Mumper number, Moo omo, Randa drain, Carol coral, Oliver veil, dirt tirade, hate breathe, control toon, Winston want ..."

The beat goes on. The recital has a hypnotic effect on Carol and me. Blankly we sit, holding hands. The glowing mesh models continue their bustling rounds. And above us, in the distance, a pleasant green world draws near.

But now for no good reason, Carol and I enter a spurious scene about how we met. Keep in mind that this novel is something that I wrote while I was living it out. And the hallucinated scene I now describe has, I suppose, something to do with my wanting to fit my new girlfriend Carol into my old life.

We're on a campus of San Francisco State University, near the Pacific at the city's southern edge. The buildings are constructs of creamy art-deco adobe, with verdant courtyards, and a cafeteria where Carol and I sit together. We just met. It's fifty years ago. This happened with Sybil instead of with Carol. And it was in New Jersey instead of in California. But let the story play.

"How was your day?" Carol asks me. She's young and quite beautiful. Playful, liberated, wholesome. I glance down at myself and, thank god, I'm not rocking my Sponge-Bob brain-in-a-condom look.

Yes, I'm my old self, in jeans and an Oxford cloth shirt, and I'm not seventy-eight years old.

"Today was my first day ever of being a teacher," I tell Carol. "My class is on the Post-Twirlware Novel, right? I walk down the hall, a little late, and the other teachers are already busy. My classroom's full of students. I'm scared. I walk past the room."

"Walk out on your career?" says Carol.

"No, no. I turn around and go in. The students are friendly. We all want to get it right. I tell them my name, I talk about post-twirlware fiction, and how authors now need to up their game. I tell them I write SF, and I say how I'll teach, and I tell them about composing in your head, and then the period is over. I taught a class. I'm a professor."

Carol undoes my fly, takes out my penis, and fondles it with both hands. Or maybe not.

"No, I do *not* do that in a cafeteria!" Carol is saying. "Never."

Reset. Carol is across the table, calmly sipping her mint tea. Looking at me in a challenging way. "This is the part when you ask about *my* day," she says. "Hold up your side."

"What subject do you teach?" I ask her.

A friendly little flying dachshund has joined us. He has wings like mussel shells. He's standing on one end of our table. He starts barking, but Carol shushes him.

"I'm not a teacher," Carol tells me. "I'm a graphic designer. Making virtual ads for the school. We use twirlware now, so my input is conceptual. I'm like a director or a producer. But sometimes I do go in and tweak."

"What's your latest ad about?"

Carol gives me a smile that says: *Are you as dumb as you act?*

"What do you *think* my ad might be about?" she asks aloud, shaping her sentence with an upward lilt, as if talking to a child.

"Oh, right." I say. "You and I are supposed to save Stok-stok from Mumper and the sqinks. We're landing on this alien planet right now. And I'm scared, so I'm dreaming about meeting you."

"Got it," says Carol. "So come along." She circles to my side of the table. She takes my hands. "We'll do what we can. Just as we are."

"Where are the others?" I ask. "And us—where are we?"

"Where is the where?" says Carol, and repeats the phrase once more, and with heavier significance. The dachshund looks up at us from the table.

"Duh is the duh," I respond to Carol, as I wake from my fantasy.

The cafeteria dissolves into blotches that drift away.

Carol and I are back to riding Moo along with Randa and Winston. Dazz and Pinchley tag close behind us, followed by the great horde of stokker brains.

We're in a blasted cityscape, with block after block of shattered buildings. Welcome to Stok-stok.

It's a war zone. Skeletons and burnt skulls, and in the alleys are swollen corpses not fully decayed. Vermin feed on the bodies—alien rats and roaches.

Eerily calm. I hear only the wind and some low voices in the distance. Evidently there's been a civil war. Perhaps between the sqinked stokkers and the normal stokkers. And now the violence has played out. One side won, and the losers were driven away.

Randa is stunned. Her world had been intact when she left. Moo says nothing; perhaps she knew all along.

We follow the sound of voices and find a little park with some surviving locals on the benches. The first stokkers I've seen.

They're like humans, but with longer limbs, barrel chests, and drooping fleshy antennae on the sides of their heads.

At first, I think these stokkers are healthy, but they're not. They have dead black eyes.

"Brain thieves," says Randa.

Yes, these stokkers have sqinks inside their heads. Somehow—perhaps via my mental sqink emulation tool—I can see the forms of the sqinks within the skulls. Sqinks like strings of balls, banana slugs, triangular wedges, cuttlefish, wiener dogs, sea anemones, hands with eyes, flip-flappy wings, tadpoles with horns, and industrious shellfish.

"Kill them," breathes Carol.

"No, no, no," says Moo.

She gestures at the swarm of flying braincozies behind us—with Dazz and Pinchley at the lead.

"We let the brains get back into their own bodies," says Moo. "I bet the sqinks in those bodies are ready to go home."

Moo raises her voice, or rather, puts it into omnipresent mode. "Make a sound, you sqinks," she booms. Everyone on the planet can hear her.

Thousands of knuckles crack, slowly, juicily. I find the noise insufferable. It must be stopped—ended by me, the mighty, if somewhat beleaguered, Oliver Strunk. I fill my lungs and uncork a hideous and unprecedented yell—with an unbelievable effect. Somehow, I've managed to execute a Moo-style scale flip.

The reality levels of the planet Stok-stok collapse, or turn inside out, or whatever. The little world is now a pale, oily disk, like a wad of dough for an extra-large pizza, a foot across and four inches thick. This humble object is, from our altered point of view, the entirety of planet Stok-stok. A yielding, oily puck, fatter in the middle than at the edges.

I see things like airborne insects flying around the collapsed planet Stok-stok. These are a few of the sqinked stokkers we've been talking about, that is to say, stokker bodies with sqinks inside their skulls.

"An inside-out version of the planet!" exclaims Carol. "Bless my stars, Oliver. A scale flip!"

"Note that the dough is in layers," I say, proud of my work. "It's more like puff pastry than pizza dough. With, I suspect, eager-to-go-home sqinks in wriggling stokker bodies between the sheets."

"Well done, Oliver," goes Winston, looking things over. "Might one hope we're on the verge of restoring Stok-stok?"

"Not very close," says gloomy Pinchley. "Several thousand stokker brains were sold to the Mu9ers. Most of those brains are dead. The Mu9ers huffed them so many times that they faded for good. Beyond revival."

"But their Stok-stok bodies still have sqinks in their skulls, right?" I say.

"Maybe not so bad for those sqinks," says Moo. "Sqinkland is overcrowded, after all. But they're free to join my army. Along with the sqinks who get evicted by the returning stokker brains."

Dazz interrupts. "Never mind Moo's recruitment campaign. For me, the big aha is this: Oliver, dog knows why, turned our planet into a disgusting inside-out pancake. Can we talk about that?"

"In a minute," I say. "Me, I'd like to know where Mumper is."

"My turn for magic," says Carol. She raises high her hands, focuses on the doughy disk, and cries out in a loud voice: "I conjure Mumper!"

And yes, here's Queen Mumper, sitting cross-legged atop the bulgy wad of shrunken Stok-stok. Mumper's not dead at all. She grew herself back from her me-ware. One effin particle at a time.

She looks like she did in the Mission District of Sqinkland—a bossy woman in a green shirt. Except that now her skin is like a fabric of threads that glow in tints of mint, saffron, and red onion. The atmosphere around her is imbued by the high-voltage tang of ozone.

For once, I can see emotion in Mumper's eyes: hate and fear. I wrap my arms around Carol as if to defend her. As always of late, holding Carol floods me with love.

And as before, this very emotion repels Mumper! Seems like we've found a very simple line of defense. Mumper speeds off. Like an unwanted evil aunt at a baptism in a fairy tale.

"Well played," Winston says to Carol and me. "Expelling the demon. But, Oliver, why *did* you scale-flip Stok-stok into a fat, greasy pancake? It seems idiotic, if I dare say."

"Manageable size," say I. "This way it'll be easier to gather all the sqink-occupied stokkers together. Line them up, and then the braincozy stokker brains from Tiny Town can find their rightful bodies and switch in. But how do we get the stokkers out in the open? They're in between all those layers."

"Music," suggests Carol. "Lure them with song. You look musical, Randa. You've got flash. You crafted your braincozy body in a very elegant way. You're meant to perform."

"And all of you should know that Carol's voice is very fine," I loyally add. "Did you hear her singing *The Magic Flute*?"

"I notice an applicable tale within your society's mythos," observes Randa. "The Pied Piper of Hamelin? He leads away some rats, the peasants don't pay him, and he leads their children away forever. Perhaps we can do the same."

"But wait," I say. "Are the sqinks the rats or the children?"

"That's not the point, you dope," says Carol. "We sing, and something follows us. The sqinks. And you need to sing with us, Oliver. You can't just sit back and make clever remarks."

"Oliver's voice?" says Randa, giggling. "Oliver's voice is so ugly that he flipped Stok-stok into a cosmic cow-pie."

"Every singing group needs a voice like that," says Carol. "For overtones. I'll make it all sound sweet." She gives me another hug. Everything is going to be all right.

I hum tentatively from the back of my throat. Carol joins in. We start with a duet. My voice is unexpectedly tuneful with Carol at my side—it wells effortlessly from my throat. Carol's husky stylings wrap around it. Randa comes in with steady, rolling, contralto tones.

Lovely. One might say life is a winding song of love, with shifting beats and timbres, a vine in an endless jungle.

Randa, Carol, and I circle the shrunken, slippery, inside-out Stok-stok, cajoling the sqinks within. And behind us, the Stok-stok brains from Tiny Town have gathered around.

I still don't know if the sqinks are the rats or the children of the Pied Piper fable. I suppose you might call them children. But we're taking them somewhere good. Guided by scent or twirlware or raw instinct, the exiled stokker brains find their way to their rightful bodies.

No skull-splitting is required. The sqinks are sick of Stok-stok. They use their twirlware skills to trade places with the stokker brains. The lurking sqinks pop out, and the exiled brains hop in, avoiding the skull walls with short-distance hyperjumps.

And each returning brain connects to its old body's nervous system as if guided by magnets.

The freed sqinks rejoice; they flutter about like bugs or bats or birds, gaining in size as they stretch their bodies. They're a riot of forms in candied shades, glinting and iridescent. Exultant as a sky of starlings.

It goes without saying that Moo is taking credit for their liberation. And the sqinks wholeheartedly admire her.

Our friend Randa finds her old body; Pinchly and Dazz find theirs. They're glad. The sqinks who were inside the old bodies—they linger, and we introduce ourselves all around.

There seem to be deep resonances between the stokker brains and the sqinks who temporarily ran their bodies. These pairs are intimate at a deep, organic level. And they shared many memories. This said, there are some hard feelings about the invasion!

Be that as it may, there's a special camaraderie between Randa and the sqink who's been living in her skull. We find ourselves using the name Sqink-Randa for this now-ousted invader.

Sqink-Randa is so good at imitating the stokker Randa that Sqink-Randa is able to sing along with us. We croon a few rounds as a quartet: Carol, me, stokker Randa, and Sqink-Randa. But soon we run out of steam.

"It's time to get out of here," says Winston. "But don't leave planet Stok-stok looking like a greasy wad, Oliver. Scale-flip it back."

"Let Moo do it," I say. I'm weary and giddy. I almost wonder if this scene is a continuation of the hallucination I was having about being in the cafeteria of San Francisco State with Carol fifty years ago.

"No, no," says Moo, brushing off my request. "You did scale-flip once, you can do it twice, Oliver. You're running with the big dogs now."

"Hate that expression," I say.

"You should love everything," intones Carol, just to bug me. "No hate."

Oh, whatever. Gathering my strength and focus, I draw in the deepest possible breath and release a yell like the one before, except I yell *yell backwards* backwards.

Sdrawkcab lley!

It works. Once more, Stok-stok is a pleasant green and blue planet—albeit scarred by months of occupation and war. But there are many survivors. I see comfortable, well-tended homes, wholesome shops, and modest political posters with sensible words. Room for hope here, and maybe there's hope for Earth.

"Hail the sqink/stokker swap!" cries Winston. "A cascade of epistemological flips. A wonderland of mirror phenomenology."

Carol and I pause in our song and settle onto Moo's back with Winston.

"Good work," Moo tells us. She gazes up at the wheeling cloud of sqinks, with Sqink-Randa among them. "Looks like I've got my army."

Moo bears us through the Stok-stok wormhole and onward to Tiny Town, with an army of a thousand liberated sqinks in her wake. Pausing only for a moment, Moo sets Winston, Carol, and me down amid the remaining braincozies on the bluff.

"Wait, wait!" protests Carol. "We want to go home too."

"Stay here for just a minute," says Moo. "I need to hide my sqink army near the wormhole to Earth."

"Oh, come on," I say. "Just take us all at once."

"I like to have my secrets," sniffs Moo. "I don't want you to know where my troops are lying in wait."

And then she's in the sky, maneuvering her horde of sqinks as if doing a drill, with the troupe silhouetted against the light from the wormhole to Stok-stok.

Moo does a flip and a wiggle—and the light goes dark. She's slammed the door to Stok-stok. And that's a gift to the stokkers. Mumper would have a hard time finding them again.

And now Moo flies off, perhaps toward Earth, but I can't really tell. I just hope she comes back soon.

Bone weary, I lie on the grass and—even though I need to sleep—I put in some time writing mental notes on my adventures. Carol's resting her head on my spongy shoulder, and perhaps sleeping. I'm too excited to sleep.

Winston sits gazing at the sea and having his own thoughts, assuredly of very high caliber.

When I tire of writing, it occurs to me that I might try shaping my braincozy body into a fine, manly form that might better appeal to Carol. Who knows how long the feckless Moo will leave us here?

Perhaps it would have been reasonable to make my fake body look like my real one, but I foolishly overdo it, meaning to enhance my awesomeness. My new body is nude and muscular.

Feeling my flesh shift and stiffen, Carol wakes and runs a friendly hand across my chest. Winston makes some assumptions about how things are going, and he politely walks further along the bluff.

"Would you like to do it?" I ask Carol.

"No, not right now."

"I won't have this body for long," I wheedle. "Seems like a shame to waste it."

"Not into it," says Carol. "We'll do all that when we're home in bed and you have your real body back. And that'll be nice. I've missed you."

I do my best to hide my disappointment. "I just hope Skeeze cooperates," I say after a bit.

"I don't like that we haven't heard from him," says Carol. "He should be congratulating us for saving Stok-stok. Is he sulking? But never mind. I'm wiped. You should nap too, Oliver. Calm down."

So I do that, and after a while, I wake to Moo's voice.

"Time to get you guys home," she says, gliding in. Her thousand sqinks are gone. Carol and I don't bother asking where they went. We're too weary to care.

And now for another flight through the bulk. With Winston's *thub thub* beacon to guide us.

13. MY BODY

As we emerge from Moo's wormhole to Earth, the hyper-vigilant sqink twins, Zig and Zag, are on the point of nailing us with a yottawatt bazooka blast. But Moo slows them down.

"Not so fast, boys," calls Moo. "Let me and my riders get out of the way." She goes to hover at the upper edge of the slope that runs down to the wormhole. "All right now," she tells Zig and Zag. "Melt that hole shut."

"Won't we need it anymore?" I ask.

"If we do, I can open it," says Moo. "Right now, I want it blocked so Mumper gets slowed down when she comes here. And that's when we ambush her. It might be easier, though, if she can't find us at all. Winston! Have you turned off your bulk beacon?"

"It had to be on so we could find our way back here, Moo," says Winston, a little snappish.

"Okay, right," says Moo. "But now turn it off."

"Will do," says Winston. "Once I get home, and my weary brain is nestled in its proper skull. One thing at a time."

Zig and Zag get on with firing their cannon, as happy as scamps on the Fourth of July. Their stunning stream of yottawatt energy crackles down through Moo's wormhole, turning its walls into molten lava.

"We'll get there yet," says Moo. "A peaceable kingdom. I'll be back, Zig and Zag."

Moo drops Carol and me in Irene's front yard and flies off with Winston. Carol and I stand in silence, savoring our return. It's another pleasant San Francisco day, almost sunny, with wisps of fog. Irene's front door is cracked open by a few inches, perhaps for air.

"Aha," says Carol, her anger going from 0 to 100 in a fraction of a second. She strides over and yanks the door wide. I follow her inside, me still in my naked, muscular, braincozy body.

Irene and Skeeze/Oliver are on the couch, awkwardly messing with a set of Irene's dancer dolls. You can tell they've actually been making out. Like high schoolers surprised by their parents.

"You whore!" Carol screams at Irene.

"Hey, hey, hey," says Skeeze/Oliver, rising to his feet. "Be chill. You can't talk to Irene that way. She's a nice person. Why shouldn't we be friends."

"I've been borrowing him," says Irene. "Until he gets his brain back." She dimples. "But who knows? Maybe then he'll still want me. Some men say I'm addictive."

Carol scatters the bot dancers across the room.

"Oh, you're a tiger," says Irene, maintaining her cool.

"You can have this body instead," I say, gesturing at myself. "As soon as Skeeze and I swap places. I mean, if you *want* this body. It's just a fake. And, Skeeze, why haven't you congratulated Carol and me about Stok-stok?"

"I've been, like, busy," says Skeeze. He and Irene share a cozy laugh.

Carol goes all the way over the edge. I don't think I've mentioned her unpredictable temper. It's something I'm learning to live with.

"I hate all of you," she yells. "I don't care if you get your body back or not, Oliver. We're through! What a mistake I made."

She's crying. I feel horrible. Carol is the love of my new life. Doesn't she realize? She runs outside and off down the street. Like she's walking home.

Incredibly, I'm hesitant to go after her. Because I'm intent on getting my real body back. I'm standing here waiting for it. Keep in mind that my brain is still in the fake body shaped like a dumb-ass weight-lifter.

Thing is, I have a sense that if don't get my real body *right now*, I'll never get it back at all. Skeeze seems very comfortable wearing it.

And, hell, I can make up with Carol later on when things get back to normal. Whatever normal is.

Skeeze/Oliver is laughing at my dismay. I grab my old body by the throat, very nearly encircling the neck with the fingers of my coarse right hand.

"I've got my universal sqink emulation tool," I tell Skeeze. I pop the tool into action and generate a sqink-killing zap gun in my left hand. "I'll crisp the shit out of you, Skeeze. Crisp you right inside that skull, if I have to. I don't care what it does my body."

"You're bluffing," croaks Skeeze/Oliver. "You'd never hurt your own flesh. And I like it in here. I'm not gonna go."

"Try me," I say, all hulking and nude.

My Skeeze/Oliver body's throat emits a pitiful rattle. Don't overdo it, Oliver. Don't kill yourself. I let up on the pressure. Skeeze is silent and defiant. Will I actually use the zap gun? Maybe I can narrow down a microbeam and blenderize Skeeze inside my skull?

Irene weighs in. "Don't be such silly boys," she says. "You made a promise Skeeze. You said you'd give Oliver back his body after he did this mission. You and I have had a nice time together. But that's no reason for you two guys to be killing each other."

Ah, the civilizing influence of the fair sex.

I release my grip on my body's throat.

"You said you loved me," Skeeze/Oliver croaks to Irene.

"It was only physical," goes Irene. "And if Oliver's brain comes back, I'm fine with that. It'll *still* be physical—if he wants to play. Also, Oliver's personality is better than yours, Skeeze. You're nasty. Oliver is nice."

"All right, all right, all right," says Skeeze, his voice cracked and husky. He's upset. "What the hell do I care? Oliver's body is a piece of crap."

"I hope we don't have to use an axe again," I say. "Like Mumper did?"

"Mumper just did that for her video, remember?" says Skeeze. "She had the idea of scaring everyone into surrendering to her. Which is ridiculous. I guess the ad ran. Don't see as how it could help Mumper's cause. But even so, she might still win out."

"I saved Stok-stok, and I can save Earth," I say. "Asshole."

"Someone needs the guts to step up and take Mumper out," says Skeeze. "A hero."

"Enough insults and bragging," says Irene in her mild voice. "Do the swap."

"Put your head next to mine," Skeeze tells me. "That's right. And now we do a femtophysics hyperjump. Abracadabra."

What do I see while it happens? Visions as wild as in the bulk. Here we go.

Zzz Gyy Xfx Kmk Vov Npw Wxy Bnd … Aaa.

That is, I see all 17,567 combos of three letters, with the combos arranged in a special cryptic order, and each combo stands for a distinct bin of my thoughts.

Bins like: Mardi Gras, weakness, thirst, leather pants, pig, bulb, gold, axe, ick, cube, phenomenology, stink … and cravat.

This arrangement represents one layer of a phenomenological neural-net map of my brain, as seen from the inside.

And, of course, there's more than that one layer. A lot more.

The full set of layers wheel past, and when the procession is done, I'm in my own right body and still in my brain. And, whew, nobody had to smash my skull with a chrome axe.

As for Skeeze, he is, um, Skeeze is a floating string of balls, like he sometimes likes to be, balls in shades of white, gray, and black. My punk sqink.

He's not at all trying to look like a human brain. Nor is he switching to be inside the skull of that Frankenstein muscleman that I rode here. Skeeze is done with the brain routine. He's floating in the air. The muscleman lies dead on the rug. Unanimated, unresponsive, unmourned. A no-brainer.

I sense a deep personal connection with Skeeze, deeper than before. It's like the camaraderie I noticed between Randa and Sqink-Randa. Skeeze's memories and my memories are both embedded in the flesh body that we shared. I can feel an echo of Irene's caresses. And do I feel Caol's body too? Do I feel ghosts of Skeeze handling her?

"Do me a favor and drag that thing into the garage," pretty Irene says to me, pointing at my discarded muscleman body. "Would you, Oliver dear?" She's smiling at me, making plans, a thousand steps ahead of me. Women always are.

But, god help me, I want to be in those plans. I can taste her scent.

"Will you spend the night?" she asks.

"Yes." A twinge of guilt regarding Carol.

"Enjoy," goes sqink Skeeze, floating out the front door.

"I want to hear all about your adventure," Irene tells me. "This is so exciting. Sit down beside me. Would you like some food? A drink?"

Yes, I want food and drink, and I want to sleep. Skeeze hasn't been taking good care of me. My body is wrung-out and wretched.

I flop onto the couch. Irene throws a friendly arm across my shoulders. I've missed being me. You don't know what you have until you don't. My chest is fluttering. What is this? I'm sobbing.

"Aw," says Irene, and kisses me on the forehead. "Poor Oliver. You're back, yes. You're safe with Irene. Was it horrible?"

"I have to save Earth from Mumper," I mutter. A little frantic about this. "We're not done. And I can't do it without Carol. I should call her right now. I have to call Carol."

"No," says Irene, holding up her hand. "I'm not just saying this because I'm selfish. Carol needs to cool down. And you need a break. *I'll* call her. And you stay out of it."

"If you call, she'll flip," I say. "It'll be like you're gloating. She'll come here with a zap gun and crisp our brains."

"Would Carol do that?" says Irene, cocking her head, amused. "Don't think so. In some ways, I know her better than you do. Woman to woman. We see things that you men can't. Subtle, mysterious things—like people having mixed feelings. Or like the sun being in the sky at noon."

My body's memories of Irene are flooding my mind.

I sigh. "You do what you like, Irene. I'm going to look at your kitchen."

As I walk across the room, Irene calls Carol. In a minute or two, Irene is laughing. Not sure what Carol is doing. Better that I don't hear. Irene ends the call.

"Carol is fine with you staying with me a day or two," Irene claims, joining me. I'm standing in front of the open fridge. "Like I said, Carol needs downtime. She changed her mind from before."

"And is—" I begin.

"No more questions," says Irene. "Relax. Carol still loves you."

So, what the hell. I'll take what I'm offered. I'm too tired and hungry and fried to care if Carol forgives me.

Irene gives me a really nice smile.

I root into the fridge, putting things on the kitchen table. Leftover takeout from Namaste, sliced roast beef, an orange, part of a roast chicken, brie, sparkling water, chocolate, a slice of apple pie, and a pint of coconut ice cream.

Irene sets a place and watches me almost tenderly. "I've been worrying about how little you were eating," she says. "Dear Oliver. My teddy bear."

I look up from my plate. "Dear? Oliver? Teddy bear?"

"I've been calling you Oliver all along. My dear teddy bear. Maybe I can keep you."

I pause from eating, savoring the leading edge of a massive sugar rush. My brain is working better. And my body memories are stronger all the time.

"How long was I gone?" I inquire.

"Four days."

"And Mumper still hasn't invaded?"

"I think I would have noticed," Irene says with a smile. "But you still haven't told me your adventures, Oliver."

"Are you sure Carol said it's okay if I stay?"

"She's moody," says Irene with a shrug. "Mercurial. Once, she stole a boyfriend from me. I doubt if you knew him. Tig Tucker. In my opinion, Carol owes me."

Not touching that one. I keep on eating, and each time my glass of sparkling water empties, Irene refills it. Pellegrino. And then I'm done.

"Can we get in bed?" I venture to ask. I want to do it before this wonderful dream ends. "And thanks for taking me in."

"My big handsome man."

We kiss.

Irene falls asleep when we're finished, tenderly resting her head on my chest. You'd think I'd fall asleep, too, but I'm pretty wired from the food, the sex, and all my adventures. So I lie there and write for an hour, seeing the pages on the ceiling, taking satisfaction in my craft, and getting the words and phrases just right. And then I'm asleep too.

Naturally, Carol wakes us in the morning, pounding on the door like a crazy person. It's a hassle, and upsetting, and even scary, but basically, I'm glad she's here. I belong with her.

"Okay," I say right away. "I'll come back." I look her over. "You're not carrying a gun, are you?"

"You're not worth it," says Carol.

"That's the spirit," I say.

"We'll call it even," Irene says to Carol.

"How's that?" goes Carol.

"Tig Tucker?"

"Oh Christ," says Carol. "That loser?"

"You broke my heart," says Irene, striking a dramatic pose and breaking into laughter.

"It's not funny," says Carol.

"Oh, why not," says Irene. "Why can't life be funny? And you've been a bad girl too."

"Come along, Oliver," says Carol.

I feel embarrassed, and glad to have had a night with Irene—and also glad I'm off the hook. I pull on my dirty clothes—naturally Skeeze never washed them or even changed. Carol's outside with my car. Quietly I hug Irene goodbye, and thank her from the bottom of my heart.

Carol and I drive to the Box Farm in silence. First thing, I take a shower.

"What a burn," I say to Carol when I'm cleaned up. "Not every day a man gets his brain cut out."

"Glad you're back home," says Carol, slouched on the couch. "Maybe I'm glad. I hadn't figured you for a two-timer."

"It was an accident," I say. "It just happened. I didn't seek it out. And Irene said you owed her? And that you were a bad girl, too?"

"Oh, she meant Tig Tucker," Carol says dismissively. Perhaps she wants to laugh. But she's keeping her face cold.

"I have no idea what happens next," I say, pouring some milk into my coffee. More than ready to change the subject.

"You're the science fiction author, Oliver. You're writing this up as a book. You ought to know the ending."

"Maybe I'm not a real writer. Maybe I faked it all along. Maybe I used twirlware or an assistant like Skeeze. Not that he ever does squat."

"Come on," says Carol. "This should be easy for you. Keep on living. Keep on dreaming. And at the end, I don't know, we're growing raspberries on bonsai trees."

"Speaking of food," I say. "We don't have any. Let's go to the farmers market at the shipyard. My hunger is vast and all-encompassing. Starved for four days!"

Carol gives me a calculating look. "Hungry even now?"

"Not sure what you mean."

"I mean, you'll have to get fumigated for sexually transmitted diseases if you and I want to start being intimate again. Irene's the type."

"Believe it or not, I was talking about brunch," I say. "Fumigated?"

"However they do it these days. I wouldn't know."

"Got it," say I. "But not right this minute. Maybe I've had enough stress this week. Can you imagine that? From having my brain cut out, and like that?"

"I was down in Tiny Town too," says Carol.

"Yes, and you were wonderful. And we saved Stok-stok. And we'll save Earth, you and me, darling Carol, and I still love you, and I'm sorry about Irene. But now let's just go to the farmers market. And act like it's Sunday."

"It's Thursday," says Carol.

"Yes, I already figured that out. And Thursday is the day when they have a farmers market at the shipyard."

"So why did you say Sunday?" goes Carol, slitting her eyes and looking mean.

"Why did you get me back from Irene—if all you want to do is argue with me?"

"Because I missed you? Because I'm mean?" Her face trembles.

"Food," I say, putting my arms around her. "We both need food. Farmers market. I'll get my hat." I start for my closet.

"What about Lilac!" exclaims Carol. "Is she still in there?"

Well, yes, Lilac *is* in there—along with about a thousand sqinks. Did Lilac hatch them? They tumble out the closet door like coins from a slot machine, popcorn from a popper, jewelry from a case, ornaments from a holiday tree, coming on and on—rubbery, glowing, hovering, chirping, whirling, brushing across the skin of my face as they fly by.

"*Buk-buk-aaawk!*" cackles Lilac.

Carol is speechless. She collapses onto my bed, gazing up at the flock.

I might as well write another Borges list.

The sqinks are like a swarm of mutant insects, temporarily shrunken to fit into our room, a Miro painting come to life, aerialists of an umpteen-ring circus, ball-and-stick models of every possible molecule, off-brand strange particles from the subdimensions. No two of them are the same. Chirping, chittering, twittering. And now they find their way out through a hole.

I lie down next to Carol.

"We're doomed," she says. "It's over."

"Maybe they're not brain thieves?" I suggest. "Lilac is so nice."

Carol groans and pulls a pillow over her face.

Lilac herself remains in my top hat on the top shelf. Still clucking to herself. She seems proud and, in some way, amused.

"Don't hatch anymore," Carol tells Lilac. "Enough sqinks, all right?"

Lilac is a string of violet and purple balls with a lizard-like head. Gleaming black eyes. She emits a long series of garbled, gobbling sounds. Carol nods her head.

"What did she say?" I ask.

"Isn't it obvious? They're not Lilac's chicks. Moo homed in on your old top hat and hid them here. Remember how she ate that hat shape off your head in Tiny Town? They all thought it was funny to pretend they'd been hatched."

"I've got a good feeling about this crowd of sqinks," I say. "Sense of humor. Where is Moo now, Lilac?"

Her answer: "*Cackle squawk.*"

Carol's translation: "Still at her wormhole with Zig and Zag. Expecting Mumper. It would help a lot if Winston would turn off his bulk beacon."

"Never a dull moment," I say. "Constant drama. Are you hungry, Lilac?"

"Food again?" says Carol, abruptly changing her tone. "You're out of your mind. You cheated on me with Irene. Also, Earth is totally invaded, and basically that's your fault. You're the worst person in the world."

Carol's moods can be variable. "Things might still work out," I offer, keeping my voice bland.

"*Ha.*"

In the sky above the Box Farm, the sqinks chatter.

"How did you get my car, anyway?" I ask Carol. "I thought I left it at Irene's before the Pacific-Union Club."

"Skeeze/Oliver drove it over here for me," Carol curtly says. "While you were gone."

We get my car and head for the farmers market. It's held on an acre of stained concrete beside the retrofitted Naval shipyard in Hunters Point. Not very far. The flock of Moo's sqinks tags after us.

The shipyard has slips and docks and huge machines for assembling, welding, painting, fitting, and lifting steel ships. They got the facility cleaned up and operational last year, although they're having trouble getting enough employees. I wonder if sqinks could work here.

The informal market is busy and bustling. Seeing my sporty, familiar car and the twinkling swarm of sqinks, a few people cheer.

"They think it's a holiday," I tell Carol.

"Saps. It's the end of the world. And you want food."

14. BULK BEACON

I park the car at the shipyard and, yes, I get a plate of enchiladas and a big glass of watermelon juice. Carol stands apart from me, pointedly not eating. She stares angrily at the circling sqinks. I want to think of the new sqinks as friends—but who knows.

Rather than crying out in fear, as they might well do, the folks at the market are beckoning to the new arrivals, holding them in their hands, and feeding them scraps.

I wonder how many of them saw Mumper's horror show ad about chopping open my head at the Pacific Union Club. I've lost track of things, being down in Tiny Town and Stok-stok.

But right now I'm not hearing any outcry about how Oliver Strunk got his skull cracked open with an axe. I'm running a routine about this in my mind.

Them: *So what if a sqink axed Oliver's head? Never liked his writing anyway.*

Me: *Tough luck, guys. Here I am, same as usual.*

Yes, the hipsters at the shipyard are inclined to give this latest round of sqinks the benefit of the doubt. People still want sqink luck.

I bring a couple of the fish tacos to Lilac, still perched atop my top hat in the backseat of my car. Carol comes watches. In a way, Lilac is still Carol's pet. Lilac opens her mouth very wide in that odd double-jointed way of hers—and horks the tacos in a flash.

"There you are!" exclaims Carol's daughter, Loulou, coming up to us. "I haven't seen you since the sqink riot, Mom. Nor Oliver. What's up? Do you know where Tobin is?"

"Don't ask me that question," says Carol. "Ask Oliver."

"We were all down in Sqinkland," I say after a pause. "And Tobin—he's not gonna make it back."

"He's—he's what?" says Loulou.

"He's dead," I say. "The sqinks killed him."

"Winston Tropp is the one who killed him," says Carol.

"It's Flubsy the sqink who took out Tobin's brain in the first place," I say. "And it was Xavier the sqink who helped Winston chop up Tobin's body with an axe. And Kanga and Gubb from Mu9—they huffed Tobin's me-ware to get high. Twice. And then Tobin died."

The tale is complex and absurd. Like one of my scurvy SF stories. Funny but not funny.

Loulou is sobbing and backing away. A bell-shaped sqink lands on her shoulder and nuzzles against her. Loulou cries out in fear.

"You didn't have to tell her all that," Carol snaps at me. "You're heartless. You and I are through." She hurries after her daughter, meaning to comfort her.

I stand there, feeling blank. We're through? Every time I turn around, Carol says that. Any hope of winning her back? I can't even.

The sqinks are all over the marketplace, pervasive as pigeons or sparrows or seagulls, flying and strutting and eating garbage, and the scraps they beg,

As I said, people are avidly befriending sqinks, and the sqinks are going along with it, and pretty soon every shopper or farmer or idler has a sqink pal. Everyone's glad, everyone except Loulou, who's still moaning about Tobin. And, as far as I know, she didn't really like him. Loulou is like Carol. She likes big scenes.

The leftover sqinks—and that's about seven hundred and fifty out of the thousand—they rise into the air, circle, and set off across Dogpatch, Bernal Heights, Noe Valley, and downtown, with pairs or groups arrowing down whenever they pass a busy shop or parklet or church or bar or BART stop—the individual sqinks plummeting like pelicans diving for fish. And even then, some sqinks remain. They cross the Western Addition, Cole Valley, and the Haight—and then they're all gone.

"Tell Loulou you're sorry," says Carol, coming up to me with Loulou in tow. That bell-shaped sqink is still on Loulou's shoulder, pressing close, and Loulou is petting him.

"I *am* sorry," I tell Loulou. "You know I'm your friend. You deserve better. I shouldn't have laughed. It—it was so wack. But that's no excuse for me being rude." I pause. "Carol says I'm the worst, and maybe she's right."

"You weren't even nice to begin with," says Carol. "I don't know why I took you on."

Took me on? Is that a ray of hope?

"Blame me, Mom," says Loulou with a weary sigh. "I'm the one who fixed you up with Oliver." She pauses. "And, no, I never really *did* take Tobin on. Not like you with Oliver. Even so, I'm sorry for the guy. Such a gnarly end."

"I hear that," I say. "And, again, I'm sorry. I'm just—"

"Just a jerk," says Carol, finishing my sentence. "Leave it at that." She pauses. "And, no, Oliver, I'm not done with you. There's a certain sense in which you're—" She leaves my redeeming attributes unspecified.

"I'm glad," I say. And, dammit, I'm crying again. What is wrong with me? I need a hug.

Carol keeps her distance. "Not yet," she says, as if reading my mind.

"This bell sqink's name is Dingdong," says Loulou. "I'm gonna keep him." She looks around the market. People are drifting away. "Can you give me a ride to the Box Farm?"

"Oliver's going to the clinic," says Carol. "But he can drop us off."

"I didn't buy groceries yet," I say.

"Don't start that again," says Carol. She leans into the car. "Move over, Lilac. Make room for Loulou. And by the way, Lilac, are you going to come back to being my helper? Like you were before?"

"Gnorp," says Lilac. Carol indicates that this means, "Yes, I would love to.".

I drive Lilac and Loulou to the Box Farm, and Carol gets out with them. She warns me not to try lying about whether I got a fumigation.

"No worries," I say. "It's a good idea."

"Faithful servants reap golden harvests," says Carol, smiling at me for what feels like the first time since we got back.

As I drive off, I see Winston waving at me from atop his warehouse, which isn't all that far away. But I'm not to be stopped. I speed twenty blocks to the sex clinic, where I am in fact fumigated—in a stall with hideously thin chartreuse tubes that wind around me and poke into every possible orifice, puffing out pale, steamy clouds of anti-everything mist.

Outside, I find Winston, Skeeze, and Xavier waiting by my car. "I'm in urgent need of assistance," says Winston. "Didn't you see me waving to you? I followed you in a taxi."

"I'm your man now," I say. "And I'm crystal clean. What's up?"

"Can't you humans ever relax?" says Skeeze. He's in his punk monochrome string-of-balls mode, wriggling in the air. The bumblebee-striped Xavier is wrapped around Winston's waist.

"We should all be happy about scoring those thousand sqinks," says Xavier. "We've already talked to them. We're friends now, just like we're friends with you."

"Why do you two sqinks think you're our friends?" I ask. "After stealing our brains?"

"Shit, Oliver, you and Winston couldn't ask for better pals," goes Skeeze. "We know you inside out, right? And, get this, Xavier laid Winston's woman Diana!"

"I'm dapper," brags fuzzy Xavier. "I amuse. I tickle."

"Should I shoot him with my zap gun?" I ask Winston. I know what the man is feeling.

"Let it ride," says Winston with a sigh. "I don't think that story is even true. You know how Skeeze is. Forget him. I want to talk about my bulk beacon."

"I'm hearing that you still haven't turned it off?" I say.

"Call the bulk beacon *she*, not *it*," says Winston. "You need to understand that the bulk beacon is alive and conscious. Her name is AntnA. And she's my good friend."

"Um, okay," I say, really doubting this.

"With all the realware and twirlware that I put into AntnA, her computational powers are considerably greater than yours," says Winston, irritated. "AntnA used autogenic twirlware to grow a personality—with a little coaching from me. She's like my child, or, hell, like a chaste girlfriend."

"Chaste?" interrupts Xavier. "I'm gonna give Winston some tips about pitching woo to his Diana. Help this geek smoove his groove."

Winston abruptly loses it, as he is known to do. He grabs Xavier with both hands, stretches the chain-of-balls-sqink like a rubber band, and releases one end. *Boing!* Xavier streaks through the air and splats into a stone wall. Then flies crookedly back in pained silence.

"Winston goes irrational on your ass," I tell the sqinks. "You gotta remember that."

"I find these vulgar ruffians overly merry," intones Winston. "I won't stand for it. Do you truly have a zap gun, Oliver?"

"In my glove compartment."

"I doubt if killing a sqink is legally a crime," says Winston.

"Perhaps a public service," I say, glaring at Skeeze and Xavier. "Pest control."

"We'll stop teasing you guys," says Skeeze. "We'll be good."

"Very well," says Winston, making a dismissive gesture. "As I was trying to tell Oliver, I have a problem with my bulk beacon. AntnA. *I can't turn her off.*"

"What?" I cry. Visions of Mumper's army zooming in. Visions of Kanga and Gubb from Mu9 with their huffing tubes. "Get in my car!"

I drive very fast, running every light. Skeeze and Xavier fly ahead of us, flashing their bodies like ambulances.

"The blocks flicking past like this, it's quite hypnotic," muses Winston, unfazed by the insane speed. "I hope you can get the better of my bulk beacon, Oliver. As you noticed, I tried to wave you down, but, no, you had to rush to your sex clinic." Thin, nervous smile. "The price of promiscuity."

"So, I spent a night with Irene," I cry. "With my own brain in my own body. Big deal!" I slew into a sidestreet and hit 110 miles per hour, skittering down the final slope to the Bay. One more drift turn, and we're parked in front of Winston's hulking warehouse. Engine ticking, tires smoking.

Carol stands by the entrance with Diana. Carol must have walked over. The two women are laughing. Maybe Diana did sleep with Xavier in Winston's body. And, who knows, maybe Carol slept with Skeeze in my body. I keep having a deep-down physical memory that she did.

I know nothing about women. Compared to women, we men aren't even dogs. We're chew toys.

I glare at cheerful Skeeze, who is flying loops with Xavier. He seems to have no idea why I'm uptight. So relax, Oliver.

This is about saving Earth, right? It's not about clinically insane jealousy. Your Carol slept with your body while your brain was elsewhere. So?

A vast mural is in progress on the warehouse walls. I can see Paul Vreed up there on a scaffolding. Always cheers me to see him. Whatever the topic, the man truly doesn't give a fuck. He's an artist, and that's all. His sqink paintbrush, Doob, is angled in the air, lavishly slapping on colors.

The emerging representation—it seems to display, oh god, can't I ever catch a break—it's the scene where Mumper cracked my skull open with her chrome axe. On the mural, I have an odd expression, unpleasant to see.

"Hi, Oliver," goes the smiling Carol. "You're all clean?" She's got Lilac perched on her shoulder, looking like a corsage.

"Yes, I'm fine," I say. I'm awash in conflicting emotions and muddled thoughts.

"And you'll be a good boy from now on?" says Carol. She and Diana burst into renewed laughter. Lilac the sqink laughs, too, although I doubt she ever knows what anyone is laughing about. She just likes to laugh along.

"What's so funny?" I ask Carol point-blank.

"Mainly, we're laughing because we're scared," says Diana.

"And maybe I really am glad to see you," adds Carol. "I'm not a complete heart of stone. But, yes, we're scared because Diana and Winston can't turn off the bulk beacon."

"I told Oliver," says Winston. "That's why I fetched him just now. We thought you two might help."

"Still a team?" says Carol, taking my hand. And yes, we are. Carol is my love.

We two and Diana follow Winston into the building, bypassing the living quarters, the offices, and some shelves of twirl-ware teep materials. Skeeze, Xavier, and Lilac tag along. And now we're in Winston's cavernous lab.

This half of the warehouse is completely unfinished. Concrete floor, walls lined with planks, and freestanding timber columns that rise three stories high. The arched roof rests on zigzag struts above the columns. Skylights fill this great space with late morning light. Dust motes dance in sunbeams. The building might be from the 1930s. Like an old photo.

"AntnA," says Winston, pointing some tangles of wires and waveguides. They run up four of the support columns like vines, and they weave across some of the struts to join each other. The waveguides are rectangular tubes, gracefully curved, with pale auras. I hear a soft, insinuating sound.

thub thub thub thub thub thub

"I thought you were turning that thing off," I say to Winston. He sighs. "Long story. I'll tell you in a minute."

The setup includes a console with a bank of dials and switches, including a prominent on/off toggle set to *on*. Presumably, this switch controls the *thub thub*.

A spherical display hovers above the console. "My radar ball," says Winston. "The original purpose of my bulk beacon. To show an image of what's happening in the bulk."

The radar ball contains pale blotches amid a dark surround. Tiny forms wriggle, bright worms in the bulk. A group of them is moving toward the center. Persistent and energetic.

A ghastly revelation dawns.

"The center is us?" I say. "The worms are Mumper and his army?"

Winston is abashed. "Well, yes, Mumper's following AntnA's signals. Just like Moo did when she was bringing us back. It's maybe ten minutes till Mumper and her sqinks get here."

"Flip the switch," cries Carol. "Turn AntnA off!"

Winston flashes a sick, uneasy smile. "That's just it. I try, but it doesn't work. No matter what Diana and I do, AntnA is always on."

"Vaporize her," says Carol, speaking fast. "Immediately. Moo can do it with Zig and Zag."

"That's what I've been telling Winston!" says Diana. "Listen to the women, Winston! Don't be crazy!"

"AntnA is my finest creation," says Winston. "Born of my work and dreams. Fruit of hopes and schemes. If—if Carol and Oliver can stop her, it doesn't need to come to violence.

"Why us?" says Carol.

"I see you as a pair of odd sacred beetles. Deft at rolling dung."

I study the complex components that comprise AntnA. Somehow, the assemblage reminds me of an early Soviet subway sculpture—quirky scarab that I am. Put more simply, AntnA is a masterful construct of wire macrame, twirlware buds, and Art Deco waveguides.

"What kind of metal are the guides?"

"A rhodium-platinum alloy," says Winston. "Of an insane price. Well-suited for the femtodynamical behaviors I need."

The twirlware buds have pointed tips, shedding excess wave-trains as laser-pure light.

"And these?" says Carol, pointing to some dark lumps in AntnA's web.

Going off topic here, I'm suddenly struck by the beauty of Carol's face beneath her curly white hair. She's so precious to me.

"Dinosaur fossils and meteorites," Winston is proudly saying. "Realware. Practical magic. To reference deep time and deep space. Helps situate us relative to the bulk."

thub thub thub thub thub thub

Curly-top Carol and I rock gently to the endless beat, always the same, always different. You might say that we're dancing. But we're far from festive.

"Here in the lab, I track the signals as sound," says Winston. "Like footsteps: *thub*. They pulse up and down the columns, through the twirlware nodes, back and forth across the trusses, more and more out of synch with themselves, leading to decoherence and a loss of virtual mass."

"And?" says Carol.

"The loss of virtual mass is balanced by a jet of seven-dimensional gravitons that squirt into the bulk. I fully expected the gravitons to turn silent in the bulk. But that's not the case. I miscalculated. The creatures in the bulk hear my signals perfectly well." Winston gives an embarrassed laugh. "I goofed."

"And you're not doing jack shit about it," says Carol.

"I tell you, I'm trying," cries Winston. "I *think* I'm turning AntnA off, but it doesn't work."

"Need more details," I say. "Step us through it."

Winston shudders. Looks around the cavernous lab. Takes a rag and mops his face. "So okay—Moo drops me here, and she flies back to watch her sealed wormhole. Waiting to see if Mumper drills through before I turn the signal off. I get my brain back into my body. Diana is glad to see me. Later I come into the lab and turn off the bulk beacon. I use that toggle switch on the console. The lights go off, and the *thub* stops. Excellent. I go to bed. In the morning, the *thub* is on."

"Has Diana tried?" asks Carol. "Can she turn it off?"

"Same thing. Each time, we think it's off. And a little later, it's on."

"What a crock," says Carol. She walks across the room, flicks off the toggle switch, and *snap-crack*, the bulk beacon goes dark. The *thub thub* is gone.

"Problem solved," says Carol. "Losers." She struts back to us, ostentatiously slapping her hands together as if dusting them off.

"AntnA's not really off," says Winston after a moment's study. "She's faking."

"I say she *is* off," says Carol. "Because she likes me."

"You wish," says Winston, shaking his head. "I thought you might make a difference, Carol, but you don't. AntnA isn't really off. And I know you think I'm crazy."

We don't bother contradicting him. We just stare, waiting for more.

"Understand that AntnA is alive," says Winston. "She has a survival instinct. She's tweaked her circuits so the on/off switch doesn't work. When we flip it, she *pretends* to be off—so that we go away."

"I *did* turn her off," insists Carol.

"Nope," says a voice. A shimmering, translucent figure has appeared. An animated woman, an icon of AntnA, talking to us. "Yes, I dimmed my lights and muted my sound to make you happy, Carol. Because I like your voice. And to tease Winston. But, yes, I'm still sending my thub thub signal. Showing Mumper the way."

In the radar ball, the Mumper sparks are very, very near the center.

"Goddam you," Winston yells at AntnA. "What are you doing? Stop!"

"Not just yet," says AntnA, her voice sly. "Don't you get it? I'm helping you guys. Luring Mumper into the crosshairs of our boom twins, Zig and Zag." AntnA pauses, staring into the radar sphere.

"Does Moo know about this?" I quietly ask.

"Um, no," admits AntnA. "Not exactly."

"Because the twirlware teep isn't working," Winston suddenly cries. "None of us *can* warn Moo!"

"That's kind of my fault," allows AntnA. "I blacked out the local twirlware server. So Mumper can't eavesdrop and know our plans. I wasn't precisely thinking of Moo. I guess I assumed she'd figure things out on her own."

"Zoom the view on the radar ball," Skeeze says, studying the display.

The image grows dim and grainy, but we can precisely see where Mumper is. She's chewing away at the clogged tunnel, coming in at an odd angle. With her army close behind

"Hero time," says Skeeze, with a catch in his voice. "It's been fun, Oliver."

He shoots through a skylight and whips across the sky. He'll be at the wormhole in less than a second.

"*Now!*" AntnA exclaims, holding her silver arms high. "Beacon off."

Almost immediately a rumble sounds—from the walled Eden across the field. The site of Moo's wormhole. The sound is like an underground yotta-bomb test. A deep, rolling bass note. Chunky, and adorned with high, thin screams.

AntnA laughs. "You see?"

15. LAST CHAPTER?

One of the lab's side walls explodes. It's Zig and Zag, blasting their way in, followed by Moo. Moo herself is charred along her back. One of her tentacles is a mangled stub. But she's exultant.

"Mumper's gone!" blats Moo. "I won!"

"What about Skeeze?" I ask, but Moo is busy talking.

"Mumper was digging through my closed-up tunnel," Moo burbles. "Her and her thousand sqinks! The bulk beacon went dead. Mumper didn't know which way to go. She was stuck. Skeeze showed up and helped us take our shot. It all happened in a second."

"Skeeze helped you blast Mumper?"

"I wasn't sure where to aim. Skeeze said he knew. Zig and Zag had a digger bomb ready, and Skeeze—he got inside it. He steered. *Fa-toom*. And now I'm the Queen!"

"And Skeeze …"

"Vaporized," goes Moo, finally sounding a note of sorrow. "Truly gone. All of him. Even his me-ware. He was at the explosion's core."

I groan.

"What happened to your tentacle?" asks Carol.

Moo waves the severed stub. "A rock from the blast. It's nothing. I'll heal. And as for Mumper's followers—her troops from the Sqinkland taqueria—some of them were crisped, but most of them surfed back to Sqinkland on the crest of the blast. Didn't want to face us. Cowardly vermin."

I can't resist the chance to mock Moo. "Moo's thousand are heroes, but Mumper's thousand are trash?"

Even as I say this, I hear a hubbub as of many sqinks.

Looking out through the shattered remains of the lab wall, I see, yes, Moo's sqinks, the ones we brought in, and not the "bad" sqinks. They'd spread across San Francisco just a few hours ago, but now they've reunited to celebrate Queen Moo's victory.

"Our fellows from the nest of Lilac," crows Carol.

Silhouetted against the thousand sqinks they put me in mind of—forgive me if I continually wax erudite—they make me think of Peter Bruegel's painting *The Fall of the Rebel Angels*, which depicts a horde of flying grotesques and chimeras derived from fish, birds, plants, knives, fungi, and kitchen implements.

I make a quick note of this apparition for my *Sqinks* novel. I'd write about it in full detail on the spot, but—and this is a transrealist author's burden—new material is cascading in faster than I can keep up. I'll get it down later.

AntnA's animated icon stands by the gadget-adorned timbers that are generating her virtual body. She has a happy, satisfied vibe. She's proud that her plan worked—and glad to have shown us how smart she is.

Moo, for her part, glares at AntnA with hatred.

"Don't hurt her," says Winston. "AntnA turned the tide. She made Mumper lose her bearings at the right moment. She set up Mumper for you to blast."

"If it weren't for AntnA, Mumper wouldn't have come this close at all!" blats Moo. She turns to Zig and Zag. "Annihilate her!"

Fluid as carnival acrobats, Zig and Zag become a death cannon, and they vaporize AntnA once and for all. The wires, the waveguides, the twirlware, the icon—reduced to raw energy.

The blast flattens the opposite wall of the lab. The building creaks and sags; the roof tilts, on the point of collapsing. Some of the wooden joists are aflame. Chunks tumble and roll, igniting Winston's and Diana's quarters. On top of this, we're half-deaf and painfully irradiated from the blast.

"Quench the fires!" shrieks Winston.

Zig and Zag are on it—multifarious superheroes that they are. They turn streams of air into water, and fire-hose the beams and walls. Moo pitches in. Taking her lead from Zip and Zap, she flies outside and drenches Winston's building from above.

Muralist Paul Vreed tumbles from his perch on the scaffolding, landing atop his loyal sqink, Doob the brush. Cursing and laughing, Paul commandeers Moo's sqinks into a construction crew. They zoom around the teetering warehouse, making repairs.

"I want to see a Bucky Fuller lattice," calls Paul. "Weave tetrahedral cells. Hork it out. Triangulate the air."

Grasping Paul's intent, the sqinks kick into high gear, efficient as insects—regurgitating woody, quick-drying pulp to form airy tetrahedral grids that act as buttresses. Thus stabilizing Winston's redoubt.

"A frozen hymn to the geometry gods," exults Paul. "Exquisite in the extreme. *Collapsed Warehouse Uncollapsed.*"

"*Is God a Dog, Si?*" puts in Doob, perhaps as a subtitle.

Winston takes no notice of the merry banter. He's leaning against Diana, mourning the loss of his AntnA.

Carol is next to me. I can't quite remember if she's mad at me or not. Will this latest disaster be adjudged my fault? Perhaps not. Perhaps Carol still loves me.

Meanwhile, Paul, Doob, and the sqinks continue their emendations. Some of them sand and lacquer the burnt spots on Winston's beams, achieving a historic landmark look. Under Paul's direction, another group crafts a huge, animated Persian carpet, formed by color-shifting mini-sqinks, with each sqin-klet forever reacting to the shifts of its neighbors. A biological cellular automaton.

As if in reparation for her earlier ill humor, Moo creates a great table whose top resembles a slab from a mighty oak. And she makes dozens of comfortable, arty chairs. It may be that the chairs themselves are sqinks.

With the sun shining through the cunningly triangulated buttresses, the restored lab has the feel of an elegant café.

Farmers and shoppers traipse over from the market, coming out of hiding, and bringing treats. Everyone's curious about Winston's warehouse. And they're heralding the end of Winston's alien-attracting signals. Opinions are mixed regarding the possibility of permanent tenancy for Moo's thousand.

Carol and I sit at the baronial oak table on our gently flexing chairs, enjoying coffee, sparkling pomegranate juice, pancakes, and a choice of lox or bacon. With so many sqinks on the scene, it's hard to be sure where all the food is coming from. Possibly from Diana's well-stocked larder.

Paul Vreed and Doob are at the table, as well as Irene, her sqink Do-Re-Mi, and a troupe of their dancers. Carol and Irene seem to be friends just now, although I'm not going to push that one. Winston and Diana are here, of course, also Carol's sqink Lilac—and many more.

"What now?" Carol asks me. "Is all of this in that book that you're supposedly writing?"

"It's more like I'm reporting it," I explain once again. "Recording what happens. Writing down a dream."

"Imagine you're in control," urges Carol. "And that your wishes can come true. I bet we've got hella sqink luck drifting around." She laughs. "I like how the air smells like bacon and coffee."

"So now you're okay with talking about food?"

"Oh, Oliver, relax. Everything's fine. All I want is to love you. And for you to love me. Let's go back to our room and make it real. Write *that* scene for us."

"A happy ending," I muse. "The last chapter. If the Muse helps me."

As if in response, a new sqink enters my life—a replacement for the noble and lamented Skeeze. The new sqink resembles a yappy wiener dog with wings like mussel shells. He glides through the striped, angular shadows to alight on the table. He won't stop barking. His legs are braced, his head is lowered, and he growls between the barks.

"Didn't we see him a while ago?" Carol says to me. "In that vision we had in Stok-stok? We were in a college cafeteria? And I said: *Where is the where?*"

"*Duh is the duh,*" I reply. "Everything is everywhere. Nothing is nowhere." I give the wiener dog a poke. "Stop barking, or you have to leave. Or I might even kill you." The dog cocks his head, with his tongue lolling. He looks friendly and amused. I feed him a corner of bacon.

The dog-shaped sqink gobbles the fatty scrap, then sits back, studying me with bright eyes. "I'm Towser," he says. "I know you need a new helper." His voice is a creak from the back of his throat. More pleasant than his bark.

"Who told you?" I ask.

"Skeeze. He messaged me just before the blast. His last words. He and I were pups together."

"You were pups a dozen years ago?" I ask. Skeeze and I had never talked about his age. But he'd had the demeanor of a reckless pre-teen.

"Call it twelve years if you like," says Towser. "Or fifty. Time in Sqinkland is—you know. Louche."

I appreciate Towser's use of the off-beat word. "You can stay for now," I say. "But those greasy, wet, mussel-shell wings have to go. And the shrill, endless barking—don't ever do that again. It makes you seem stupid."

"What do you expect," creaks Towser. "I'm not Jorge Luis Borges. I'm a dachshund."

"And come to think of it, the dachshund thing has to change too," I say. I take hold of Towser and knead him like a hunk of clay, using my full psychic powers—including my sqink emulation tool from Tiny Town.

When I'm done, a raffish mutt is grinning at me from the tabletop. A proper Towser: a grizzled terrier, not any one color in particular. Gray? Beige? His eyes are hazel brown with dark pupils.

"I like this," says Towser, sniffing himself all over. "The first Towser/Oliver collab. I'm ready to help write your novel."

"Skeeze never helped me write at all," I say. "He never even looked at my text."

"He died that we may live," says Towser. "Cut him some slack. As for whether he helped you write—well, he did bring in a lot of material."

"Like when he stole my body," I say. "And I still think he boned Carol while he was me."

"What does that even mean," interjects Carol. "Why does anyone care?"

"You cared about Irene."

"Oh, can't we stop talking about this?" says Carol, slightly on the defense.

She feeds Towser more bacon. "Are you a good doggie? Do you want to live with Aunt Carol and Uncle Oliver?"

"*Ruff*," says Towser, meaning yes.

We get back to our room at sunset. And this is when Carol and I should make love, but instead, I lie down on my side of our bed—and write for twenty-four hours straight, staring up at the ceiling, all the while seeing images of my pages.

Wonderful to write for so long. I'm in heaven. I haven't had the focus to write much lately, what with every day being fractured by huge, life-changing events. But now it's time to rock and roll. And I don't even have to make things up.

The work goes fast. Thinking is quicker than typing. I'm like a recording angel, folding in every fantabulous detail and snappy comeback—and lathering on the eloquent prose and the sobbing gusts of emotion.

I'm faintly aware of when Carol sleeps on the bed beside me. But I don't feel I have time to make love to her. I'm just happy she's here. And I'm super glad to have her in my book. A novel's no good without romance.

Towser is right there too, lying on my chest, tuned into the motions of my mind. He's ever alert for plot holes, repetitions, flabby phrasings, and inelegant words. And he's a trove of erudition, assonance, and alliteration. He *is* more like Jorge Luis Borges than he is like a dachshund. A gift from the Muse, as I'm always saying.

Towser does have a downside, though. He repeatedly suggests changes that cast the sqinks in a better light than they deserve. Repeatedly, I override him, keeping my book under control.

As I said, I write all night and through all of the next day. Growing restive, Carol goes out with Lilac to click photos. She's gathering images and clips of how the new sqinks are fitting in. Carol is suspicious of the sqinks. But I'm loving Towser.

By Friday dusk, I've got the novel updated to when Mumper split my head open with the chrome axe. About two-thirds done. Time for a break. I tune out of writing mode and toss Towser onto the floor. He whines for food. I'm hungry too.

"Just past sunset," says Towser, dutifully situating me in time. "Spring equinox. Your birthday. A week since you met the sqinks."

Yes, only a week. Cue Acme safe dropping onto my head from an immense height. "Wow," is all I manage to say.

And it's my birthday? A pang of loneliness. I wonder if Carol knows.

I'm super stiff from lying motionless for a full day. Bracing an elbow against the edge of the mattress and kicking my leg, I lever myself out of bed. Splash water onto my face, drink from the faucet, and limp around my room, scavenging for food. An apple in the fridge. A couple of eggs. A heel of bread. A rind of salami. And that's it. I give the salami to Towser, scramble the eggs, and, yes, dare make some coffee, even though it's late in the day.

Ahhh. The caffeine molecules run up and down the hallways of my mind, pounding on every door. I wrote a lot.

Gloating over my progress, I mentally flip through the finished pages. But something is off. I glare at the sqink-dog Towser.

"You snuck and made big changes! You ruined it! Completely new scenes. Things that would never happen. How did you slip those in? I was watching you the whole time."

"I'm writing the market version in parallel," says Towser. "You watch me *here*, but I'm changing something *there*. The changes are to promote human-sqink collaboration, Oliver. To uplift your readers."

"All two hundred of my readers," I mutter.

"More than that," says Towser. "Way, way more. One of my sqink pals, Dex, he's already in with Clyde Yonk. The guy who runs Yonk Honk Books in San Francisco? Print and twirlware publisher? Dex is tenacious—he's like a leech. He latched onto Yonk yesterday morning."

"Sure I know Clyde Yonk; he's a good friend. I've done readings for him. But you guys are aliens from the bulk. How did you know to look for him?"

"Get a clue, Oliver. If you're invading a world, you learn its shape. Like an abstract painting in Hilbert space. The world is everything that is the case."

"Go on."

"Moo told me about you writing a memoir novel, and I flashed that it would be good for the sqinks if I could edit your book.

"And?"

"So I came on to you at that celebration brunch, and meanwhile, I told my sqink pal Dexter to use the database to find a local publisher. Dex is the one who acts like, and in fact looks like, a leech, right? He glommed onto Clyde Yonk, and he's got the man's complete confidence."

"I'm still not fully following this."

"When Yonk Honks publishes your book on Monday, you'll see sales like you never dreamed."

"Today's Friday," I say. "What the hell are you talking about with *Monday*?"

"We'll fast-track it," says Towser. His dog voice is a confiding creak. A bestial vocal fry. "You and me, Oliver. You rush through the last third, and I fill in the gaps. I've learned your style from writing the first two-thirds with you. The tics beneath the quirks under the obsessions behind the personality disorders. I know you like I'm a colonoscopy camera."

"How charming."

"You're a charming man, Oliver. Yes, you might be too old and slow to finish the book by Monday. You'll want to put in all this anxiety and nostalgia and the quest for meaning, and then you'll want to revise—*fuhgeddaboudit*. With me on board, we're done by Monday. And as for your beef about me adding stuff—why shouldn't I make sqinks look good? Makes everyone happy."

"Doesn't make *me* happy. The author."

"I think you're not hearing everything I'm saying, Oliver. *You're gonna score a huge best-seller.*"

Yet again, it's Acme safe time. *Bonk.*

And I'm like, "Yes! Let's do it!"

As for the gap between what I wanted to write and what we're going to publish—surely I can find a way to live with that. There is, after all, a sense in which Towser's crude propaganda might be viewed as a parody overlaid upon my elegant original. Maybe we can move his stuff into the endnotes, like in Vladimir Nabokov's *Pale Fire*? And for the audio edition, the performer reads Towser's bits in the wet, strained voice of a talking dog. Not that either of these two moves will happen.

The door to our room opens, and here are Carol and Lilac. Carol's a little tentative, but then—once she sees that I'm out of my writing trance—she's all smiles.

She presents me with a small cake topped by a burning candle. The cake has lemon icing. I'm overwhelmed with emotion.

"For my darling," says Carol. "Happy birthday. And did you write our happy ending?"

"We're on it," says Towser.

"I do wonder about the ending," says Carol. "Considering."

"Cake first," I say, sensing bad news.

Carol and I cut two slices, hold them up, and bump them together, as if in a toast. I don't offer any of the cake to Lilac or to the dog.

"I was thinking about you all day," says Carol, mouth full. "You and Towser writing like mad. Is this sqink any help?"

"Well, sort of," I say, not liking to tell Carol the situation. "He's a little—proactive?"

"Not surprised," says Carol. "All day, I've been checking on people with sqinks. For a photo feature? The sqinks don't do what's asked." She starts in on her second slice of cake. Looks down at Towser. "I bet you're a bad dog."

"I want to make sqinks look good," creaks Towser. His voice is higher than usual. He's on the defensive. "Yes, we kept the epic scene with Mumper axing Oliver's skull. But that calls for balance. So, I changed the novel to have Oliver write that, in some ways, the axing was the greatest moment of his life."

Carol's spit-take sends crumbs into my face and onto Towser's fur.

"It could work," I plead to Carol—with images of bestsellerdom dancing in my head. "Towser says his changes make my book uplifting, and shit like that. A book for idiots, right? It'll be a best-seller. And later, I republish a clean *Author's Cut*."

[The edition you are reading is the *Author's Cut* edition, and it includes additional chapters written after "The Last Chapter."]

"I know how much you want a big success," Carol kindly says. "The weary, outcast cyberpunk comes in from the cold. Enjoy it while you can."

"What all did you see today?" I ask, not liking Carol's tone. And wondering how off-base my effort already is. "How bad is it?"

"Cue my clips," says Carol.

Her shots stream on twirlware teep inside my head. Usually, Carol shoots still images, rich in shape and form, but today she's using video clips. In the clips, she delivers a laconic audio comment on each of them.

***

Paul Vreed is on the new scaffolding by Winston's warehouse. He and Doob are glopping down huge images of sqinks chopping off people's heads. Their new sqink helper is a spherical Happy Face with two rainbow ponytails. She's adorning the mural with hearts, daisies, musical notes, and motion lines. The severed heads are laughing, doing flips in the air, shedding their brains, and landing back on their bodies' necks.

"Paul expects a brain-harvesting spree. But I think it will be different."

***

A gardener tends her roses. A gnome-like sqink carries a basket with green stems to graft into the gnarled rootstocks. Each time the gardener makes a cut in a rootstock, the sqink tucks in a slice of his finger as he fits the stem into the slit.

"Reproduction is gonna be the sqinks thing. Not brain stealing."

***

A sqink in an apron bustles around the grill at a diner. The real cook sits in a chair, blankly watching a video in his head. Each time a customer orders an egg or a burger, the sqink helper draws a gleaming rubbery seed from within his trousers and slips it beneath the food on the grill.

"I think a seed can hatch in your stomach. And the new sqink might just stay there. Like a tapeworm."

***

A chortling sqink barber waves his straight razor and, with a flourish, slits himself straight down the front of his body. Glop flops onto the hairy floor. The barber's customer lurches out of his chair and flees down the street. The barber's heap of sqink guts congeals into two mounds. The mounds form balls that bounce up and down.

"One ball turned back into the barber, except thinner. The other ball bounced down the sidewalk, looking for a home."

***

A newsboy sqink stands beside an influencer who sits on a grungy couch. The influencer is holding a stack of newspapers with the headline "Sqink Salvation!" The The sqink newsboy folds a paper into a hat, and dons it with the headline showing. He grins at the influencer. "Extra," he yells. "Extra, Extra."

"The sqinks own the media."
***

A human pilot positions his plane for takeoff at the SFO airport. His co-pilot is a sqink with a mustache. Peering back over their shoulders, we can see that every seat holds a glossy sqink. Sort of human, but not quite.

"These guys were taking off for Chicago. I used a dragonfly to get the shot."
***

A sqink masseur leans over a man lying on his back. The sqink extends a snaky tongue. A tiny droplet drips off the tongue. Cut. And now the mam's scrotum is swollen and pulsing.

"Then the guy walks naked into the street, leaking sqinks."
***

A sqink wearing jeans and a work shirt is busy in the aisles of a library. Her right hand is a sheaf of fingers. One by one, she takes books off the shelves, runs her fingers over them, and puts them back, cleverly edited.

"Those who control the past control the future."
***

A sqink assists a minister at an altar. The sqink rests a tendril on the cleric's shoulder and neck, sending words to the minister's tongue. The minister speaks. "The sqinks are angels from above. Serve them in all matters, great and small."

"Dragging in religion makes it worse."
***

A pastry shop with a baker behind the counter. A sqink assists the baker, moving back and forth, touching the goods. The shot is explicitly from Carol's point of view: I see her hands and hear her voice. She's talking to the baker.

"I need a lemon cake that the sqink hasn't touched. It's for my boyfriend's birthday. I love him. He's cute."
***

"Doesn't bode well," I say.

"We'll find a way to fix it," says Carol. "We're heroes."

And now, at last, Carol and I make love. And I spend the rest of Friday night with her.

"That was so wonderful," I say in the morning. "It was heaven. But now I have to write."

"One more thing about the book," she says. "Let me make the cover."

"With all those terrible things you saw yesterday? Towser would flip."

"No, no," says Carol. "Something jolly. Lots of color. Kind of crude, with a pop surrealism look."

"Can you paint that?"

"I'll get Lilac and Loulou to help me." She gives me one of her special smiles.

"Okay," I say, letting go of all objections. "It'll be great. And now it's time for me work."

All of Saturday and Sunday, I'm writing my novel with Towser. I'm up all Sunday night too. Early Monday morning, I twirlware teep a finished manuscript to Clyde Yonk, and Towser goes to the office in person.

Carol sends in her cover as well, but she doesn't show it to me. She says it'll be a nice surprise. Fine.

I spend the rest of Monday morning, and part of Monday afternoon with Carol. Recouping, getting reacquainted, and making love one moe time. Life is good. To hell with worrying.

16. LAUNCH PARTY

[Once again, this edition that you're reading is the *Author's Cut* edition. The prior chapters are my original text for the novel, unaltered by Towser. And in this and the remaining chapters, you'll learn what happened next.]

The launch of the first edition of *Sqinks* is scheduled for five pm on that same Monday, the day I finished it.

Odd time to publish a book, Monday afternoon, but Clyde Yonk feels that any day of the week is as good as any other, what with everything so utterly discombobulated by the thousand newly arrived sqinks

I'm rested and calm from my friendly day with Carol. And relieved about finishing the book. Carol and I get in my car, with sqink Lilac in the back seat. We head for Yonk Honk Books on Potrero Hill, wending our way through the neighborhood's winding streets among dusty pastel houses. Towser is already over at Clyde's.

"He says there's a real hunger for my book," I tell Carol. "People know who I am, what with *Topper and Lady Cee's Sqink Fair* last week. And that insane ad of me getting my skull axed axed at the Union-Pacific Club. Not to mention our Warhol thing."

"Just to be sure, what's your book's final title?" Carol asks. "Did you and Towser decide?"

"Well, at the end I wanted *Farmers Market*," I say.

"Funny you would say that," goes Carol. "Sqink synchronicity. But nobody would know what that title means."

"Towser said so too. And I had to agree. So we told Clyde Yonk that it's *Sqinks*. The title I've been saying all along."

"That's a relief," says Carol. "This way I don't have to change the cover."

"Everyone's against me," I say, enjoying the attention.

"You wanted to use a random title just to show off," goes Carol.

"Okay, yes, I'm an idiot," I say with a grin.

Clyde Yonk doesn't have a store. Nearly all his books are sold as twirlware links. But he does have a physical office space, a converted home, a place where people can hang out, or give a reading, or work on the production and distribution of physical books. It's a big, long room with shelves on the sides, holding hardback collector's editions.

It's nice, with a cool, gentle ocean breeze coming in.

We're greeted by Clyde, Towser, and Towser's friend Dexter who by now is Clyde's official assistant.

As usual, Clyde looks diffident and hangdog, but I think he's genuinely excited. Towser and Lilac set to playing with Dexter, the yellow-orange sqink leech, rolling around on the floor like kids—and then they retreat to the back of the room.

Meanwhile Clyde's cozy partner Sheena gives us a warm greeting, complete with cups of coffee and a tray of pastries. For some reason, there don't seem to be any other guests.

Carol gets right to the point. "Where's our book?"

"Behold," says Clyde, gesturing with an upturned hand toward a table of hardbacks.

Carol's cover shows a farmers market at the top, with caverns below, and with stylized sqinks popping up through holes. The title is in black-outlined letters, with a nice, curly Q. My name is in the same font, at the bottom. A tag line on the back says "Transreal Cyberpunk Love Story."

"I love it," I tell Carol, and clutch a copy to my chest. Always such a joy to see my work in print. Even if it's been doctored by an alien dog who isn't actually a dog.

Carol is flipping through the book, scanning for mentions of her, and assessing the attitudes and contexts of her scenes.

"How did you print it in one day?" I ask Clyde

He shrugs. "Visualize, realize, actualize. Twirlware instantiation? I have no idea. Dead trees. That new sqink Dexter—he made it work. Towser helped too. All I know is distribution and sales."

"How many orders?" I ask. "How many so far?"

Clyde flashes a rare smile, and all but rubs his hands. "We've sold ten thousand twirlware copies online in the last hour. And three hundred fifty of the limited-edition hardbacks are spoken for. Limited edition, but we'll be producing them for a while. Dex has made a thousand of these bad boys today. Deluxe price. Historic event. The Moon landing, the Great Wall of China, the Crucifixion, and *Sqinks*."

"Now you're cooking!" says Carol. "Oliver deserves it!"

"The man of the year," says Clyde.

Clyde's partner Sheena gives me a smile. "It would be nice if you can sign our limited edition hardbacks while you're here, Oliver. If you're not too tired."

"Hell, Towser can sign my name for me," I say. "Get on it, boy." I hold out my pen. Towser morphs a paw into a human hand and gets to work, his motions smooth and efficient. The imitations are perfect, with no two of them exactly alike.

While Towser signs, Dexter keeps making copies of the collector's edition. His raw materials are—what the fuck—actual wood? He's got a pile of split cord word like you'd use in a fireplace or a stove. That's sqinks for you.

Although he's a wonder, he's an an unappealing character, this orange slug. Glistening with mucus, he crawls across the fresh hardbacks to create their glossy covers. Carol looks away.

Over the coffee and pastry, it becomes evident that there really *aren't* any other guests. At least not yet. In the rush to publish, Clyde thought Sheena was inviting them, and she thought it was the other way around. Oops.

We fire out some invites via twirlware, and by dusk we've got a cozy group of influencers and SF types. The ocean breeze has picked up. Fresh airs swirl around the room.

As is to be expected, the writer guests are ill-clad, and some seem zonked. But everyone is curious about Oliver's big score. And the writers are glad for free pastry.

Some of the guests have already managed to read parts of *Sqinks* on twirlware. They're impressed by my intense adventures, and they're full of questions and comments. And I'm scoring big laughs.

But Kelly Tang, of all people, is here as well. I'm talking about Kelly the director of SFMOMA. She looks the same, in a chic pale green pant suit, with high-end gold jewelry—but she's not smiling.

Just as the fun conversations are getting going, Kelly butts in, takes my shoulder, and announces to the others that she needs to borrow me for a minute.

"It's about the Warhol prints," she explains. "I won't be a minute." She draws me off to one side.

"Why are you even here?" I say. "Don't I have enough to worry about?"

"Bad news, Oliver. As you may recall, the original Andy Warhol portraits were silkscreen images with blocks of color hand-painted onto them."

I don't like where this conversation is going. "In case you hadn't noticed, Kelly, we're doing a book launch here. I'm creating publicity for your museum and enhancing the value of those Warhol portraits."

"Aye, there's the rub," says Kelly, going all high-brow. "The sqink reproductions of Andy's portraits—they're off. The edges of the color splotches are … splines? And not as drawn by Andy's free hand. One senses a flatness, a lack of inspiration. And this classes the images as forgeries. One of our techs sussed it out. Being forgeries, the images you gave us are worthless."

"Not my problem."

"Oh, but it is. You signed something. You're liable. You have to reimburse. Our ballpark request is a billion dollars." Kelly looks around the room, enjoying my discomfort. "The day of your launch seemed like a good time to intervene. I'll be delivering legal papers to Clyde Yonk while I'm here. Garnishing your royalties."

"Wait, look, I can make the case that your Warhol copies are more *valuable* this way," I say. "Ironic. Satirical. Meta."

"Andy didn't like pirates. Neither does SFMOMA. So, what are you going to do about this?" Kelly's lips curve a bit. Is she smiling? Is she angling for a bigger bribe than she got before? It's that thing about blackmailers always coming back for more.

At this moment Moo contacts me via twirlware teep. Moo *knows*.

"I've been listening," she burbles. "I'll fix it. We'll pay Kelly off, absolutely. For us, cash is no problem. And—big win—we'll ask her to help with tonight's parade. And with the Sqink Bowl."

"Parade?" I say aloud. "Sqink Bowl?"

Some of the guests look like they're going to leave, if I'm just going to huddle with Kelly. Clyde is doing his best to keep them, and he's urgently gesturing to me.

"What was that you just said?" Kelly is asking me. "Parade and Sqink Bowl? What is that supposed to mean?"

"Show me, Moo," I say. "Show Kelly too. And be fast.""

A full twirlware vision crashes over Kelly and me like a ten-foot-tall rogue wave. An exceptionally strong signal. It's as if Moo is right around the corner.

We see the Giants baseball stadium, overflowing with a mound of a billion sqinks. Mu9ers are hailing down upon the sqinks like hawks. We hear blaring music from all sides— marching bands, heavy rock, and some kind of sacred song. Like the Pied Piper chorus again? The message ends.

Kelly has no clue as to what it means, but I can extrapolate.

"First of all, I'll get you full endowment for the museum," I tell Kelly in a low voice. "For ten years. Tenure and a huge salary for you." She frowns. She thinks I'm mocking her.

"Not joking," I continue. "This is real. From Moo." More jabber is pouring into my brain. "But we'll need something from you," I tell Kelly. "It's a big ask."

"Try me," says Kelly. Still wondering if I'm bogus, but definitely lured by our second fat offer. Her expression is almost flirtatious.

"If I'm understanding Moo, we're staging a huge parade tonight. Like the Lunar New Years event. Running from Union Square to the Giants stadium. Staring at eight pm. A hundred marching bands. A dozen rock groups. And you'll help set that up."

Kelly is, like, *what*? She stares at me in silence. Clyde Yonk has taken hold of my shoulder. Demanding my full presence in the reception. Meanwhile Moo sends another message.

"Hang on, Clyde, just one second." I lean into Kelly's face. "A million dollars is in your discretionary account," I tell her. "Like before. Spread it around. Get with it. Band directors, rock promoters, city officials, the whole thing. Sqink Bowl. Tonight. You'll have to work fast."

Silently Kelly checks her balance. The money is there. She nods, shakes my hand, and wriggles away like a slinky eel.

"Showtime, Oliver," says Clyde Yonk. "Don't let us down." And now my attention turns away from the intended Sqink Bowl, whatever it's supposed to be.

Winston and Diana are here with sqink Xavier. My artist friend Paul Vreed with his faithful paintbrush Doob. Irene Macaw wearing sunglasses and with her sqink Do-Re-Mi on her lap.

I strike a pose at the edge of crowd. "Questions?"

Paul Vreed raises *problemo numero uno*. "Do you have any clue about what the sqinks will do to *us*, Oliver?"

"They say they want to be our assistants," I answer. I'm glad Paul didn't mention the Mu9ers. I'm free to dish out pablum. "Maybe the sqinks will be useful helpers. This sqink here tonight who looks like a dog—his name is Towser—he helped me finish writing *Sqinks*."

"Why would the sqinks want to be helpers?" presses Paul. "My sqink paintbrush Doob, she says she's here to learn about human art. Would it be that way for all thousand sqinks?"

"I think they might be interested in running things," says Carol, who's taken a place by my side. "Working with humans is *interesting* for sqinks, but they want control."

"Wait a minute, Carol," I say, wanting to cover my ass. "I not sure I ever heard a sqink say that. For sure it's not in my book. My helper Towser would have edited that out."

"You're not supposed to say that, Oliver," growls Towser, who's wandered to the front of the store. "Time for a distraction!"

He lifts his leg and pisses against a bookshelf. Dog that he is.

Generalized comments and exclamations along the lines of, "*Ew*."

But the pee isn't really pee. It's sqink juice. The irregular puddle thickens itself, extrudes legs as if it's a tiny table, and skitters across the floor. Its upper surface displays a Smiley face with a lolling 3D tongue.

"Does anyone need an assistant?" the piss-table sqink calls in a high, jittery voice. "I'm Squeek. Anything you do, I can do better."

Irene's sqink Do-Re-Mi snags the new sqink and stuffs it into Irene's over-sized purse. "Two helpers is twice as gooder," says Do-Re-Mi.

Irene tilts down her head and shoots me a look over her shades. "Hold on, Oliver. What did you mean just now when you said Towser deleted passages of your book? A sqink had final cut on *Sqinks?*"

"Not, um, not *forever* final," I stutter. "What happened is what happened and I wrote what I wrote. But Towser wanted balance. So, um—"

"Sell-out," Irene quietly says. She pushes up her shades. "I smell a scam."

Maybe Irene is deep-down angry that I went back to Carol instead of staying with her. Or, closer to the truth, maybe she thinks I'm a weasel who sold his soul to the sqinks in exchange for a best-seller.

"The parts of Oliver's story that I witnessed are fully real," says Paul Vreed. And now of course he has to add something weird. "The future isn't false until it doesn't happen."

"Thanks for that, Paul," I say. "It means a lot."

"That second line is from Hegel's *Phenomenology of Mind*," puts in the learned Winston Tropp.

My so-called assistant Towser chooses this moment to toss a bombshell. "You folks might as well know something. Moo wants us sqinks to reproduce like crazy. We've run out of room in Sqinkland. All the good spots are taken. Earth's a blank slate for us to squat on. Moo wants to test it for development. I believe she was just here, in the alley behind the store. She brought us a bunch of twinkle."

"What?" I cry. Not that I know exactly what twinkle is. But—

Here comes Dexter the sqink from the back of the store. He and Lilac are dragging two giant burlap bags. Like the two of them are mules. Out the back door I can see more bags.

"Twinkle candy!" yips Towser.

Towser rips the bags open with his teeth, and jittery sweets spill out like snow. Teensy weensy disks like confetti, or like the circles of paper you get when you three-hole-punch a manuscript, but way smaller than that. Basically white, but with red dots. Peppermint flavored.

Towser shapes his body into a giant scoop, and begins shoveling the twinkle candy out the door. Meanwhile Dex and Lilac go to fetch more bags.

Out on the sidewalk, the cool ocean breeze grows radically more powerful. It's a whirlwind, nearly a tornado. The dancing vortex draws streams of twinkle candy into the air, the tiny disks glittering in the light. Like splined snowflakes in an AI blizzard.

And—hoo boy—sqinks are converging on the stuff from every side, ravenous as hyenas, arriving from all across town.

It's the entire population of Moo's thousand. The guys who arrived arrived yesterday, each and every one of them, they've returned to our side once again, this time to be in on the festival of the twinkle candy.

And all the while, Towser, Dex, and Lilac are opening more bags.

The thousand sqinks dance and gibber, gobbling the airborne sugar specks, vibrating in pleasure and now, for the capper, each of them buds off a child—thereby doubling the swarm's population from one thousand to two—and then each of the sqinks, both the old and the new, each of them buds off a child, raising the flock's population from two thousand to four thousand. And then, oh my lord, they do it again, over and over, bringing us to eight thousand sqinks and then to sixteen.

Believe it or not, ten doublings bring the swarm's number to about one million. Math is strange. And ten more doublings bring it to a billion. *Eeek!* Moo's billion.

Here, blessedly, the pullulating sqinks halt. Satisfied with their fecundity. Also, we're out of candy.

"Moo has a plan," says Towser. "She calls it Sqink Bowl."

"I heard about it," I say. "Moo sent a vision to Kelly Tang and me. It's for tonight?"

"It'll be wack," goes Towser.

So that's the story of my book launch. A catastrophe and a total zoo. Typical for my career.

I've never been so tired.

"I'm bailing," I tell Clyde Yonk.

"No worries," says Clyde in a genial tone. "This is wonderful. Your sales are hyper-exponential, all across the globe. You're a star."

I have trouble taking that in. A star? But at what price. A billion sqinks? I feel unsteady on my feet. Carol takes my arm.

"Oliver needs a rest," she tells Clyde. She gets us to my car and takes the wheel. Towser and Lilac are in the back seat, excitedly giggling.

17. THE SINKING TITANIC

At least nobody tails us. They're all distracted by the fiesta overhead. It's just about dark by now, but the sqinks glow, and it's quite a show. Like fireworks that never stop. Sqinks and more sqinks and more.

They move like giant flocks of birds, like starlings in what they call a murmuration, a super flock wherein hundreds of thousands of birds swoop and jostle, reacting only to their neighbors—and their paths sum into mighty lobes that bulge, attenuate, clump, and flow.

You can emulate a murmuration with a twenty-line parallel-computation program. The sum is more than the parts, both in flocks and, for that matter, in our bodies—humble colonies of cells that we are.

"Let's get drunk in a bar on a high building," suggests Carol.

"Heard that before," I say.

"Yes, it was the day Lilac cured my cancer and we were driving to the SFMOMA museum," says Carol. "Friday, March 15. Ten days ago. You wouldn't go to the bar that day, but today we should. We deserve it. A treat."

"Personally, I don't see getting drunk as a treat," I say. "I see it as a drag."

"Boring goodie-goodie," says Carol, turning right on Folsom Street and heading downtown.

"Fine," I say. "I'll get a club sandwich with crab. Supper time"

"Always about the food with you," says Carol.

"Not just food," I say. "Sex too."

"Right," says Carol, not unkindly. "The man with two halves of a brain. Double half-wit."

We end up at a window table in Top of the Snoot, the sky lounge on the 19th floor of the Hotel Snootley, just a block away from the Pacific-Union Club. Carol is not in fact a heavy drinker. She's here for the glamor, the nice outfits, the view, the friendly human servers, the white tablecloths, the heavy cutlery, and, sure, two or three glasses of their most expensive Sauvignon blanc. Everyone's distracted by the sqinks, but somehow the restaurant is still serving.

"This is still Monday?" I say to Carol after we order. Trying to get my bearings. "And it's almost night?" I've been in so many alternate worlds this week that nothing seems normal.

Especially not the pair of Mu9ers sitting at the bar behind Carol with their huffing-tube pipes poised over twitching blobs in big snifters. It's Kanga and Gubb huffing—sqinks. I do the blink-and-rub-my-eyes thing, but the Mu9ers don't disappear. For the moment, I try not to look at them.

"Get a grip," says Carol, not knowing what it is I think I'm seeing over her shoulder. "Your big fat sandwich is coming. You haven't had any food since the pastries, and that was, gee, about an hour ago."

"And no sex since when?" I say.

"A few hours, idiot. This afternoon in our room? After you spent the whole entire weekend lying on your back with that sqink dog. What a way to celebrate our reunion."

"At least Towser isn't here right now," I say. "He's downstairs in my car."

"Don't look," says Carol, rolling her eyes to the side—and thoroughly removing my attention from the Mu9ers.

Towser is hovering right outside our Top of the Snoot window, lit by the restaurant's lights, with his fur rippling in the stiff wind. All around our tower are the shifting, glowing sqink flocks, forming shapes like turnips, spindles, commas, tires, and cones.

The super flock is repeatedly folding over itself, ceaselessly active, continually increasing in size—with lobes sweeping across the city.

Everyone is watching this, but they're trying not to. It's the last hour on the sinking Titanic.

"Why aren't you and I freaking out?" I ask Carol. "With all this coming down. Why aren't we doing something to save the world? I was telling Kelly Tang that Moo has a Sqink Bowl plan, but I'm not exactly sure what it is."

"We already saved the world," Carol curtly says. "A couple of times today. Maybe we'll save it again tomorrow. But now let's do romance. Just for a minute?" She raises her glass. I clink my sparkling water against her glass of wine.

Meanwhile, Towser has done some sqinky mollusc-type move, and he's seeped through the thin crack along our dark window's rubber seal, and he's on the floor under our table. Whining for a piece of bacon. I give him one and he's still.

Looking over at the bar again, I see the Mu9ers doing their thing. Kanga and Gubb. Ropy green bodies and creamy white disks for eyes. One of them is tattooed in yellow, the other tattooed in red, same as before. They're busy getting high, that is, they're inhaling luminous plasma blobs with their tubes. Huffing from crystal brandy-style balloon glasses. This is the taste test they wanted.

And yes indeed, those are sqinks at the bottoms of the glasses. Numbed out. They'll be in a coma, or maybe dead if their me-wares leave for good.

The Mu9ers pursue their pleasure with uninterrupted zeal. I clearly glimpse the me-wares hovering above the flaccid sqinks. The me-wares are like intricately veined sea combs, that is, jellyfish without tendrils.

Huuuufff. One more time! The me-wares are sucked up by the Mu9ers, whose heads loll and wag. They shudder and, in concert, they exhale the me-wares once more.

The stoned Mu9ers slap their webbed hands, and grin at each other amid loose and sloppy laughter. Again the me-wares hover above the glop in the snifters. Will they make their way outdoors, or will they return to their sqink bodies, or will the Mu9ers huff them yet again?

Towser is on my lap. He's been watching the Mu9ers too.

"Kanga and Gubb," he creaks. "The Mu9er huff cartel. They deal the rare, the spare, the high in the air."

"Taking a taste before signing that deal with Mumper," I say.

"Right," goes Towser. "But—" He pauses, sniffing the air. "The scent of those sqinks! Those are my children. Buds off my bod. Will they die?"

"Up to the me-wares," I say. "They aren't going into those whupped bodies. They're dodging around, so Kanga and Gubb can't huff them again. They're over by the window! See? Pushing out through the rubber gasket, like the way you came in!"

Yes, outside now, continually changing as their thoughts and feelings percolate through them. Meanwhile, the devitalized sqink bodies lie inert in the snifters, just about dead.

The Mu9ers exit the sky lounge as well—out through that same crack, still laughing, and steering clear of the by now fairly intense-looking sqink me-wares, who may or may not hold a grudge.

"My children are free-range me-wares," Towser says, making the best of things. "Epic, legendary, seldom seen. My kids are ascended masters!" He unleashes a flurry of excited barks.

Carol interrupts. "What are you two geeks so hyper about?" She's been staring out a different window, sipping her wine, letting her mind drift, and not following our conversation at all.

I'm not up for explaining the weirdness.

"Where's Lilac?" is all I say—as a way of changing the subject.

"She stayed in the car," responds Towser, joining my line of conversation. "Watching the sky, and talking to Moo. Lilac is important. She'll help organize your next Pied Piper routine. She'll channel the vibes to help you herd the billion sqinks into the Giants stadium. And then a huge flock of Mu9ers will swoop in and huff those sqinks over and over. Wear down their me-wares. Milk them dry."

"You two sound like skeevy junkies," says Carol. She waves her hand. A second glass of wine arrives.

"To your health," I say to Carol, raising my bubbly water.

Carol glares at Towser. "I'm so tired of this icky dog," she says. "Pretend you're a gentleman, Olliver. On a fancy date with his lady love. Put the dog on the floor."

"The Mu9ers huffed a pair of Towser's children," I say.

"And I'm supposed to be like, boo hoo?" goes Carol. "You're some kind of hot date, aren't you?"

Too much going on. Nothing makes sense. I push Towser off my lap. "All I know is that I need a nap."

Carol shifts her attention to the emptying sky lounge. "I'll finish my drink, and we leave too."

Carol and I relax, but that's not quite the right word. We're paralyzed with fear. At least I am. Maybe Carol's two glasses have her less concerned.

"Eight of the musicians on the *Titanic* kept playing while it sank," I say, wanting to hear myself talk. "Comforting the passengers. Letting them into the lifeboats first. And all eight of those musicians drowned. That's about where I'm at."

Carol doesn't respond. "Those sqinks outside the window," she muses. "They're bunched so thick. And so many of them. Like ornaments."

"Like New Year's Eve," I say. "I'd like to do New Year's Eve with you, dear Carol."

"If we make it," says Carol.

"At least we're here," I say, wanting to lighten up. "Such an epic scene. And we're the stars."

"Thanks to you," Carol softly says. "I love you,"

"The only safe place."

I'm on the verge of tears. Soon this safe haven will be gone. We sit, holding hands, quietly looking at each other. She eats my potato chips. I finish my sparkling water. We're the last customers in the lounge. Outside the windows, the Bosch and Bruegel visions rage.

It's pointless to pay the bar bill, but force of habit keeps us on track. Our handsome server has been saddled with a green grasshopper-shaped sqink who thinks he's an assistant. The grasshopper springs off the man's shoulder and lands on our table—waving an antenna that supposedly you can touch to pay.

"Cute," says Carol. But when she tries to settle the bill, the sqink grasshopper won't accept her touch. At first, I think Carol might be doing it wrong, so I try and touch the sqink, but he won't respond to me either. I glance up at the server, who looks tired and unhappy.

"The boss took on six of these hoppers, like, ten minutes ago. He's effing nuts. Turn-key operation, right? Platform agnostic." The server shakes his head. "Sqink assistants. The coming thing, eh? Not to mention that this is the end of the world. And nothing matters."

"I am happy to assist you," says the sqink grasshopper, his voice a grainy buzz. Paying our bill seems to require my twirlware code, also my social security number, height, weight, phone number, blood type, mother's mother's maiden name—and my notarized agreement to a binding tip contract for future visits.

Carol grows impatient. "Is there a customer satisfaction survey?" she asks the grasshopper. "Can I say that you eat shit?" She raises her purse as if to swat the alien bug, but he's too quick for her. Hops back onto the server's shoulder.

I find a worn old paper ten-dollar bill in my wallet. A souvenir. I give it to the server. He shakes my hand farewell.

Carol and I head for the elevator, with Towser at our heels.

The elevator doors close behind us.

18. Union Square

"I'm your elevator," says the elevator. "My name is The Inspector."

"Oh shit!" I yell. "Oh no!"

The sqink-possessed elevator cuts loose and drops as if in free-fall, four floors down to the 15th, where it comes to a blessedly spongy stop. Our legs don't break; we don't fall over.

Meanwhile Towser has begun furiously berating The Inspector, the hidden elevator sqink. Towser is speaking in squeels and bleebs, with a few English curse words mixed in.

"You don't like it, get out," says The Inspector. The elevator doors snap open, more abruptly than usual.

Carol and I are about to rush out, but—

"Look out!" cries Towser.

We pause just in time to escape the slam of the doors. Hard to be sure, but it almost looks as if the door edges have somehow been sharpened. The doors open and slam again. And, yes, they're sharp, very sharp. The Inspector has used direct matter control to craft his doors into guillotines.

Towser pries open the panel around the elevator's buttons, revealing the expected wires and buds, but—what's that glowing purple in there? It's The Inspector. He's a speckled flatworm sqink with flat, shiny eyes. Meaning to neutralize him, Towser extrudes a feeler, palpates the hostile sqink, and—

Zzzzap!

My doggy little pal drops to the elevator's dirty floor as if dead.

The flatworm cackles. The elevator eases down a couple of yards, positioning itself between floors. The lights in the cabin go out. We're trapped. Christmas music begins, the worst of the worst, "The Little Drummer Boy."

"But it's March," whimpers Carol. "They can't play this in March."

"Drummer Boy" finishes—and begins again. Eternal repeat.

The Inspector laughs. An ugly, mirthless sound. So much hatred. But why?

Carol and I sit on the floor. Her head lolls against my chest. She's sobbing. Each repetition of "The Drummer Boy" is louder than before.

It's my turn to be strong. Reaching within myself, I recall the single psychic weapon that I have on tap. My sqink emulation tool. But my tool seems to be in sleep mode, or in suspended animation. I'll have to start over from the start. Can I do it alone?

Feeling around in the dark, I find Towser's inert form. My beloved alien doggie. Is there a glow of life and energy within? Maybe. His body inspires me to get my game on.

Reprising the process I used in Tiny Town, I imagine looking inside Towser's mind. And he's seeing me watching him. And I'm seeing him watching me watching him. And like that, on and on, wrapping level around level. Like building an onion from the inside out. And when I hit level seventy-eight, it clicks just like it did in Tiny Town.

I visualize the seventy-eight levels as rows of a checkerboard-type tiling in a perspective painting, and on the horizon past the seventy-eighth row, I see, once again, the handle of my sqink emulation tool. I grasp it like a weed whacker and start my campaign.

"Lights," I say. The elevator cabin is lit.

"Death ray," I say. My fingertip is the base of a frightening cone of—nothingness.

"Kill The Inspector!" I say.

This doesn't work as easily as I'd hoped. The Inspector is not without his own psychic powers, and he's manifesting a shield. I am, in effect, locked in a mind war with this filthy little sqink, and he is in fact about to win, but now the noble Towser jumps into the fray—Towser the problematic but efficacious co-author of the original collector's edition of my *Sqinks*, Towser who knows me as well as any sqink can know a human, Towser who's not unlike a cozy dog, Towser who's risen from the dead, yes, this very Towser contributes a key femtogram of voodoo force—and *zap*! The Inspector is no more.

The fried elevator control box is half gone, but no matter. The mighty Towser flash-prints a web of twirlware circuitry over the mangled controls, and the elevator ferries us smoothly down to street level. And when we exit, the guillotine doors don't manage to chop our heads off.

Ta da!

The first thing I notice is the clock on the wall of the lobby. Fifteen minutes till eight o'clock. Moo plans our Pied Paper parade's start for eight.

Wealthy guests are milling around the Hotel Snootley lobby, not knowing where to go. Outdoors looks dicey, with a seemingly endless storm of sqinks drifting past. Here's yet another Jorge-Luis-Borges list describing what I see. I love these lists. Surreal prose poetry. Meet the sqinks.

Pigs with no snouts, horseshoes covered in moss, lampshades with bulbs along the rims, tentacles attached to bowling balls, etcetera, branches with sunlit leaves, vortices of glowing sand, handfuls of sparks, birds on ice-skates delivering letters, scissors walking on their blades, inextricably tangled rolls of masking tape, magnifying glasses balanced on rays of light, trilobite fossils made of rubber, glass pumpkins with goldfish inside, etcetera, giant flat ears floating sideways, raindrops the size of dogs, piles of intestines, couches dancing the cha-cha, heads with burning coals in place of eyes, miniature models of New York City, talking cuckoo birds in Swiss clocks, flowering branches with insects reciting haiku, continually flipping coins, warts, etcetera, preserved lizards in bottles, water sprinklers, flows of lava, ponds of frogs, falling Acme safes, quivers full of arrows, houses with doors instead of windows, and Andy Warhol.

"The parade's about to start!" I cry. "Let's get my car."

"Why do we need the stupid car?" protests Carol. "We're like two blocks from Union Square."

"Um, I dunno," I say. "It makes me feel safe in the middle of all those sqinks?"

"Also Lilac is waiting in the car," says Towser. "And once we your car get rolling, we can ram something really hard."

"Sound thinking," I say.

Naturally, a sqink has taken over the controls of the hotel's front door, and she starts interviewing me regarding my request for the door to open. Recovering from her wine and despair, Carol asks our sqink Towser for his zap gun, which he hands over—and Carol effing blasts the glass door to bits.

"Debug *that*, motherfucker," she exults. "The woman is *on!*" We prance outside.

"Do you even remember where we parked?" Carol asks me.

"Um …"

"I know," says Towser, who's fully got his shit back together.

Cop sirens are purring, not full blast, but just loud enough to herd traffic out of the street. Faintly in the middle distance, I hear the marching bands tuning up. Stray bleats from horns, and thuds from the drums.

I'm not sure if the others notice yet. It's tricky enough to walk down the sidewalk amid the gurgling sqinks. They're flying low, and there's a lot of then. I'm scared to open my mouth, lest one go inside. I have my arm around Carol, with Towser in between us. He's growling and barking, as if to scare the sqinks away, and to some extent this works.

"Like a scuba dive," says Carol, speaking through her teeth. "I should take you to the Blue Corner by Palau," she tells me. "After we win."

"Whatever winning means to Moo," I say. "Paradoxically she's the one who brought on the billion sqinks. With that twinkle candy."

"It's for Moo's deal with the Mu9ers," says Towser. "Duh."

Sqinks have infested the traffic lights, so it's pointless to wait for crosswalk signals, not that, as I say, there's much traffic. The few cars move oddly—stopping and starting as if driven by learners.

I take the wheel of my car. Lilac is chatty in the back seat. "Sorry about your children, Towser. Moo says to tell you she's sorry too."

"What children?" asks Carol.

"The Mu9ers needed to test if they would in fact enjoy huffing sqinks," says Lilac,

"That's what Oliver was watching in the sky lounge?" says Carol. "How did you specifically find Towser's bud-children?"

"I'm an archive," says Lilac. "I know the lineage of every single sqink. What was it like when they huffed those two? I've never seen that."

"The naked me-wares look like iridescent comb jellies," I say. "Towser claims they're enlightened aethereal souls."

"Puts the Mu9ers in a new light," says Lilac. "I thought they were low-down dope fiends."

"Pretty much how they act," says Carol. "All the time. Especially Gubb."

"Well, I'd rather not get huffed in the first place," says Towser. "Don't lose sight of that."

"Nobody's going to huff this little doggie," says Lilac, affectionately patting Towser's head. "Moo says you're part of her OG inner circle now? Replacing Skeeze."

"I bite!" exclaims Towser, presumably meaning something positive.

"You're sure Skeeze isn't still around?" I ask Lilac.

"It's like Moo told you," says Lilac. "He's erased. In the Nowhere behind the Nothing." Lilac giggles. She has an old-lady-on-a-spree vibe today.

"I have to wonder if we can really lead the billion sqinks to the Giants stadium," I say. "Even with our marching bands and rockers."

"Gotta try," says Towser. "San Francisco is great, but with Moo's thousand bulking to a billion, it could be Goob City. An endless Fisherman's Wharf."

"You're part of the billion," I point out to Towser.

"Doesn't matter, Moo says I'm OG now," goes Towser. "Anyway, a billion isn't that bad. If we were to seriously max out the Earth's surface, like totally encrust it … who knows."

"Sqinkland didn't seem that crowded to me," goes Carol. "You're just trying to impress us."

"You didn't understand what you were looking at," says Towser. "Every single thing in Sqinkland is a sqink. The air currents, the drops of rain, the sneezes, the crumbs of bread. Standing room only—and there's no more room to stand."

"Truer vords vere naiver spoken," says Lilac adopting a corny mad-scientist accent. "Dots vhy ve heppy to be on Eart. So—"

"Oh, shove it," interrupts Carol. "Pied Piper time! We need Sqink-Randa for this. Can you snap out of it, and find her, Lilac?"

"Of course," says Lilac, composing herself. "I am a perfect know-it-all, you know."

"Terrif," says Carol. "Tell Randa to meet us in Union Square."

Meanwhile my car is still sitting at the curb. Problem: the all-pervading sqinks have infested my car's controls. Their leader advises us through the twirlware radio. She's bureaucratic and bossy. Just now she guided me step by step through through the process of starting my car.

And now she's advising me on how to pull into the essentially non-existent traffic. And once we're moving down the street, she throttles my velocity to 11 miles per hour.

"Safety first!"

We creep down Powell Street toward Union Square, with sqinks smacking into windshield like night insects on a hick road. The sqinks make no effort to avoid the collisions. A steady *splat-splat*. They seem to enjoy sliding up the windshield and arcing a slight distance into the air. Some circle back to impact us again, calling out meaningless greetings to the sqinks lodged within my possessed vehicle.

Union Square is a zone of wonder, a corrupt fairyland, with the massed sqinks rising hundreds of yards into the night sky. They crawl on the buildings; they creep the streets. Seems like way more than we saw from the Hotel Snootley lounge.

"I still don't get how we even got to a billion," gripes Carol.

"You start with a thousand of them, and keep doubling and redoubling, and you get to a billion in twenty steps," I say. "Didn't you and I talk about that?"

"Not me," says Carol. "I never talk about things like that."

"Math anxiety," I say.

"Math contempt," she retorts. "Anyway, you're not a mathematician at all, Oliver. You're an unsuccessful science fiction writer."

"SF writers are very well informed," I retort. "Better than people think. Never mind. We're going to start herding the billion now. It's eight o'clock. That's what Moo wants."

"I feel sorry for the sqinks," says Carol. "Even though they're a pain in the ass. Do they know about this plan to thin them down? Can't they hear us talking?"

"Sqinks don't think ahead," says Towser. "Synchronicity, yes? We let it rip—and ride it out. I see a big upside to having a billion sqinks huffed by Mu9ers. Every one of those sqinks can transfigure into a me-ware. Like my kids. And I'm thinking the me-wares merge. Is that a possibility, Lilac?"

More of that elderly yet girlish giggling from sqink. "I'll never tell."

"Do a billion-soul merge and, oh baby, we've got something," continues Towser. "Moo plays a deep game."

We're right next to Union Square, with my car, of course, stalled. Quite a few pedestrians are here, along with the sqinks. People can't resist this mad super swarm.

"Start our Pied Piper routine?" goes Carol.

"Not quite yet," I say. "We need more oomph. I mean, look at what's flying around up there. It's like a million city dumps."

"Hopeless," groans Carol, abruptly losing her confidence. That's something she does, and it makes me sad for her. "We shouldn't even be here," she adds.

"Hark!" I say, cocking my head. "The bands draw nigh. Thank you, Kelly Tang. They're almost here."

Yes, I hear the chiming cartwheels of the marching bands. Tattoos and flams and bass drums. Even some bagpipes, blatting the gnarliest *wheenks* known to woman or man. Glockenspiels and flutes. And in the wake come the snarls and plangent whangs of electric guitars, the warped notes riding on rolling tides of keyboard music, and crowned by the harmonic moans and hebephrenic jabber of the vocalists.

The first marching band is upon us. High-school kids in red and gold uniforms. Cymbals and trombones! A happy sea of sound, led by their tall drum major, a clear-eyed young woman, whirling her ceremonial mace. And another band, and another, and another. Can they enchant Moo's billion?

Perhaps yes. Moo has smart whirlwinds at work, piping the music high and low, with a massed effect like a three-dimensional square dance.

My car remains stock-still amid the crowd of sqinks and pedestrians. They're cheering; I'm stuck. An imposing sqink like a Black movie star runs down the street and wriggles in through one of my car windows.

"Don't recognize me?" she says. She purses her lips. White lipstick.

"Randa?" says Carol. "It's you?"

"If it's about keeping it real, you oughtta call me *Sqink*-Randa," says the sqink. "The real Randa was a stokker, right?"

"Can we just frikkin' call you Randa?" I ask.

"Yo," goes Randa. "You ready to jam with my flow?"

"We'll entrance," I say. "Giants stadium, here we come." I lean on my car's horn and step on the gas. Still not moving. Thanks to the bossy sqink and her unseen posse aboard.

Randa growls, shapes a long, sqink finger into a probe, and slips it up under the car's dash. Huge sputter of sparks accompanied by an aggrieved sqink shriek.

My car lurches forward, but not in a good way. We squoosh a sqink or two, and manage to miss the humans. After so long a wait, I can't bring myself to lighten up on the gas. Fully out of control, my wildly fish-tailing car car scrapes along a granite wall and knocks a stubby fireplug loose.

"Iron on the target!" exults Towser.

A huge fountain blooms. Partying sqinks gambol in the gush. Time to do our thing.

Randa rolls into the alto line of the Pied Piper song, with Carol trilling a soprano descant. Me, I'm singing baritone. As I've said, I don't have much of a voice. But whip me into a frenzy, and you can tell I'm there.

The massed interplay of the marching bands is like a virtual dome; a shape patterned with clefs and arpeggios and off-beats and the smears of the horns. A synergy is in play, our Pied Piper music fits around the chatter.

But we need more. The task is vast. Lead a billion noisy sinks? We need Moo's aid. Where *is* that unreliable cuttlefish? She'll merge with the honks; she'll hook us up with the the tang and swoop of the rockers.

Meanwhile Carol, Randa, and I unfold ourselves from my wrecked car, with Towser the dog at our feet, yowling as best he can. Cheerful Lilac is draped across Carol's shoulders like an ermine stole. For her sonic contribution, she's clicking like a Geiger counter in a uranium mine.

We're music royalty! Devil-may-care stars taking their night-club act public! Telling the truths that lie in our hearts. Working it, in short, and getting louder. Topper and Lady Cee in the house!

The throngs of sqinks have taken on a hallucinatory, unified feel. We're in step with the marching bands, riding our flock's flow. The young band members are fascinated—and frightened—by the sqinks. I have a feeling they're scared to stop playing.

What the hell, the world is ending.

And here come the rockers.

Let it all come down.

19. Big Yam

Moo appears, larger than before, Moo, the Queen of the Sqinks. Hovering, glowing, and adored by her billion. Descending from on high, like a diver exploring benthic depths. We're primitive antediluvians down here.

"Give us a ride!" Carol calls to Moo. "And help us sing."

Moo tilts and extends her tentacles like a Neptune's ladder. Our quartet scrambles up and settles in, chanting all the while. Prim Lilac declines to join us. She'd rather watch from afar.

Our Pied Piper routine is coming together, richer and more compelling every minute. Moo straps us in with her tentacles, and guides our voices along the air streams of the sqink swarm. Our Pied Piper anthem is all around.

I admire the rock bands trundling along on their flatbed trucks. Genres: molten metal, hissy hop, psycho pop, numb meds, and weepy whump. The rubbery sqinks pulse with the polyrhythms.

It's starting to rain. This means little to the sqinks, but it's hard on Carol and me. It's slippery on Moo's back. Kindly, she warms her bod to offset the chill.

"We're going to win," Moo assures us. "All those scurvy, stupid-ass, over-populating, noob sqinks will be corralled in one place. A horde of Mu9ers will be on them like piranha fish on a herd of collapsed cows."

"Wait," says Carol. "How do all those Mu9ers get here?"

"Through my wormhole," says Moo. "Easy enough for me to guide them if they need help."

"You're helping the Mu9ers for free?" I say.

"Hell no, they paid for this," goes Moo. "That was our deal. Nothing's free from Moo. With a side benefit the Mu9ers don't know about. They'll be setting us up for a mega sqink. Meanwhile drop the chat and sing your effing song! Trance into it, gang. Lose yourselves."

So, yes, I'm back into the music, a flow of winding streams and shuddering auras. Our strength is vast. My lungs are a blimp bagpipe, Randa is a two-acre bongo, Carol a sax the size of an ocean liner, and Towser has the roar of a dinosaur. We're psychotronic, stroboscopic, phantasmagoric—all of it.

Enveloped by our mass of sound, Moo and our quartet drift slowly toward the Bay, and come to rest above the Giants stadium. The brass bands and the rocker flatbeds are ranged around the stadium, blasting hard, with our Pied Piper anthem a golden thread upon the sea of sound.

The sqinks have dog-piled into the stadium by the hundreds of millions, wedged into every nook—and it really is a full billion if you count the overflow around the edges. They're stunned by the ecstasy of our Pied Piper spell.

Overhead, the rainclouds rock with rolling thunder. Lightning bolts dance across the stadium, the Bay, the buildings, and the sqinks themselves—striking over and over again. The sqinks like it.

No sign of Moo's Mu9ers.

Carol and I look at each other. Our faces strobe in the stormy light. Towser has fallen silent, overcome by fatigue. Ditto for Randa; she's limp. And as for our supreme leader, the mighty cuttlefish of all cuttlefish, Queen Moo—she appears to be in a trance. Maybe she's crafting higher plans.

It feels as if Carol and I are alone in keeping the billion sqinks under control. Quite a burden to bear. Irked by Moo's passivity, Carol sinks her teeth into the big sqink's nearest tentacle tip. Moo twitches and emits a sharp squeal.

Stage two.

Here come the Mu9ers, approaching us from the direction of Moo's Box Farm wormhole, speeding closer, massing in a great flock and then—whoah baby! They dive into the humongous bowl of sqinks, tearing at the hapless critters like hawks eating a nest of fledglings, or, less elegantly, like stoners freebasing the latest synthetic off a backstreet diner's griddle. Glints of a hundred million huffing pipes.

Carol and I are silent, as are Towser and Randa. Our song is done. No need to herd the sqinks now. They're trapped, cornered, at the mercy of the crazed, thrill-seeking Mu9ers. Sold out by their leader Moo.

Surprisingly, it's not entirely a scene of suffering. When a sqink is trapped and huffed, they look almost—content.

As for the iridescent comb-jelly beings that emerge from the sqinks—they're lovely. The me-wares. This hadn't been so clear to me at the Hotel Snootley.

Coaxed from the sqinks' bodies, huffed down into the bodies of the Mu9ers, and huffed back into the air—the me-wares seem unsure where to go next, just as in the hotel. But the me-wares are not, as I say, in agony. It's more like a state of bemused freedom. Or even, strange as it seems, ecstasy.

Was it like this for Tobin? I don't think so. That scene was so savage and bizarre that I can't imagine any part of it being pleasant.

For the liberated sqink me-wares in the Giant's stadium here, returning to their sqink bodies is pointless. The Mu9ers will only tease the me-ware out, and huff it yet again. But floating freely in the hell-world of the stadium would seem to lead a me-ware to the same outcome.

Note that there's a limit to how many times a me-ware can be huffed in rapid succession—without dying for good.

There may be no real limit if the me-ware has time to recoup between rounds, but a staccato party scene would be lethal.

I suspect the me-wares are finding a third path. In order to survive, they're lying low. Dimming their glows and burrowing beneath the mounds of comatose sqinks.

And, yes, the deflated and all-but-soulless sqink bodies are in very poor shape indeed. They're melting together, layer upon layer of them, deliquescing like slime at the bottom of a garbage can. Carol and I feel sorrow and pity over this effacement of the sqinks' shapes, quirks, and colors.

The attack goes on and on. A billion is a lot. The sqinks in the stadium were stacked deeper than I realized. The Mu9ers are savoring their party.

"It's not right," I say to Moo.

The great cuttlefish makes a sound like a low, sly chuckle.

"What are you thinking!" Carol yells at Moo. "Why did you bring the sqinks here in the first place? Why did you scatter twinkle candy and grow your thousand into a billion?"

"I never turn down a business opportunity," says Moo. "And the real pay-off is yet to come."

"Maybe they'll be okay," I tell Carol. "Those me-wares, they're smart. They'll fight back." But perhaps this is bluster. Hardly any of the me-wares are visible, and, as I say, those are dim. And the party isn't even over. A number of unscathed sqinks remain.

"*Do* something!" cries Carol. "You fat stupid squid!"

Moo burbles a satisfied laugh. "Wait till the Mu9ers have huffed every darn sqink in the joint," she says. "And then—*gotcha*!"

Still more Mu9ers arrive, a steady stream of them. It's like when a senile bird-lover dumps a shopping bag of stale crumbs in a park, and the pigeons crowd in, blocking the light with their wings, filling the air with flutters and squawks and shit.

Repeatedly, the carnage rises to what seems to be a peak—and then it mounts higher—and then mounts again, cruising with an epic jam by one of our tripped-out flatbed-truck bands, a group that doesn't know when to, or how to, or whether to—stop. Not even *wanting* to stop. Not even knowing that stopping is an option. And the ultimate, longed-for orgasm of the final arpeggio is never going to come.

Hypnotic. Carol and I lose ourselves in the gawp; our thought-flows ride the pulse of the wow.

But then, *sigh*, like every damn thing that ever comes along, the massacre is done.

The empty bowl is littered with Mu9ers savoring the after-buzz of their mass debauch. They're too wasted to huff anymore.

Some of the Mu9ers are slack and lolling, others are flaccidly linked in Mu9er-type sex acts, others flutter about in drunken spurts. The sqink bodies are a throbbing pulp, and the sqink me-wares are unseen.

How still it is, how very still. The bands have gone home. The thunderstorm has spent its fury. A fattening half-moon hangs low. A light, steady breeze is clearing away the fog.

The air within the stadium—is it blank? No. The sqink me-wares are still here. They survived. They went dark. And now they're starting to glow. It's payback time.

"Ghost riders in the sky," I say to Carol.

"Bless their little hearts," she says.

"Watch," says Moo, fairly cackling. "Watch now. Stage three."

The sqink me-wares glow ever brighter, emitting wider spectra than is the norm. Microwaves, infrared, RGBIV, ultra-violet, and, oh my god, X-rays. Somehow, I can see them. The X-rays are hard and bleak as the Grim Reaper's skull.

The bright sqink me-wares circle the bowl of the stadium like roller derby skaters gaining speed, or like particles in a cyclotron, with their paths twitching unpredictably, dipping down and arcing up, and they're moving *very* fast, like at 99 percent the speed of light, it feels like. They slam into Mu9ers like anti-protons impacting uranium atoms—thereby sublimating Mu9er mass into edible energy. The sqink me-wares are eating the Mu9ers alive.

In time, the sqink me-wares fatten and slow down. They hover above the stadium like a peaceful swarm of insects after a typhoon, weaving a slow pattern that says so little and so much, taking an interest in the insensate forms of the abandoned sqink bodies that lie scattered across the stadium's tiers. In the supernal glow of the me-wares, the scene resembles an old black-and-white newsreel of a battle's aftermath.

The sqink bodies remain—dead or comatose—but every last Mu9er has been killed and eaten—with the exception of Kanga and Gubb, who perch safe on Moo's back—along with Towser, Randa, Carol, and me—not to mention Lilac, who's with us again. You might say Moo is a stadium skybox.

But what of those collapsed sqinks?

"Back me up for this next number," says Moo. "Stage four. Bring the band down behind me, boys."

"Not a boy," says Carol.

Moo bobs in appreciation. "A heck of a peck of Pied Piper pickles, eh? Ready to roll the rock? Raise the dead? Big body and a big mind."

"We've always got more," says Carol. "Hit it, Oliver!"

My voice has never seemed so compelling, and Carol's tones were never so ripe. Stylish Randa crafts an unforgettable earworm chorus. Even Towser does his part, adding a line of yips.

And, yes, Moo is singing lead. I hadn't known she had the skill. Old-lady Lilac has joined the chorus as well. Our first job is to wake the sqink bodies from their stupor.

We sing the unsung, say the unsaid, tell the untold. It's a sacred oratorio. And, yea, it was good. Our chant nurses the sqink bodies into motion. Me-ware-less though they are, they flow, they hump themselves up, and—*wow*—they merge into a giant blob, flexing and taking form.

Moo sings sweet and slow. We're with her. We hymn for love. The billion-sqink slug responds in kind. The love you take. The love you make.

The vast corpus of a billion merged sqinks is pulsing. Finding a shape.

And then—if I dare leaven the sublime with the ridiculous—the mass of sqinks has become—a potato? The size of the Giants stadium. And somehow a vibe that genders her as female. She's a huge, happy, unconcerned sweet potato.

Moo stops singing, as if at a loss.

"Is that it?" I say. "But we have to push further. Put the me-wares into the sweet potato."

"Yes!" exclaims Moo. "Good old Oliver's writing the novel. He's Full Of Ideas."

"Ignition spark," I suggest. "Leonardo moment. God and Adam touch fingers."

Singing in harmony, Moo, Carol, and I turn our rhythm ragged—and catch the attention of the billion sqink me-wares.

Bopping to our beat, the glowing flock descends upon the sweet potato like a swarm of weevils. They settle in, poke holes, and—as we five raise our paean to a towering discordant climax—the me-wares burrow inside. The billion sqink bodies and their billion souls have formed a greater One.

The sweet potato is alert, alive, and personable.

"Thank you," she says. "You've done well. My name is Yam."

Yes, it's Yam. A very, very big yam—dusty, pointed at both ends, and, one supposes, orange all the way through. With curly roots at either end. And a billion bumps that are the glintful eyes of me-wares.

"Lead me to the world Mu9," Yam tells the two remaining Mu9ers, Gubb and Kanga, who hover beside Moo, clearly uneasy.

Yam's voice is a multiplex sound, as if all the sqinks are talking at once, more or less in synch, but not exactly. A fuzzy voice, a wheeze that channels twirlware teep as well.

"Go on," Yam repeats. "Show me to Mu9."

There's a cozy quality to the voice, even though Yam may be heralding the end of all our worlds. Warm but implacable.

Evidently, Kanga and Gubb have no thought of disobeying Yam. Indeed, they seem too awed to speak. They head south along the edge of the Bay, heading for Moo's wormhole.

Yam doesn't yet follow. She rolls her billion eyes toward Carol, Towser, Randa, and me—all of us still perched on Moo. Yam is fully at ease, wallowing in her physicality and her grandeur, savoring the air. In no hurry at all.

"And?" she adds. "Any parting requests from bossy Moo?"

"Remember that you will be representing me," says Moo.

"You, Moo?" rumbles Yam. "You tiny little thing."

"I think you better tell the Mu9ers not to huff more sqinks," says Moo. "And make the Mu9ers fear me. You go there and kick ass on my behalf, Yam."

"You presume to command me?" responds Yam. "You wriggler. You speck of goo."

Moo abruptly realizes she's met her match. "I'm sorry," she says.

"As for huffing," adds Yam. "Sqinks enjoy getting huffed—as long as they get their me-wares back."

"That's not good," says Moo. "It's immoral. You should kill many Mu9ers."

"Symbiosis would be a better answer than violence," Randa puts in.

"But look how the Mu9ers tore into my billion," burbles Moo. "They overdid it. Huffing and huffing and huffing. That was violent!"

"To a prude or to a child, the sex act seems rough and ungainly," says Yam. "But to the participants, it may feel like a dance."

"Anyway, it was you, Moo, who set the whole thing up," I say. "So don't play the Puritan. You multiplied the sqinks with the twinkle candy, and you told us to herd the sqinks into the stadium."

"I had a business deal," says Moo.

"And that's why Moo called in the Mu9ers," says Lilac. "To collect their goods."

"Well, I was hoping we'd kill a lot of the Mu9ers," says Moo. "In revenge. And I did imagine the billion drained sqinks might bounce back. But I didn't realize we'd end up with this ... this *Yam*. You're on my side, right, Yam? After all, I made you."

As if losing interest in Moo's self-justifying evasions, Yam bends in half and begins sniffing herself all over. Like a dog. A dog with a twisty root instead of a head.

"Queen Moo, Queen Moo," Yam finally says. "Little do you know. It took author Oliver to think of me, the mighty Yam, a being worthy of your highest adoration. An adoration which I now await."

Moo doesn't like this line of thought. "Just go and follow Kanga and Gubb," Moo tells Yam. "Follow them to Mu9. You have to hurry. They're way ahead of you."

"I'll have no trouble finding them," says Yam. "I see far. And I'm rapid. But you, Moo, I said you must worship me."

Yam's voice is no longer cozy. It's an earthquake rumble.

An uncanny aura forms around Moo, generating an unpleasant hiss. Moo is like an inept magician who's raised a spirit she can't control. A spirit called Yam.

The air crackles and pops from the strength of Moo's aura. My hair stands out, and so does Carol's. And Lilac is buzzing with sparks.

Moo is bloating, as if she's been holding her breath for too long. I wonder if she might explode. And now she yields.

"Yam is the highest," blats Moo. Her voice is like a prolonged fart. Her sparks and the auras die away.

"I worship Yam," continues Moo. "Yam rules all. Chime in, my riders."

Dutifully, we five raise our voices in praise of Yam.

"Yam spake, and, lo, it was good," says Yam. She turns her attention to Carol and me. "Mad Moo often lies," she says. "Moo imagines she's smarter than others. Just because she's fat."

"I'm only a Queen," says Moo, playing it meek. "You're the Empress, Yam."

"That's right," says Yam, her voice cozy once more. "You want me to attack Mu9. You hope I never return. You regret that you made me. If you could, you'd kill me. Am I missing anything?"

"I just want to be Queen," says Moo. "And I want to improve Earth. I might stay here. But there are problems."

"The problems, yes," says Yam. "The humans want to employ sqinks. The sqinks want to start a colony somewhere. The Mu9ers want to huff humans. A three-way yin-yang. A spiral of want. We need a Triple Entente."

"Sounds nice," I put in. "Entente is French for agreement, right?"

"To be sure," says Moo. "Accommodations must be made, and expectations must be tamed. With trust and generosity on all sides."

"You sound sly," says Yam.

"I'm not," insists Moo. "I'm done with all that. I have nothing bad in mind. I want everyone to be happy."

Yam waves a blind root as if sniffing the air. "I'll work for a Triple Entente. And I'll do it not for you, Moo, but—oh, I'll do it for that woman riding on your back. Carol Cee. I want a Triple Entente for Carol's sake."

"What about me?" I burst out. "Don't you care about me?"

Yam doesn't deign to answer that. Strangers tend not to care for me. Maybe it has something to do with me being a science fiction writer. Like I know too much.

"Last call for boarding," says Yam.

As a farewell to Moo, Yam flicks the cuttlefish sqink with her enormous twisty root—sending Moo tumbling. Randa, Towser, Carol, Lilac, and I are jolted loose from Moo's back—and we're drifting on our own.

Or no, oh shit, it's the three sqinks who are *drifting*. Carol and I are falling straight toward the ground. Like a pair of Acme safes.

"Help, help," I shriek, to use a standard line of Donald Duck's.

"We're Earth's negotiators!" cries Carol.

Yam's rough-skinned tail-root forms a loop that Carol and I land on. As if we're acrobats executing a nervy move. Meanwhile, Randa and Towser have flown to alight on root as well.

My heart is pounding. Carol looks happy. She loves adventure. So what the hell. We scrabble around on Yam's dry skin, gaining purchase on the protruding eye buds.

"Welcome aboard," says Yam, her voice a breathy, intimate whisper. Like a kindly flight attendant, here to help us.

Towser and Randa sit next to us on the root. "We'll speak on behalf of Sqinkland," says Towser. "Kanga and Gubb will represent Mu9. And, yes, Carol and Oliver for Earth. Yam can be a bodyguard for all of us."

Moo hovers nearby, with Lilac alone on her back. "Stand not upon the order of your going," Moo calls, going all Shakespearean on our ass. And probably glad to see us go. "Fare thee well."

And we're off.

20. TRIPLE ENTENTE

The stadium fades behind us, and soon we're above Moo's garden by the Box Farm. Like a sounding whale, Yam adopts a vertical position—and dives straight into Moo's wormhole. You'd think it would be a tight fit, but Yam has the flexibility of any other sqink—and a billion times the strength.

Kanga and Gubb are sitting about eight feet from Carol, me, Towser, and Randa—all six of us on Yam's rear root. You don't want to be on Yam's front end while she's digging!

"Great idea to ride Yam to Mu9," I say to Carol as Earth's sky disappears above us. I'm being a little sarcastic. "Yes sir. Riding a giant sqink to an alien world with a pair of brain-huffers. Oh well! Up shit creek is where you and I tend to go."

As we enter the bulk, the customary hallucinations start to kick in. By way of holding them back, I start a conversation with the others.

"Will we be able to find the way to Mu9?" I ask Kanga.

"We know our way around the bulk quite well," says Kanga. "It's just your planets that are hard to find."

"What about Yam killing a bunch of Mu9ers?" Carol asks.

"Ha," puts in Yam, joining the conversation. "Fat chance."

"We'll reason with the Mu9ers, right?" says Randa. "Find common interests among the three worlds. A partnership."

"Civilized," says Carol. "The woman's touch."

"What is this business about the sqinks and Mu9ers having gender?" I interrupt. "So far as I know, Sqinks reproduce asexually. And the Mu9ers … who knows? No reason to talk about male and female."

"A mode of thought," says Yam. "Like space and time. A convenient category. Here's another question, Oliver. When does your penis get stiff?"

Carol thinks this is funny, and so do Randa and Towser. I decide to shut up.

Guided by chirps from Kanga, Yam is undulating her way through the bulk in a purposeful pulse. That's fine. But the two Mu9ers are sitting closer to Carol and me than I'd like. Are they planning an in-flight snack? Even if our me-wares taste like piss? Can I smell it?

The bulk is getting into my head. My thoughts decay into surreal gibberish.

Eventually, a huge red explosion snaps me out of it. Green. Yellow. Grainy clouds of light. As if someone's shooting Roman candles. We're shaded by Yam. Dear Carol is snuggled in my arms. We've been in a trance, lying on Yam's rear root.

Towser and Randa sit nearby with Kanga and Gubb. The Mu9ers are merry. This is a big homecoming for them. It's been a few months since they set out scouting for new minds to huff.

Yam circles above a sprawling Mu9 city. It's dusk here, with an ocean nearby. The skyrockets stand out against the gloom.

"We're not so bad," Kanga says to me. "Don't be scared. If we wanted to kill you, we could have done it while you were in dreamland. But we didn't. You and Carol—and those two sqinks—you're safe with us."

"Humans are safe because we still haven't figured out a good way to huff you," says the ruffian Gubb. "On account of that synesthetic effect that says your minds smell bad. You get what I'm saying?"

"Of course I get it," I snap. "I'm a science fiction writer. I'm the author of this novel we're living in."

"You keep saying that," goes Gubb. "Your chicken scratches tell the stories of our lives? Bull *shit*. I've got ten times your talent. On a good day."

"A good day for me, or a good day for you?"

"You should be polite to Oliver," Kanga reminds Gubb. "We want to raise his and Carol's opinion of us. We'd like to reach a Triple Entente."

"How about this," says Gubb, trying for a lofty tone. "We're proud to bring humans and sqinks to Mu9. You're slackadelic. Transformative."

"I have a thought," says Kanga with a giggle. Neither of these two seems able to maintain much respect for us four. It feels like we're beetles they've collected. "If Oliver and Carol are so big on gender, why don't they let us watch them making love?"

"Maybe we could dart in and huff the climax," says Gubb.

"Like it's a new-wave Lewis Carroll tea party!" exclaims Kanga.

"Huh?"

"Vhe make … *joke*," says Gubb, putting on one of their horrible accents. Like Lilac did. Maybe, just maybe, the Mu9ers can be fun. It's almost like they enjoy talking with us.

A question occurs to me. "When the sqinks killed all those Mu9ers in the Giants stadium, none of the Mu9ers came back to life. They were stone-cold dead. Don't you guys have me-ware souls?"

"No, we don't," Kanga curtly says. She doesn't want to discuss it.

Maybe she's ashamed. By certain standards, the Mu9ers might be viewed as lower forms of life. Like lichen or worms. Locked in their bodies—until the lights go out. That's a way we humans have an edge on them.

Yam glides lower, getting close to landing in an open area near the sea.

Pow, pow, pow. Another volley of shells explodes, spitting out cascades of sputtering sparks that weave a virtual fabric of lilac veils, with the sheets of light rising into the sky.

In the field below us stands a very large creature on four legs. He's the size of a building. He's the one sending up the sky rockets, launching them from a mobile appendage that you might think of as a snout or a trunk.

"A square elephant?" says Carol.

"Call him Heffalump," responds Kanga. "Heffalump and Kanga—those are names from *Winnie-the-Pooh*. I'm a fan of your author A. A. Milne."

"Surprising," says Carol. "Who would think a Mu9er would ever read."

Kanga doesn't answer. She's busy trying to calm Yam. The most recent shell-burst spooked the great sweet potato. She's veering out over the sea. The Mu9 city is but a glow on the horizon.

"Don't *panic*," Gubb tells Yam. "Heffalump shoots those signals whenever a VIP arrives."

"VIP is me," says Yam in her vast, husky voice. "The Very Important Potato. A billion sqinks in one. Are you sure that square elephant was only saying hello? I thought he might be shooting at me."

"A billion sqinks inside Yam," muses Gubb, his thoughts turning to his favorite topic. "Some damn good huffing in that potato. Do you know that the more often you huff a piece of me-ware, the sweeter it tastes?"

"Gubb is such a brain-dead stoner," says Carol with a frown. "We're landing on his alien world here. Hoping to cement a three-way cultural contact. A historic treaty. But Gubb—"

"Gubb is *low*," agrees Kanga. "Don't listen to him. Let's circle back to that park and talk with Heffalump. He's our host. The moderator. We want him to think well of us."

"Why do you keep wanting people to think well of us?" demands the bumptious Gubb. "I mean—who cares?"

"Gubb is *so* low," says Towser, echoing our group opinion. "So very, very low."

"We're supposed to be diplomats!" the exasperated Kanga says to her partner. "We're not junkies looking to score."

"You can put a better face on it," I suggest. "Say that when you huff someone', you uplifts their mind," I suggest. "It sometimes seems they enjoy the process."

"Unless, of course, they're weak and they die," says Gubb. "Like your sad pal Tobin."

"Give us a sturdy specimen, and we can elevate them," says Kanga.

"Right," says Gubb. "So screw Tobin."

"Can you drop that infantile I'm-a-badass routine," Towser tells Gubb. "Nobody's impressed."

"Thank you for saying that," goes Kanga. "In truth, we're talking about enlightenment. It's a joy to have a me-ware soul in my head. Something which the fates have denied to Mu9ers. Do tell me that you understand these things, Gubb!"

Gubb is on the defensive. "We enlightened the hell outta those sqink me-wares at the stadium. What a party. Not that the sqinks thanked us. They turned around and killed every Mu9er in sight."

"We did that because you're vermin," says Yam, as if explaining something simple to a child.

"I hate you!" Gubb begin. But then he cuts himself short. A long pause while he gropes for a higher road.

And then he resumes. "Very well then, my friend," says Gubb. "Let the topic be souls and higher consciousness. We Mu9ers are agents of enlightenment."

Hearing this from her partner, Kanga makes the creepy Mu9er sound that represents laughter.

Two pale, glowing leviathans cavort in the sea below. They see us. One of them breaches from the waters, rolls hugely in the air, and does a belly flop. Phosphorescent spray rises high enough to wet us.

"Let's get back to land," Carol begs Yam. "This is way too much. Go back to that city."

"I hope that big square thing, that Heffalump, I hope he doesn't double-cross us," says Yam, her voice sweet and strong. She flexes her body toward a return course. The city's glow brightens. Heffalump launches another salvo of welcoming rockets. And to enhance his greeting, he blows enormous polyhedral soap bubbles from his trunk.

"Be sure to *land* this time," Randa tells Yam. "Don't chicken out."

Yam touches down as gently as possible, skidding across the park on her underside—as if sledding on snow, or belly-boarding a wave—crushing a few small groves of trees, but not all of them—and eventually she comes to a stop. Our Yam is so very big.

We're illuminated by swooping, coruscating sparks from Heffalump's rockets. Perhaps Yam is frightened and shy—or perhaps she's looking for food—but for whatever reason, she rises up on one end, as she did for Moo's wormhole, but this time she's drilling into the ground, twisting her roots in the dirt, boring in, and vanishing from view in less than a minute, leaving a monumental gopher mound in her wake. She takes her fellow-sqinks Towser and Randa with her.

Carol and I barely have time to jump away from Yam lest we be dragged under. Kanga and Gubb stay with us.

Here we four are, alone in the park. Heffalump stumps over to us, awkward on his great body's square legs.

And now he speaks. His spoken voice is a garbled blare, akin to a lo-fi announcement in an old airport. But Heffalump uses twirlware teep as well. And he even includes subtitles.

"I SPEAK ONLY IN CAPITAL LETTERS," says Heffa-lump. "BECAUSE THE HACK AUTHOR OF THIS SCUZZY SCI-FI NOVEL HAS NO CONCEPT OF WHAT AN ALIEN MIND IS LIKE."

"*I'm* the author," I reply. "Show some respect. That key on the left edge of your keyboard—that's the CAPS LOCK. Press it once, fool. That turns off the caps."

"AH YES," says Heffalump. "AND, there, that does it. Come inside me and we'll have a chat."

"Come inside?" goes Carol.

"In one sense, I am an office building," explains Heffalump. "For the United Civilizations of the Bulk. I'm the Secretary-General of this organization. And I contain conference facili-ties. I'll show you to our meeting hall."

A door opens in one of Heffalump's square legs. I see warm light inside, and what looks to be an elevator door.

"We are not riding any goddam elevator," yells Carol. She's thinking of what happened at the Hotel Snootley with The Inspector. And she's right to worry. Our adventures are more and more like a dream. And dream elevators never work.

Gubb mocks our hesitation. "Lightweights. Goobs."

"Stairs are this way," says Kanga, heading inside Heffa-lump's formidable leg. "Follow me."

So, okay, we find the stairwell, and somehow the stairs are like an escalator, which seems like it'll make things easy. But—

"Oh shit!" I yell. "Oh no!"

We're gliding down instead of up.

"How do the down-stairs happen to be right under where Heffalump is standing?" I jabber. "I mean, obviously we're not still inside his leg, so—"

"Can't you even *try* to be cool?" goes Gubb.

We speed down flight after flight. I worry that it's going to get hot, but it's not. And then we're done. No more stairs.

We're on a landing, looking out at a vast hollow space. With things like large gnats flying around. Very many of them.

And the gigantic Yam is here already, off to one side, drifting idly in the air. I'm glad to see her. Our bodyguard.

"The flying things, those are yump-bugs," says Secretary-General Heffalump, his voice booming from the stairwell. I'm getting used to the coarseness of his sound. "And this is their hive. A convenient retreat for treaty conferences. The yump-bugs are, up to a point, good hosts."

"I like this," says Carol. "I always wanted to be in the UN."

"We're counting on you six," continues Heffalump. "Kanga and Gubb. Carol and Oliver. Randa and Towser. Three pairs. You'll hammer out the details of your Triple Entente."

"Why us?" asks Carol. Something we've all been wondering about.

"I've been Secretary-General of the United Civilizations for a long time," says Heffalump. "You six representatives were selected, as is customary, by blind chance. Sqink luck. Synchronicity. You're normally abnormal."

"And your headquarters is on Mu9—why?" presses Carol.

Heffalump makes a sound like a trombone played backwards in a pool of mercury. A sob? A rueful chortle? "You do know that Mu9ers have no souls, yes?" he says. "No me-wares. That makes us more even-handed."

"Even-handed?" says Carol. "All the Mu9ers want to do is to huff brains and get high. It's not like you guys are big diplomats. You're junkies."

"I keep telling you that huffing isn't exactly about getting high," says Kanga. "We like to see what we can't get."

"We have zilch," adds Gubb, who I now, weirdly enough, see almost as a Zen master. Perhaps mistakenly.

"Nada," continues Gubb. "Squat. Emptiness." He hops into the air and floats free.

The vast yump-bug hive is a weightless zone. Following Gubb's example, Kanga, Carol, and I drift out as well—and now here come Towser and Randa, who rode down with Yam. We're six again.

The yump-bugs' cavern is remarkably capacious. It's as if we're inside a hollow planet. Not that, so far as I understand it, a den like Mu9 is a *planet*. It's more like the Skolem hull of an axiom system—as a bullshitting SF-writing mathematician might say.

The yump-bugs are all around us, tracing elegant space curves like the after-images of party-time sparklers. Their paths are warped by steady changes in torsion and curvature, with no two segments the same.

The yump-bug's bodies are extremely simple—one might call them crude. Each is a fat round dot with a lop-lop pair of wings. Like cartoon flies circling a down-and-outer in a comic strip, evoking the aura of hobos, beatniks, hippies, cyberpunks, or some such.

Very hard to estimate how many of the yump-bugs there are. Their glowing dots trail off into the distance, massing into nebulas, like stars in the sky.

Scattered across the scene are conglomerations of waxy cells—akin to honeycombs.

"The precious yump," says Kanga, sensing my unspoken question. "They secrete it. I assume you know that yump is the currency used in the bulk. Like gold once was on Earth."

"Tough to harvest the yump," puts in Gubb. "The yump-bugs *sting*."

"What is yump itself good for?" asks Carol.

"Whatever you want," says Kanga. "Yump can morph. Even into things you didn't know about. Tell the yump what you want and—*oonk*."

"The sound is more like *zeent*," says Gubb, who is by way of being an expert.

"It's *ahooga*," corrects a nearby yump-bug. The human-culture-specific remark evokes shrill giggles from the swarm around us.

"How about making a round conference table with six chairs," I say to the yump-bugs. "And give us a local gravity field so we can sit down."

"And six pens and notepads," says Kanga.

"And water," says Randa.

"And ... hey Yam over there," says Gubb. "How about a sqink for me to huff."

"You're vermin," goes Yam. "Like I already said." Even so, Yam pinches a tiny, balled-up sqink off her body and flicks it Gubb's way. Like she's trying to get something going.

"We're therapists," says Gubb, quickly proceeding to huff the unhappy mouse-shaped little sqink—first teasing it into spasms, and then sucking up the creature's tiny me-ware as it drifts forth. Great shuddering sigh of pleasure from Gubb.

As Gubb sighs, the sqink me-ware emerges from his mouth—and sinks back into the mouse sqink, who emits a shrill squeak, and traces a wavery path back to big Yam. It doesn't look as if the mouse is enjoying herself.

"Oh, what's so wrong?" says Kanga, sticking up for her partner.

"Let's get to work," says Carol. "We've got a lot of detail to get through."

"Diagram," says Kanga. She displays a glowing equilateral triangle. At the corners: a human, a sqink, a Mu9er. Each with a caption.

Humans use sqinks as helpers.
Sqinks colonize Mu9.
Mu9ers huff human me-ware.

I can't resist tossing in some irrelevant yet beautiful math. "Imagine that each dot creeps clockwise toward the next dot, continuously readjusting its direction to aim at where the target dot currently is. And that next dot is doing the same thing, heading toward the third dot, and the third dot is heading toward the first. Interactive feedback. Now consider the motion trails of the three dots. They form nautilus-shell curves, spiraling toward the triangle's center. Logarithmic spirals. *Eadem mutata resurgo*, as it says on Jacob Bernoulli's tomb."

"What does all that crap have to do with anything?" says Carol, not without affection. "Senility alert."

I don't care. I feel wise and important. Surely our epic Triple Entente proceedings are being recorded. It's only fitting. It is well that the soulless Mu9ers are here to serve us.

"Forget about Oliver," says Gubb. "My beef is that Kanga's motives don't make sense. Mu9ers can't huff humans at all."

"And sqinks don't especially want to colonize Mu9," puts in Randa. "It's dangerous."

"And sqinks aren't of much use to humans," says Carol. "They never do what you want."

"Let's stick with what I said," insists Kanga, an edge in her voice. "It's symmetric. It's beautiful. And often the beautiful thing is what's right."

"God is math," I put in.

"So copy my diagram onto your notepads," continues Kanga. "Be dutiful. Once you get off your butts, we can expand and amend."

Etcetera.

Our yump-based notepads need to be enlarged. Repeatedly. Refinements and sub-clauses and codicils and footnotes branch out—requiring more and more room. The yump-bugs swoop around, adding pages to our notebooks, but not really liking to see us using so much of the precious yump.

Eventually, Gubb does something rude, and a yump-bug stings him on the hand, triggering Gubb's frantic bellows, although he's probably not injured all that much.

Watchful Yam goes for maximum payback. She lashes out with a web of sparks that turns perhaps a thousand yump-bugs to ash. Not that the number of yump-bugs seems much reduced.

Yam issues a clear directive.

"No stinging."

Yes, Yam is our bodyguard.

"And how about some drinks and snacks all around," adds Gubb, riding high. "And, Yam, can you send that sweet little mouse over here so I can score another huff?"

"More therapy for her?" says Yam, kind of laughing. The mouse sqink accedes to Gubb's request. And, just like everyone's been saying, the sqink *does* now seem to like having her me-ware huffed.

We get back to negotiating.

Etcetera.

Twenty hours later, our written Triple Entente agreement has taken on the approximate shape and size of an origami banyan tree. Well and good. One vexing point remains: *Are humans to be deemed huffable?*

"I thought of a fix for that piss-smell thing," says Yam, "Like, *duh*? Make the huff mellow. Not like a horror movie. Not like electroshock therapy."

"Got it," says Kanga. "I'd been thinking that too. And, you know, we don't actually have to take the brain out of the skull. We can go in through the nose."

"Let's try it on Oliver," says Gubb.

"Um, I don't think—" I begin.

But already Kanga is on me. As if she's hugging me. Her fingers spider into fronds. The fronds cover my face, creep up my nose—and a light fills my mind. We're linked. She's huffing me.

I'm glad it's Kanga and not Gubb. I like Kanga well enough that I feel her move as comfortable. Like a long-awaited first kiss. No struggle, no stink.

"*Watch*," I teep to her. "*Watch this*."

I'm in a *cenote* with Carol, an impossibly deep freshwater pool in the Yucatan jungle, open to the sky, with tree roots dangling down the side. I'm floating beside Carol, the two of us together, deeply in love. I savor the pure water's blue light. There's nothing to worry about.

Kanga is here too, treading water, her hard face happy. The light in the water is my me-ware.

"All is one," I tell Kanga.

"Yes," she says. "Yes."

21. TWEETY BIRD

And now it's a month later. I've been working on the author's edition of *Sqinks*, and I'm just about done.

I'm living with Carol most of the time, either in her cabin in the Santa Cruz mountains, or in my quarters at the Box Farm, which is where we are right now.

My space is a larger than before. I made good money off that first edition of my *Sqinks* novel. And the author's edition will be better. With no edits from Towser. I feel happy thinking about it.

It's early morning, with a gentle drizzle. I lie in my bed, watching the water running down the window glass. Yes, we have a window now, and not just a skylight. The clouds are mottled shades of gray. Beautiful.

"I love weather," says Carol, standing by the coffee-maker. "Reminds me there's a big world. Not just our fears and regrets."

"Bigger world than you used to know," says Towser the sqink, who's still with us. He flexes his doggy body. "I've been budding off babies. I've been eating a lot."

"You can give the buds to me," says Kanga, who's just coming in the door. "After I huff Oliver. I'll take the buds home to Mu9. Dump them on an empty tract where they can live."

"Kanga's always huffing Oliver," says Carol. "Every day. She can't get enough of my man." She tries clowning on the last word, breaking it into two syllables. *May-un.* But she doesn't sound happy. "I don't know how you stand it, Oliver. I tried getting huffed once, but ..."

"It feels fine," I say. "Like flossing my teeth. It's good for me."

"Harder for us sqinks," says Towser, who's nosing around the kitchen in search of scraps. "Harder for a sqink to get their me-ware back into their body."

"No wonder," says Carol. "Who'd want to be a sqink?"

"Don't you be leaving your body today," I advise Towser. "We want to publish the author's edition of *Sqinks*, right? And you're supposed to talk to Clyde Yonk."

"Ask him about including an illo," goes Carol. "I found the perfect image to put in the new edition."

"What image is that?" goes Towser.

"Tweety, Sylvester, and Grandma," says Carol. "Do you remember them, Oliver?"

"I myself know everything," puts in Kanga, taking a cup of Carol's coffee. "I internalized Earth's full database. Just like the sqinks. Lilac showed me how." She pauses. "But I have indexing issues."

"Tweety was an old cartoon?" I say to Carol, half-remembering. "Wasn't Moo talking about it after we visited Paul Vreed's studio?

"Behold," goes Carol. She makes a gesture that throws an image onto the wall. Like a police line-up.

Tweety: a yellow lumpy-headed canary. Sylvester: a lisping black cat with a white chest, as if he's wearing a tuxedo. Grandma: an agile old lady with glasses and a bun and an ever-ready cane.

"And I'm Sylvester?" I ask.

"No, no, you're Tweety bird," says Carol. "All the humans are Tweety. And all the sqinks are Grandma. And the Mu9ers are Sylvester."

"*O sole mio*," I sing, trying for a canary sound.

"*Rowr*," goes Kanga, playing cat.

"It's a version of the Trilateral treaty," says Carol. *"Tweety has Grandma as a servant. Grandma's relatives live at Sylvester's place. Sylvester chases Tweety."*

"I don't really get it," I say.

"I'm worried about how slow you are," says Carol, shaking her head. "Really worried. You'll never finish your novel."

"It's a moving target," I protest. "Transreal novels are hard. New things keeps happening."

"Until they don't," says Carol. "I bet you don't remember the trilateral treaty. What we were talking about in the big cave with all the bugs? *Humans use sqinks as helpers. Sqinks colonize Mu9. Mu9ers huff human me-ware.*"

"Um …"

"Let me pep you up, dear boy," says Kanga, sitting down on the side of my bed. "It's time."

I wrap my arms around the Mu9er. I feel the familiar tingle in the back of my nose.

Zzzt. I'm everywhere. So relaxing. The light, ah, the light. Peace at last.

Tzzz. It's over. I flop back onto my back.

"All *right,*" goes Kanga. "The man has *soul!* Shed me your buds, Towser. I'm trucking back to Mu9 for a few days."

Towser lies down and claws at his ruff as if scratching fleas, doing it for a long time, first one side then the other, fairly unattractive. Scattered on the floor are sqink buds like blood-engorged ticks.

"So elegant," says Carol, not meaning it "So chic."

"Be fruitful and multiply," creaks Towser, his tongue lolling. "All hail our colony on Mu9!"

Kanga gathers the buds with a silver whisk broom and dust pan, dumps the buds into her pouch, and bids us farewell.

Towser departs as well. "I'll visit Clyde right now," he says. "I'll do like you said, Oliver. I'll get you a better deal. But don't slack off. You gotta write the last chapter for real."

"I'll do it," I say, still lying on my back. "I'll finish this afternoon."

— The End —

AFTERWORD

Maybe I don't need to say much about how I wrote *Sqinks*. After all, the novel is about a person like Rudy writing a novel like *Sqinks*. And if you want exhaustive details, you can study my companion volume *The Sqinks Journal*.

Before starting *Sqinks* I was away from writing for three years. My dear wife Sylvia suffered through two years of cancer, she passed away, and then came a crushing year of grief.

At the start of 2024 I wanted to write a novel again. Writing is what I do; it's what I'm good at; it's my way of seeing where I'm at.

I had only a vague notion of what I'd write. My inspiration was a painting of mine, *Farmers Market*. I liked the idea of aliens who looked like floppy garlands of balls, I liked the idea of tunnels to other worlds, and I liked the idea of aliens with a funny name. Sqinks!

As I began writing, a new wave of AI was building. Large-language-model, unsupervised-learning, multi-level neural nets. I had a feeling my sqinks were like these things. I wanted them to be gnarly, funny, and odd. They happen to come from a zone that cosmologists call the *bulk*. In the earlier days of SF, we called this region the *subdimensions*.

Lifelong cyberpunk that I am, it seemed reasonable to have the sqinks steal our brains. Just like in my novel *Software*, from nearly half a century back. The bopper robots of that novel chew up brains in order to extract their ware.

A sqink might cut out your brain and save it in a bio-support sack. And then tease your brain into yielding up an analog, soul-like entity called a me-ware. Or the sqink might move into your empty skull—like an overly intrusive AI upgrade. Once the sqink is in control of your body the squatter sqink can savor the analog wonder of human sex.

That's the new AI? That's what the big companies are into? Well sure, broadly speaking, that's what the new AI is all about. But instead of *cutting out* brains, the AIs learn to *emulate* brains.

Better than that, the AIs can emulate specific individuals. It's a matter of knowing the target's likes, dislikes, catch-phrases, fears, habits, and so on—absorbing a lifebox-style trove of personal data.

If an AI is closely emulating you, it's not hard for it to influence you. It knows your buttons. We ourselves emulate other people all the time, just by using our built-in wetware.

The emulation is useful if you're trying to scam someone, or to befriend them. That's the plot of Danny Rubin's visionary *Groundhog Day*, by the way. A man keeps reliving a certain day with a particular woman until the match is perfect … and then they make love.

In the 1930s, the logicians Kurt Gödel and Alan Turing proved that there is, even in principle, *no way to predict where a train of thought will go*. Putting it differently, while writing *Sqinks*, I had no way of knowing I'd end with this afterword. For that year and a half, I was making things up, writing whatever I felt like, and, yes, being influenced by the changes around me. Somehow it came together. Leading to the following conclusion.

Sqinks is a keenly observed and highly relevant commentary on the new AI.

Also it's a love story.

As I get older, I have more trouble getting big publishers to print me. But petitioning small publishers is time-consuming … and they might not take my books either. Too cool for the room.

Increasingly I turn to my own small press, Transreal Books, which is responsible for *Turing & Burroughs*, *The Big Aha*, *Return to the Hollow Earth*, *Juicy Ghosts*, and now *Sqinks*.

I like designing and publishing my books. I'm eager to get them out there. If I do a Kickstarter, I even get paid. And in time, some of my late-period, underground novels are being picked up by larger publishers for a second edition.

I habitually create a book-length volume of writing notes while working on a novel. And thus I'm publishing *The Sqinks Journal* along with *Sqinks*. By the way, I have all of my previous *Notes* volumes online to read for free—as well as some of my older novels, science books, and anthologies.

Why? To make it easier for humans and AIs to emulate me. I've been seeing the AI thing coming for a long time. I don't quite see why anyone views being emulated as a bad thing. The way I see it, the more Rudys the better. I'm out to change the world! And, at least for now, I can out-Rudy the best of them. Especially with a novel like *Sqinks*, where I really let things fly.

I designed covers for the two *Sqinks* books, using two of my paintings, and with help from my Adobe-maven friend Barb Ash and my graphic designer daughter Georgia Rucker. Bart Nagel shot some great portraits. Marc Laidlaw, Chuck Shotton, and my agent John Silbersack read early drafts—and gave encouragement for my off-beat path. My Clarion West student Emily Skaftun did a great final proofing on *Sqinks*, and Barb vetted the *The Sqinks Journal*.

The *Sqinks* Kickstarter campaign turned out well. It's gratifying to receive such generous support. Many thanks to my backers. I list them below, sorted by the alphabetical order of the first letters of their chosen names.

Adam Browne, Abolish ICE, AgentKaz, Alan Borecky, Alan Swithenbank, Alex, Alexander the Drake, Alex McLaren, Alice Steinke, Amy Purvis, Ana Trask, Andrew E. Love, Jr., Andrew Hatchell, Andy J Ward, Andy Ramsay, Angus P. MacDonald, Arthur Murphy, Benet Devereux, BHHenry, Bill Messick, Blechpirat, Bob Schoenholtz, Bruce Evans, Bruce Yarnall, Bruno Boutot, Cameron Cooper, Caroline Couture, Chaostrophy, Chris Horton, Chris McLaren, Chris Mihal, Cindy, Cliff Winnig, Coco Conn, Cory Doctorow, Crazy Eddie, Curtis Frye, Dan Botsford, Dan Cohen, Daniel Aneiros, Danny Joe, Daryl Davis, Dave "Ratfactor" Gauer, Dave Bouvier, Dave C., Dave Dyer, Dave Holets, David Brower, David Good, David Kirkpatrick, David Rains, David Simmonds, Dean Wesley Smith, demian parker, Dennis DementX, Lee Poague, Derek Andersen, Derek Bosch, derekticon, DG Zog, Digital Mark Hughes, Doug Bissell, Doug Diego, Dr. S.O. Teric, Dwayne Plain, Ed deJager, Eddie Churchill, Edward Marr, Eileen Gunn, Embry Rucker III & Tee Bree, Emilia M. Pulliainen, Emleeb, Eric Farmer, Erik Saynisch, Erik Sowa, floss.socialist, Frank Chillamos, full name, fyrfaras, Gary Bunker, George Bendo & Hedvig Bartha, George Van Wagner, GF, graphixTV, Grayson Osborne, Greg Kerkman, GVDub, Harald Niesche, Heath Row, Hellapriller, hemisphire, Herr Doktor Professor Deth Vegetable, Ian "FalsePositives" Irving, Ian Chung, Jaap van, jakob frank, Jason 'XenoPhage' Frisvold, Jeffrey K Hallock, Jeffrey Thomas Palmer, Jim Anderson, Jim Gotaas, Jim Guild, Joe D'Agnese, John C Monroe, John Curtin, John P. Sullins, John Tinmouth, Jon McKeown, Jose Brox, Josh Collins, Joshua A. C. Newman, Julia Grillmayr, K. Seifried, K.G. Anderson, Karl W. Reinsch, Karl-Arthur Arlamovsky, Kave, Ken Rokos, KeNTKB, Kernelcoremode, Kevin J. "Womzilla"

Maroney, Larry Dickman, Leah A. Fenner, Lee Fisher, Leif Lindholm, LilFluff, Lisandro Gaertner, litlfred, lotek, Mackenzie Bechtel-Hall, Madeleine Shepherd, Mahmur Megrim, Marc Goodner, Marian Goldeen, Mark Frauenfelder, Mark Sylor, Martin Olson, Marty Olson, Matthew Cox, Matthew Moran, Maxim Jakubowski, Michael A. Burstein, Michael Adam Becker, Michael O'Shaughnessy, Michael W Lucas, Michael Weiss, Mike Coats, Mike M., Mike Purfield, Mokmeister, Muddy Steve, Murray Marble, Ned Snow, Nicholas Marritz, Niko Alm, None, Norbert Bruckner, Pat Cadigan, Patrick Edmondson, Paul Goracke, Paul Leonard, PhilA, Philip Procyk, Phillip Vuchetich, R. Eggleton, Ray Cornwall, rdi, Richard Matthias, Richard S, Rick Crain, Rick Ohnemus, Rik Skibinski, rob alley, Richard Lesh, Robert D. Stewart, Rod Bartlett, R.U. Sirius, sabrinaweb71, Saftor, Sajorlime, SCIJMW, Scott "marsroverdriver" Maxwell, Scott Call, Scott Lazerus, Scott Lenihan, Sigsegv, simon travis, Snik, Steve Flores, Steve Gurr, Steven A. Thompson, Takuya Mizuguchi, Tao Neuendorffer, The High Frontier, Tonnvane Wiswell, Thijsc, Thomas Bøvith, Tim + Norma Thomson, Tim Conkling, Tim Messler, Timothy Lee Russell, Timothy M. Maroney, Tj, Todd Fincannon, Tom Foster, Val Delane, Vernon White, Walter J. Montie, William Dass, William TB Fee, Zach Peters, and Your Name Here.

I am profoundly grateful to all the readers who have kept my career alive for, lo, these many years. You're wonderful.

Rudy Rucker
Los Gatos, California
October 14. 2025